GHOST TRAIN

C. J. PETIT

TABLE OF CONTENTS

Printed in the United States of America

First Printing, 2021

ISBN: 9798701151954

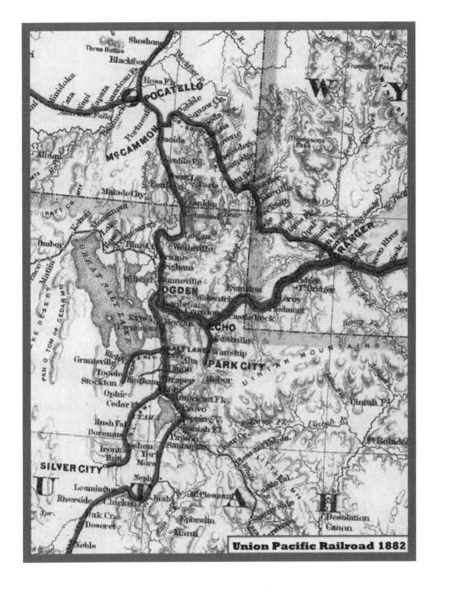

Union Pacific Railroad 1882

PROLOGUE

July 4, 1882
Cheyenne, Wyoming

Cassie Gray sat on her blanket beside her friend, Barbara Foster as they waited for the first rocket to launch into the night sky and begin the town's Independence Day fireworks display.

"I can't believe you'd do something like that, Cassie," Barbara said in quiet shock.

"It was stupid but it's over now that he's gone. I'm just lucky that I'm barren."

"Do you think Ned will find out?"

"I think he already knows but won't say anything. If I confess what I've done, he'd probably blame himself and beg me to forgive him for not being a good husband. I'm just about the worst wife God ever put on the earth."

"You're a good woman, Cassie. It's just that Ned is such a sweet man, and you, well, you're...um..."

Barbara stopped as she searched for the properly descriptive word.

Cassie snapped, "Bitch. I know what I am, Barb."

"No! No! I wasn't going to say that. It's just that you're very confident and forceful. To be honest, I always wondered why you even accepted Ned."

"For as long as I can recall, my mother told me how to behave around boys and men. I was never to contradict them or show any signs of temper. I was to be sweet and demurring. The other girls in school were like that, so that was how I behaved. Ned was well liked by my parents and came from a very good family. So, when he wanted to be my boyfriend, I fell into my coquettish role. I even giggled, for God's sake!

"We were married when he returned from college and accepted the job with Union Pacific. He was so proud and happy that I had to keep my true nature in hiding. It was growing more difficult each month and it didn't help that I failed to conceive. He worried about me constantly and treated me as if I was an invalid. There were times I wanted to throw something at him, but I knew he was just being considerate. When he got the assignment to Cheyenne, at least we were away from his family, and I thought he'd be less fawning. But if anything, he became more of a sycophant than a husband."

"When did you first meet Tom Richardson?"

"Two months ago. I guess he saw how frustrated I was and took advantage of it, so I don't blame him either. He left Cheyenne for Denver because he got into some kind of trouble, so he's gone. I won't make that mistake again. I'm just going to have to at least start acting like myself a bit more to see if Ned can adjust to it."

"You can be the bossy wife," Barbara said followed by a short giggle.

"I don't want to boss him around, Barb. But I don't want to be treated like a fragile, porcelain doll, either. I want to be more than a bedmate, cook and housecleaner. I want to be a true partner and feel free to express myself. I want to be able to argue without making him cry."

"He cries?"

"Sometimes. What makes it more obvious about how poorly we were matched is that I've never shed a tear since we've been married."

Barbara looked at her friend for another few seconds before turning her eyes away in expectation of the first rocket.

Before Ned struck the match to the fuse, Barbara said, "At least he won't be crying tonight. He was as excited as a little boy with a new toy when they asked him to launch the fireworks."

"He was like that all week after John Chalmers had to leave town and they asked him to do it. I hope he doesn't trip and fall into that big crate of rockets in his excitement. A lot of folks would be disappointed if he breaks those tubes."

"I'm sure that he'll do a good job."

Cassie nodded but wasn't so sure. It wasn't that Ned was overly anxious, it was that he was clumsy. She could almost picture her husband lighting the first fuse and stepping backwards too quickly then falling into the crate with the rest of the rockets.

Two hundred yards from where Cassie and Barbara sat, Ned nervously approached the big rocket. He was well aware of his clumsiness and had ensured that he had a clear path behind him. He was confident that once he launched the first one, the others would be easier.

Before he'd gone, John Chalmers had instructed him on the proper technique for having a successful show. He'd been asked to fill in because he was a structural engineer for the Union Pacific, and everyone agreed that he was the best choice.

He'd taken the first of the two dozen rockets from the crate, pushed the long launching stick into the ground and trailed the fuse closer to him. He glanced back at the open crate to make sure it wasn't behind him. Then he took a deep breath, bent at the knees, struck the match on the flat rock he held in his left hand and touched it to the fuse. When it ignited, he quickly stepped back and watched the fuse burn.

Ned forgot about the burning match until the flames licked at his fingers and he tossed it away before jerking his fingertips to his mouth. He kept his eyes on the fuse as it neared the rocket and waited for it to woosh into the sky.

As the fuse burned closer to the base of the rocket, the still flaming match he flipped away didn't land on the empty ground but dropped into the box of rockets. The bottom of the crate was covered in a film of leaked gunpowder and was crisscrossed with a web of fuses. The match's flame had almost extinguished before it hit the explosive surface, but not quite.

While Ned and the large crowd of onlookers watched the first rocket ignite and fly into the dark sky waiting for the magnificent shower of light, the gunpowder ignited in a flash that bypassed the fuses and set off the packed gunpowder in the remaining twenty-three rockets. The rocket exploded in the sky overhead but before the first onlooker could ooh or aah, there was a much more massive blast that shook the ground like a small earthquake.

Pieces of wood and rocket casing began dropping all around the townsfolk as they realized what had happened. There would be no more fireworks that night and Cassie Gray was now a widow.

———

July 7, 1882

Cassie felt like the ultimate phony as she sat in the pew of St. James Methodist Church wearing her black widow's garb and listened as Reverend Hobson extolled the virtues of Ned Gray.

6

But even now, she refused to reach the level of hypocrite and generate false tears.

What made it worse was knowing that the preacher wasn't exaggerating. Ned really was a kind, gentle and loving man. He didn't drink, smoke or womanize. For any other woman, he would have been a perfect husband. But she wasn't any woman. She was something else she still couldn't understand.

They'd only lived in Cheyenne for two years, but she knew she couldn't stay where Ned was buried. His family would be returning to Omaha tomorrow, and they hadn't even spoken to her, which was actually a relief. She was surprised that Ned's father didn't institute some legal action to take the house and seize their bank account. They never believed that Cassie was good enough for their precious son, and they were right, but for the wrong reasons.

She'd finalize her husband's affairs here and then she'd take the Union Pacific train to San Francisco if her sister agreed to let her come. After Ned's spectacular death, she'd written to Charlene and asked if she could stay with her for a while before she decided what to do with the rest of her life.

Charlene was married to a less-than-gentle husband and had two children already, so Cassie wasn't planning on staying with her for very long. She just had to leave Cheyenne. At least she wouldn't have to pay for a train ticket. She could use the pass that she had been given after marrying Ned.

There was only one thing that was absolutely sure about her future. If she married again, her next husband would see the real Cassie. She knew that there would be men who would be willing to overlook her fierce character because of her better than average appearance and her healthy bank account. But she didn't want one who just tolerated the way she was; she wanted a man who appreciated her. That would be difficult because there were few men in this world who wanted a wife who would challenge him.

CHAPTER 1

July 28, 1882
6:08 p.m.
Forty-Six Miles southwest of Granger
In the Southwest Corner of Wyoming Territory

Will Hitchens leaned through the locomotive's window watching for any trouble with the tracks ahead while Jim Kennedy shoveled more coal into the roaring flames that licked out of the firebox. He was making good speed on the downslope and knew it would take a good half a mile to stop the long train that trailed his engine. He'd made this run often and knew the rails were in pretty good shape, but with the surprisingly long heat wave, he was worried that some may have buckled.

They were taking the Union Pacific's southern branch out of Granger and would stop at Echo in Utah before a longer stop in Ogden where he and Jim would be replaced by a new crew. They could use the rest.

The noise in the locomotive's cabin was intense as it usually was, but Will found the sound soothing because there weren't any hints of a malfunction. It was when there was a new sound added to the normal cacophony that he wouldn't be so content. Number 373 was a fairly new locomotive, and he didn't suspect anything to break yet. He had inspected it at the stop in Granger and he and Jim had greased anything that needed lubrication. His only concerns were with the two ribbons of steel that stretched out in front of him and continued all the way to the Pacific Ocean.

They were approaching a long curve and Will pulled the throttle back. His practiced hand drew it back just enough to scrub five miles per hour from their current speed of almost forty. He didn't see any problems ahead, but the tracks disappeared halfway through the curve as it entered the forested area. He knew that the train could handle the curve at this speed, but he slowed it another five miles an hour because of the heat wave. He'd had a few problems with buckled tracks before and almost lost one train. But he was able to get it stopped just in time with the cowcatcher hanging over the bowed steel rail.

———

Among the trees at the other end of the curve, ten men waited with their Winchesters. Their leader, Jack Rodgers, had devised an outlandish plan that had taken months to put into operation. After a lot of hard work, they were finally about to reap their rewards.

"Remember what you're supposed to do! We want to get rolling in less than an hour!" Jack shouted as he heard the train approaching.

After hearing assorted confirmations, Jack turned his eyes toward the east. They weren't worried about the train derailing, but it wasn't going to get past them either.

———

He may have been looking for buckled tracks, but when his locomotive was halfway through the curve, he spotted something much worse. One of the rails had been removed from the crossties and was just laying across the tracks more than fifty yards from where it had been removed.

He shouted to Jim, "We're gonna be robbed!"

Will yanked back on the throttles to throw the wheels into reverse and applied the new air brakes. The locomotives drive wheels quickly began to rotate in the opposite direction, screeching loudly as they threw up sparks.

The passengers were thrown out of their seats as Will tugged on the whistle's cord. They didn't realize that the blasts from the whistle weren't to prepare them for the sudden stop, but to warn them of the potential danger.

In the two passenger cars the men, women and children were tossed out of their seats and many suffered head injuries as they slammed into the back of the bench seat before them. Even those who weren't knocked dizzy were in no shape to do anything even if they did realize the danger. There were six men wearing sidearms, but it no longer mattered as the gang was already moving.

Before the train lurched to a stop, Jack and his gang exited the trees and rode quickly to their assigned targets. He knew that the engineer and fireman were unarmed, so he sent his least experienced shooters but well-trained railroaders, Mick Gifford and Joe Smith, to handle them. He and Big Bob Post would head for the express car where they expected to meet their only resistance while the others took care of the passengers and the conductor. All their time in preparation and the railroad background of most of his men gave him confidence for the success of his bold plan.

He wasn't worried about witnesses hearing any gunfire because the closest town was Castle Rock which was four miles behind them, and Jack knew that the train hadn't even had to slow as it passed the quiet station. The next stop that was large enough to have passengers board or disembark was Echo, and they wouldn't get concerned until the train was more than three hours overdue. By then, it would be dark, and they'd be ready for the last part of the scheme.

Before Will could even clamber out of the locomotive to warn the passengers, he found himself looking down at Mick Gifford's Winchester.

"Get outta the cab, mister. You and your fireman."

Will glanced back at Jim, then nodded before climbing down and wishing he'd had time to at least shut down the locomotive.

Jim followed him to the ground and each of them expected he'd soon be shot, but that didn't happen. While Mick held them under gunpoint, Joe quickly tied their wrists with pigging strings and gagged them with a long strip of cloth.

"Get over in them trees," Mick snapped.

The two captives slowly walked away from the steaming locomotive and after they entered the forest, Joe had them sit down on opposite sides of a pine trunk and lashed them tightly to the tree with a heavy rope.

As Mick and Joe were handling the engineer and fireman, the four assigned to the passenger cars had split into pairs and one entered each door to block any escape route. It was only then that the still-stunned passengers realized why the train had come to the unexpected and hard stop.

Boomer Wilson and Audie Scott walked into the first passenger car and had the men toss any weapons onto the aisle floor. After they were reasonably sure that no one else was armed, Boomer picked up the assorted pistols and after grabbing a woman's purse, dropped them inside. Then he and Audie began having them hand over any valuables.

None of the passenger doubted for a moment that the outlaws wouldn't hesitate to kill them and quickly gave them their wallets, purses and jewelry. Once they'd made the first round, they just positioned themselves at each door with their loot at their feet and kept their Winchesters pointed at the terrified passengers while they waited for the boss to arrive.

Harry Ent and Bo Davenport had followed the same procedures in the second passenger car. They weren't surprised that it had gone so smoothly. Jack Rodgers was a genius. When Bo thought of the rest of the plan, he smiled but was close to giggling.

As he'd expected, Jack was finding the express car's occupant to be their only problem. He was sure that there was only one man inside the locked car, and he refused to open the door. Short of blowing it up, which was something he had hoped to avoid, he had to convince the employee to surrender. He was losing valuable time.

He rapped on the heavy door once more and shouted, "Come on out, mister! We haven't killed anyone yet and I don't want you to be the first. I've got six sticks of dynamite out here and I'll blow that door off in five minutes if you don't open it. You might survive the blast, but if I have to waste my dynamite, I'll be mighty peeved. I'll be so mad that I'll start firing my Colt at your ankles and work my way up. Maybe I'll just start at your privates. You've got one minute to answer, then I'll get my dynamite."

Al Fitch licked his lips then glanced back at the safe in the corner. He took another short look at the two bags of U.S. mail and although he'd sworn to protect them, he didn't think they really expected him to die to keep that promise.

He didn't yell back but unlocked the door and slowly slid it open. He found himself staring down at the outlaw chief and was surprised that he didn't even have his gun pointing at him. Then he noticed the enormous man sitting in his saddle a few feet to his left and gulped. Not only was he a giant; he did have his Winchester aimed at him.

Al looked back at the gang leader and asked, "You aren't going to kill me; are you?"

"Nope. Just hop down and we'll escort you to one of the passenger cars."

Al was relieved and after jumping to the ground, he turned toward the closest passenger car as Big Bob walked his horse to the mail car and slid the door closed.

After they reached the second passenger car, Jack and Bob dismounted and waited until Al climbed the steps. Bob took his saddlebags from his horse, then followed Jack after he mounted the steel platform.

Al passed Bo Davenport and took a seat on the last bench before Jack loudly said, "Alright, folks. I want you all to just stay put and put your hands over the back of the seat rail in front of you. Nobody is going to be hurt as long as you don't start trouble."

Everyone did as he'd ordered then Big Bob opened one saddlebag, pulled out a mass of pigging strings and handed some to Bo. As Harry Ent kept guard with his Winchester, Jack

Rodgers turned and left while Bob and Bo began tying the passengers' wrists to the seat rails.

After he stepped to the ground, he took his saddlebags down, then walked quickly to the second passenger car and after entering, he made the same announcement. After Jack watched the folks place their hands on the passenger rails, he and Audie Scott began tying off the passengers' wrists while Boomer kept them covered.

While the passengers were being subdued and secured, Joe and Mick had moved onto their second task. Mick checked the locomotive to make sure that the engineer hadn't done any damage. While Mick inspected the levers and dials, Joe threw a few shovelfuls of coal into the firebox to keep the fire going. Then he and Joe left the locomotive and headed back down the track to repair the damaged they'd created earlier.

They looped ropes over each end of the rail that they'd left across the tracks to stop the train, then slid it back to where it belonged. They didn't even need to lift it from the rails, but once they reached the gap, they just let one end drop to the first of the empty crossties. They lifted the other end and rotated it until they could lower it back into place.

It didn't have to be perfect, but once it was close, they left the rails and headed into the trees where Joe picked up the burlap bag with the missing spikes while Mick grabbed the heavy sledge and their spike puller. Both of them had spent years helping to build the railroad before Mick became an engineer and Joe a fireman, so now they'd make better use of those earlier skills.

Joe began inserting the spikes into their original holes as Mick walked behind him and hammered them back into place. He'd left the spike puller by the side of the tracks before he began because they no longer needed it. They didn't care if the next train derailed. All that mattered was that their repair job held long enough to allow their train to pass over the rails.

By the time all the passengers were bound and their booty had been moved to the express car, Joe and Mick had completed the repair and after Joe picked up their long spike puller, they returned to the locomotive.

Joe and Mick carried their tools into the cab and began preparing the locomotive to do its job.

The last task was to open the stock car and pull out the internal ramp. Without bothering to check on the horses and mules that were already inside, Bo and Boomer led their eight horses and packhorse up the ramp and tied them off inside. After replacing the ramp, they hopped back outside and slid the door closed.

The others were already waiting for them in the caboose and before they entered, Bo looked back at the locomotive, saw Joe waiting for the signal, then waved his hat over his head before trotting to the caboose.

After seeing Bo's signal, Joe shouted, "Okay, Mick. Let's get this beast movin'!"

Mick grinned then opened the throttle. He knew the train wouldn't gain too much speed before it reached the repaired rail, so there wasn't any risk of a derailment.

The sunset was already underway as the train passed over the replaced track and soon was making up some of the lost time. The entire well-executed operation had taken just fifty-three minutes.

The delayed train rolled along the rails heading southwest for its final destination. Jack knew that there were probably passengers waiting on the platform at Echo, but they would never even see the train.

When they were just eight miles out of Echo, Mick pulled back on the throttle and applied the air brakes. The train slowed much more smoothly than it had the last time. In the light of the almost full moon, he watched for the expected signal.

He was sure that Pooch and Carl had finished before they arrived, but they hadn't been able to start their work until the westbound coal train had passed. It had departed Granger two hours before their train. The next scheduled train wouldn't pass this point for another four hours and by then their train would no longer be on Union Pacific tracks.

He had the train crawling by the time he spotted the swinging lantern.

Mick grinned as he turned to Joe and shouted, "There's the signal. I hope Pooch and Carl did their job right or we'll have a real disaster."

Joe yelled back, "It'll just mean a smaller payday, Joe!"

Mick watched as the light grew closer and did more than just hope that Pooch and Carl did their job well. He actually said a silent prayer as the locomotive neared the curved rails. If they didn't, it would be harder on him and Bo than most of the others if the train rolled onto its side. The released fire and steam would turn the locomotive's cab into hell on earth.

Pooch McGregor was still waving the lantern even though he was sure that Mick had seen it. He and Carl Brown had a hard time replacing the rails after the coal train passed. Even with the setting sun and now the full moon overhead, it had been difficult work for just two men, even with Jack's ingenious lifters. Soon he'd see if they had done a good enough job.

Mick waved out of the cab's window when he spotted Pooch and waited for the cowcatcher to swing to the left. Just seconds later, the guide wheels reached the temporary curve and began following the steel path. Mick heard the loud clacks as the locomotive's big drive wheels rolled over the larger-than-normal gaps left by their crude switch, but the steel behemoth just swayed slightly as it made the turn. It was much sharper than the direction change made by normal Union Pacific switches, but Mick didn't care. He was just enormously relieved that it had worked.

He looked back at the eleven cars that trailed the coal car and watched as each of them followed the locomotive around the curve. When the caboose straightened out, Mick let out a deep breath and turned to the front to look for the last signal that Pooch and Carl had left at the end of track. With trees on both sides of the train, he didn't see it until it was less than fifty yards ahead, but the train was moving so slowly by then that he just applied the air brakes and after he pulled the throttle back to neutral, the thousand-foot-long train slowed smoothly to a stop.

After the successful train theft, now they needed to put the rest of the plan into operation.

The men were all so well prepared that as soon as the train came to a stop, those who were on board poured out of the cars while Joe and Mick shut down the locomotive.

All of them except Jack and Boomer Wilson headed back to the main track to help Pooch and Carl remove all evidence of their work. They knew that they had another three hours or so before the next scheduled train but wanted to be done much earlier. Jack's tools would make that a much easier task.

Jack and Boomer entered the first passenger car but only Boomer had his pistol drawn as Jack stood at the front of the car.

"In a little while, we'll start releasing you from your bindings. No one will be hurt unless you give us trouble. You can curse at us if you'd like, but nothing beyond that. This will be the men's car. Any women who want to stay here with their husbands can do so. You can pull the cushions from the seats to use as beds and we'll provide food and water until you're free. You'll use the car's privy for personal hygiene.

"If the Union Pacific meets our demands, then you'll be free to go to your destination and never have to leave the train. If they refuse, well, I'll apologize in advance for what we'll have to do. But don't blame me or my men. Blame the greed of the Union Pacific."

He turned and left the car with Boomer following. They walked to the second car where he made the same speech, only modifying it for the women's car. When he'd done a head count, there were nineteen men, ten women, three boys under twelve and two young girls. There weren't any children under eight, which made the situation easier to control. The men ranged in age between low twenties to upper forties, but none seemed threatening, especially now that they were disarmed. Not surprisingly, the women had a much smaller age range. The youngest appeared to be in their upper teens and except for one matron, the next oldest was barely thirty. Jack had no idea why it worked out that way, but it didn't matter. They were all his prisoners now until the Union Pacific decided how to react.

He and Boomer were joined by Joe and Mick after they left the locomotive.

Jack said, "Okay. In a few minutes, we'll start letting the passengers loose in the men's car and any women who want to

21

head to the women's car will need to be escorted before the men are taken out of the women's car. We've talked about this and if anyone makes a break, you have to shoot. Don't fire a warning shot. Do you understand?"

Joe and Mick both nodded and hoped that none of them tried to escape. It wouldn't be hard if it was a man; but shooting a woman would be unnerving.

"Okay, let's get this started."

It took about forty minutes to move the women to the women's car and the men to the men's car. Four of the women stayed their husbands and kept their children with them, so that left the second car practically empty with just eight women and two children. There was still plenty of room in the men's car, but it was another statistical oddity for Jack. He loved playing with numbers because it had been the focus of his life since he was a boy.

It took the men less than two hours to replace the two straight rails and remove the crossties and their own rails from the original railroad bed. They restored the cinders and raked the dirt behind them as they kept working their way back into the trees. Once they reached the trees, they pulled the fallen pine back across the gap. It was at an odd angle so no one could see the stump. Jack had wanted it to look like nature's work.

By the time the next train thundered past, there was little evidence of the temporary switch. By morning, even the slightest clue that it had been there would be gone. The train was now hidden among the trees six hundred yards off the main line.

Before they had finished removing the evidence, Jack had sent Carl Brown and Bo Davenport west on horseback to deliver his ultimatum to the bosses at the Union Pacific. Carl had been a telegrapher after being fired by Western Union and would use their portable set to send the ransom demand. He was sure that the Union Pacific bosses wouldn't believe it at first but wished he could be there to see their faces when they finally realized that they'd lost an entire train and its cars of fare paying passengers.

CHAPTER 2

Ogden, Utah

It was barely past sunrise when Nelson was rudely awakened by loud pounding on his front door. He groaned before he slid his legs out from under the blankets and stretched as the thumping continued unabated.

He shouted, "Stop that! I'm coming!" then stood and just pulled on his britches and his shirt.

He was buttoning his shirt as he left his bedroom, then walked down the short hallway to the front room and opened the door.

"Nellie, we got problems!" exclaimed Homer Watson, Union Pacific's Ogden station manager.

"Come inside and tell me. I need some coffee."

As he turned around, Homer entered, closed the door and followed Nelson down the hallway.

When they reached the small kitchen, Nelson said, "Sit down, Homer. You're almost ready to pass out anyway."

Homer plopped onto the closest chair while Nelson built a fire in the cookstove.

Homer quickly said, "The 7:40 from Granger didn't arrive last night. I wasn't told about it until a couple of hours ago and had them ask Granger if it left on time. It did, but Al Jones at Echo said he didn't remember seeing it."

Nelson tossed a match onto the kindling and as he added wood to the flames, he asked, "Did anyone report a derailment?"

"Nope. The next train passed through without a problem. That's what triggered them to tell me about it. Eddie asked the engineer and he said that there was nothing unusual about the run from Granger."

That did pique Nelson's interest as he closed the firebox door then stood and walked to the kitchen table and sat across from Homer.

"Are you telling me that the 7:40 just vanished?"

Homer nodded then pulled a folded sheet of paper from his jacket pocket.

After unfolding it, he said, "When I was in the Western Union office, the operator said that he got this from the Echo operator who heard it over his line. He sent it here just because it was so odd. It was sent to the Union Pacific headquarters in Omaha.

After they told me that the next train didn't have any problems on their run, it made sense. Sort of, anyway."

He slid the sheet across the table and Nelson read:

UNION PACIFIC PRESIDENT OMAHA NEB

WE HAVE YOUR TRAIN AND PASSENGERS
YOU HAVE ONE WEEK TO PAY FOR THEIR RETURN
ONE HUNDRED THOUSAND DOLLARS
ONLY US CURRENCY IN TENS AND TWENTIES
PACK IN TRAVEL TRUNK
LEAVE BY TRACKS AT MILE MARKER 18
OF PARK CITY SPUR
YOU HAVE UNTIL AUG 5 TO DELIVER
IF NOT OR IF LAWMEN SEEN
PASSENGERS START DYING
AND TRAIN WILL BE BLOWN UP

Nelson looked back at Homer and asked, "Did the operator say which line it came from and how strong the signal was?"

"I didn't ask. I figured that was your job. Do you think that they're really going to kill all those folks and blow up the train if the company doesn't pay?"

"I have no idea what to think yet. Let me get ready to go. I'll catch the 10:10 to Echo and maybe I'll have more information by then. And quit calling me Nellie."

26

"Good luck, Nel…son," Homer said before he stood, then left the kitchen and soon exited the house.

Nelson looked at the message again and noted a few items of interest already. He stood, filled his coffeepot then set it on one of the hotplates before walking back to his bathroom to wash and shave before he dressed properly.

As outrageous as the ransom demand might appear, Nelson knew that it was about the cost of the train itself, so whoever did this must have understood the finances involved. He was also smart enough to ask for only U.S. currency and not local bank notes which could be difficult to use in other territories. Even the proper use of the English language marked the man as educated.

By the time he was dressed, the water in the coffeepot was boiling, so he pulled it from the hotplate, dumped in a half a cup of grounds, then prepared a cold breakfast. He needed to do a lot before he boarded the eastbound train. Luckily, it was his habit to be ready to depart at a moment's notice. Sometimes, he'd get word of a problem that required his attention and had to hurry to make the next train. But he'd never had anything close to this odd or as grand in scope.

He quickly finished his hot coffee and cold breakfast before going to the next bedroom and selecting his weapons for the trip to Echo. Because he had no idea what to expect, he wanted to have to have a wide variety. He skipped his shoulder holster and Webley because this wasn't an undercover job, then buckled his Remington around his waist. He already suspected that there were at least eight men in the gang that had stolen the train but could be double that number. He had no intention of taking on that many on his own but hoped that the bosses back in Omaha ignored the 'no lawmen' threat.

With the U.S. mail on board the train, he knew that the United States Marshal's office and the Secret Service would both have jurisdiction. But having jurisdiction didn't necessarily mean that they had the manpower to offer any help, even if the railroad notified them. He planned on just doing some investigating and at least get an idea of where they'd taken the train.

There weren't any spurs or abandoned lines between Granger and Echo, which really added to the puzzle.

He took two long guns from his rack. His Winchester '76 and his Sharps musket. Both fired a .45 caliber round, but the Winchester's cartridge was a good inch shorter than the Sharps'. With his weapons selected, Nelson headed out of the room and walked to the kitchen again. He leaned the two long guns against the wall and donned his tan jacket and slightly darker Stetson.

After opening the back door, picking up his single-shot musket and his repeating rifle, he stepped over the threshold onto the small back porch and kicked the door closed. He trotted down the two steps and headed for his small barn. He had to move the Winchester into his big left hand that already held the Sharps to open the right-hand door, but then took it back and entered the shadows.

"Good morning, boys," he said as he passed the two dark brown geldings then laid both long guns on the bench along the back wall.

Nelson didn't have to check their shoes or anything else before he began saddling Rowdy, his older horse. He wasn't that old at nine years, but Gomer was only six. He may be younger, but he was much more docile than Rowdy who had earned his name. Rowdy wasn't uncontrollable for Nelson, but he was feisty if anyone else tried to mount him. He'd had Rowdy for four years now and had bought Gomer two years later when he discovered that he needed a pack animal for some jobs. He decided against buying a mule because he wanted to have a backup horse if he lost Rowdy. The fact that both horses were similar in build and shading helped. Rowdy was about a half a hand taller and had a white slash down his forehead while Gomer had almost no markings at all. He had a smudge of gray between his eyes that wasn't even noticeable at first glance.

He finished saddling his horses then slid his Winchester into Rowdy's scabbard and the Sharps into Gomer's. Gomer wore a modified riding saddle that allowed Nelson to hang one pannier on each side. It gave him a lot of flexibility. After hanging on his two pre-loaded packs, he added his final weapon to Gomer that he'd built himself last year. It was just an experiment after he'd seen an article about the weapon in *Harper's Weekly*. The article had included a diagram, so he'd spent three months making it. It was a mid-sized crossbow that fired foot-long bolts. Making the bolts had turned out to be the biggest consumer of his time. But when it was finished, he was impressed enough to consider it a real weapon. It was silent and after he'd practiced with it for a month, he could hit a two-foot target at fifty yards. He had John Fellows make a custom leather pouch for storing the crossbow and its dozen bolts. When it was hung on Gomer, it looked odd, but not threatening.

He led Rowdy out of the barn with Gomer trailing. The trail rope that he used wasn't hemp, but woven deerskin. He'd bought the rope from the Ute reservation when he'd had to return property that had been stolen by two railroad employees. They no longer worked for Union Pacific but didn't go to prison for the crime.

Nelson rode down his drive and turned onto Saint Street then headed for the depot. The Western Union office was next door, as it usually was, and he needed to talk to the operator. He wasn't the same man who'd received the ransom demand, but Nelson was sure that the outgoing telegrapher would have told his replacement about the unusual message.

He stepped down before the stock corral and led Rowdy toward the wide gate. There were already two horses, a mule and a large bull in the corral but the bull was in a separate pen.

"Morning, Nelson. I hear you're headin' to Echo to check on that missin' train," Charlie Nix said as he took Rowdy's reins.

Nelson wasn't surprised when Charlie had mentioned it because he was sure that it was already common knowledge at the depot within a minute of Homer's return.

"Yes, sir. I want to get out there as quickly as possible to pick up clues for the U.S. marshals or Secret Service agents when they show up."

"Homer said that they don't want any lawmen."

"I know, but I can't imagine that they'll manage to keep them from finding out anyway. If it wasn't for the U.S. mail on the train, maybe they wouldn't bother. I guess we'll find out soon enough."

He then gave a short wave to Charlie and let him move his horses into the corral. He headed for the Western Union office and soon entered the open doorway. Even though there were two other customers waiting for messages to be sent, the on-duty operator, John Hipper, waved him over.

The man closest to the counter wasn't happy about the delay until he turned and saw who the telegrapher had signaled. Nelson Cook was a well-known figure in Ogden and the man's dissatisfaction evaporated before Nelson reached the counter.

"I figured you'd be stopping by pretty soon, Nelson. What do you need to know?"

"That message. Did the Echo operator let you know which line carried it and how strong the signal was?"

"Yup. He said it came from the line to Park City and was even stronger than their station would put out. He also said that whoever sent it had a really good hand. He figured that the man must have been an operator at one time or another. He didn't recognize the hand, though."

"Did you hear any more traffic about it?"

"Nope."

"That's a lot of good information. Thanks, John, and pass along my thanks to the Echo operator."

"I'll do that, Nelson."

Nelson turned, smiled at the two men and said, "Sorry for interrupting."

"No problem," replied the man closer to the counter while the second man just nodded.

Nelson quickly left the Western Union office and returned to the platform. He checked the station clock and expected that his train would arrive soon, so he sat on the nearest bench to make some sense of what he'd learned so far. It wasn't much, but there were enough clues to give him a starting point.

Aside from the size of the gang that had pulled off this incredible crime, he knew that it had to have at least a few ex-railroaders among their numbers. He assumed they'd killed the engineer and fireman and run the locomotive themselves. But it was the empty track that the next train had taken to Ogden without any signs of the missing train that added even more substance to the kind of men who had made it disappear.

Even if they had a dozen well-trained railroad workers, that wasn't enough to figure out how to move it off the tracks. They had to have a structural engineer with them to make it work. Judging by the wording in the telegram, he was pretty sure that the engineer who had figured out how to do that was also in charge.

Before he moved on to how they could have managed to do it, he concentrated on their boss. It didn't take long before Nelson smiled because he was sure that the man who planned and executed the bold scheme was probably Jack Rodgers. He'd met Jack a few times and knew that he was a brilliant engineer. But he was also very ambitious. He had become frustrated when other, less talented engineers received promotions and plum jobs while he didn't advance as quickly as he believed he deserved.

Two years ago, a bridge that Jack had designed then supervised its construction had collapsed after just three weeks of operation. He had complained before the bridge was even finished that the beams that he had been given were substandard and had too many knots and cracks. But when bridge collapsed and took the long coal train with it, the company had placed the failure on his shoulders. They hadn't fired him, but Jack was furious and had quit.

Nelson hadn't been there when Jack left, but he'd talked to some of the workers who were at the site and they'd told him that Jack had vowed revenge. For six months, Nelson had been expecting a bridge to be blown up or tracks weakened, but nothing had happened, so Jack Rodgers had drifted from his memory. Now he seemed to have returned with a vengeance.

Once he identified the probable gang leader, he was free to try and figure out how Jack had pulled it off. He'd barely begun to tackle that problem when the whistle from the arriving train made him shelve it until he boarded.

Nelson stood and walked to the track side of the platform and glanced to the north. The train he'd be taking had just left Idaho and after stopping in Utah, would soon reach Wyoming. He'd exit the train before it reached Wyoming and start his investigation in Echo.

He soon climbed aboard the last passenger car and had to wait while the animals were loaded into the stock car and shipments were loaded into the boxcars. Twenty minutes later, the train pulled out of the station to make the short journey to Echo.

———

Forty-eight miles away, Jack sat around their smokeless campfire talking to the eleven men who had helped him steal the train. He didn't consider them a gang, although three of them were wanted by the law. Most were disgruntled ex-railroad

34

employees he had recruited after he'd finalized his plan. He'd known most of them while they still worked for Union Pacific, so he knew that they would be eager to join him. The three outlaws, Big Bob Post, Boomer Wilson and Harry Ent were added after he'd collected the railroaders. He needed them because he knew that they wouldn't have any reservations if it came to violence.

While everything had gone even more smoothly than he could have hoped, he knew that there was still a potential for disaster. After they'd moved the passengers into their cars, they'd just locked them inside by wrapping heavy rope around the doors. Whatever they wanted to do while they passed their time was up to them. The last warning he'd issued was that they'd be watched and anyone who tried to escape would be shot.

The passengers had already been given breakfast and they were behaving. Jack suspected that sooner or later, some of the men might try something but it would only happen once.

"How will we know that they won't send in the army, Jack?" Mick Gifford asked.

"They won't. The can't afford to have newspapers go crazy printing stories about how the company cared more about money than the folks who buy their tickets. If the U.S. Marshals or the Secret Service tries something on their own, we'll take them down then kill a few passengers. We'll send another telegram blaming Union Pacific and that'll ensure that they pay up."

Joe Smith asked, "How long do you reckon we'll have to wait for the money?"

"I originally estimated four days, but it could be as many as six. We've got enough food to last us and the passengers for two weeks, but as soon as they drop off that trunk and we're sure that it as the money, we'll leave."

Then Carl Brown asked the one question that they'd all wanted to ask.

"What about the passengers? They can all identify us, Jack."

Jack just shrugged. He knew that Big Bob, Boomer and Harry already knew the answer, but the railroad boys probably just suspected what would happen to them even if the Union Pacific paid the ransom. But Jack already knew before he started planning that the railroad would never be able to gather that much money in a week. He expected to blow up the train and passengers when the deadline passed. He felt no guilt about it. It was the Union Pacific's fault.

————

As his train rolled eastward, Nelson had already solved what many probably found to be the most difficult part of the puzzle: *how did they move the train off the tracks?*

He knew that they couldn't have used a real switch because they were much harder to steal and even more difficult to manufacture. But to get the train off of the main tracks without a switch meant that Jack would have to bend some rails, remove two straight rails, then after the train passed over their bent rails, they'd replace the originals. The reason it wasn't difficult for Nelson to figure out was because he'd heard of the technique.

During the Civil War, General Sherman's army, as it marched to the sea, destroyed the Confederate rail system when they found any tracks. They did more than just pull the rails from the crossties. They started bonfires, then after the rails glowed, the Yankee soldiers would bend them around trees and posts until they were pretzels. They were commonly called Sherman's neckties. His wasn't the only army to use the technique, but they were enthusiastic in the number of rails they twisted into useless shapes.

So, if Jack had his boys build a bonfire, they'd have to be very accurate when they began to shape the rails. Knowing the radius of the curve they'd need was critical and made Nelson even more convinced that Jack Rodgers was the man responsible for the disappearance.

Nelson was more perplexed about the rest of the rails that had to be laid in preparation for the train's arrival. Even if it was only a half a mile long, it would take months for a crew of eight to ten to build it. That wasn't what made it hard to fathom. It was the rails and crossties themselves that created the mystery. The crossties weren't difficult to figure out because they could just make crude ties out of logs that would suit their purpose. It was the rails that posed the bigger question.

Each rail was thirty-eight feet long, so if they were going to build their own spur line for eight hundred yards, they'd need more than a hundred and twenty rails. He knew that no one had reported any stolen rails from the Union Pacific warehouses. *So, where did they get the rails?*

The train had almost reached Echo when he at least came up with a possible answer. He was sure that he was dealing with ex-railroad men, so if one of them worked at a warehouse, he could have arranged for some to go missing. While most of the crossties and rails rarely lingered in the warehouses, some of the spurs wound up collecting too many when the powers that be couldn't decide if they wanted to continue extending the tracks down the line.

He was still visiting the issue when the train began to slow, and he knew he'd have to continue the thought process after he'd picked up Rowdy and Gomer. But first, he needed to talk to the telegrapher.

———

After everyone had taken a short nap, Jack and Big Bob headed for the express car. Jack wanted to open the safe but didn't want to use any of sticks from their one box of dynamite they'd need to blow up the train. They'd already put all of their collected booty in the empty packs they'd brought along. They now had a dozen more horses and two mules they could use to carry whatever else they wanted to take with them.

"Do you reckon you're gonna have to get that express feller to give you the combination, Jack?" Bob asked as they walked alongside the train.

"Maybe. But those boys usually write it down somewhere. They don't keep it with them because the safe stays in the car and they move around."

Bob snickered as they reached the express car and slid the door open to allow Jack to climb inside first. Bob wasn't very bright and had depended on his size and brute strength to keep him solvent. But when Jack had asked him to join him for this giant payday, he had been flattered. Since then, he'd come to hero worship the bright engineer. Jack had treated him as an equal, even though Bob knew he wasn't even close to being the man that Jack was.

Jack climbed into the car and walked to the safe in the corner where he dropped to his heels. He had no idea of what was inside. It could be just a confidential letter or a few bars of gold, but it didn't hurt to check.

As Bob stood behind him and watched, Jack began scanning for the combination's most likely hiding place. It would have to be invisible at first, but easily read once uncovered. It didn't take him long to notice a chalkboard leaning against the back wall.

He picked it up and smiled when he saw the numbers scrawled into the car's wall.

"You were right, Jack!" Bob exclaimed, but he wasn't surprised. Jack was really smart.

Jack didn't even smile as he tried the combination. If it didn't work, he'd try it backwards. But after he dialed in the last number, he turned the handle and did smile when it opened.

Bob was wide-eyed in anticipation as Jack swung the door opened. Then he softly whistled.

Even Jack was surprised to see the bundles of U.S. currency that were stacked inside. He pulled one out to check the denomination. They were twenty-dollar bills, which was as good as he could have hoped to find. He began pulling out the others and discovered that only four of the bundles were twenties. The rest were tens and fives, but the total was eleven thousand dollars.

He replaced the currency then closed the door and spun the dial before standing.

"That was a nice bonus. That'll be a thousand dollars extra for each of you even if they don't pay the ransom."

"That's the most money I ever saw, Jack. What do you reckon it's for?"

"I imagine it's a payroll for some big company down the line. If it was for a bank, then that might get the government interested. It doesn't change anything though. Let's head back and I'll let you give the good news to the rest of the boys."

"Thanks, Jack. I'm sure they'll all be real happy, too."

"I'm sure they will," Jack replied before slapping Bob's broad back and hopping down from the car.

Jack had intentionally developed a strong bond with Big Bob because he didn't trust the other two outlaws. Boomer and Harry Ent were smarter than Bob and devious as well. But Bob terrified them both and Jack needed to keep the big man happy to make sure they stayed in line.

———

Nelson left his horses in the stock corral as he walked to the Western Union office. He wasn't going to send a telegram but hoped to get more information. He may not need to send one, but he soon discovered that one was waiting for him.

When he entered, he didn't recognize the operator, so he pulled his badge from his jacket pocket as he approached the counter.

He showed the telegrapher his Union Pacific Special Agent badge then said, "I'm Nelson Cook. Have you heard anything more about the missing train?"

"No, sir. But I have a message for you that arrived about an hour ago. It was forwarded from Ogden," Tom Welch said before he turned and pulled a sheet from his box and handed it to Nelson.

Nelson quickly read the telegram and wasn't surprised that it came from the head office in Omaha.

He read:

NELSON COOK OGDEN UT

INVESTIGAGE MISSING TRAIN
DO NOT TAKE ANY ACTION
REPEAT DO NOT INTERVENE
SCOUT ONLY AND REPORT TO THIS OFFICE

WILLIAM BURNS UPRR OMAHA NEB

Nelson said, "I'm going to send a reply."

"I figured you might."

Nelson flipped the sheet over and pulled a pencil from the counter and quickly wrote down his message. He wasn't about to tell his boss that he would do whatever he thought was necessary until it became apparent that he had to act. That would only happen if he found he had an unexpected advantage.

He wrote:

WILLIAM BURNS UPRR OMAHA NEB

ALREADY ENROUTE TO SCOUT
BELIEVE AT LEAST A DOZEN INVOLVED
MANY RAILROAD MEN
SUSPECT JACK RODGERS IN CHARGE
WILL KEEP YOU ADVISED

NELSON COOK ECHO UT

He handed the message back to the operator before he turned and walked out of the office. It was one of the agreements between the Union Pacific and Western Union which were both headquartered in Omaha. He could send telegrams without cost and some of their employees had passes to ride gratis on Union Pacific trains. The difference was that his badge would allow him to ride on other railroads without having to buy a ticket while the passes the Western Union had only worked for Union Pacific rails. It was still an impressive network.

After returning to the late summer heat, he headed for the stock corral. He'd get something to eat then head east along the road that paralleled the tracks. Because the road was on the northern side of the rails, he was sure that their homemade tracks headed south.

After mounting Rowdy, he rode the gelding down the main street and pulled up in front of Aunt Alice's Diner. He's used it before and found it a good value but wasn't going to stay long.

43

When Big Bob had passed the news that they each would get another thousand dollars over the five thousand they'd each get from the railroad, it had created an almost party-like atmosphere.

Inside the two passenger cars, it was more like a wake than a celebration. The more crowded men's car was gloomier as some of the men who'd given up their sidearms stewed in their inability to do nothing but wait. The men who had their wives and children with them were in a better frame of mind but were still worried about what would happen to their families. But even the disgruntled men didn't dare think about trying to escape. It was no use.

While the mood in the women's car wasn't as depressing, it was still far from cheerful. Most of the women were still lying on the seat cushions that had been laid down the aisle. Two had their young daughters snuggled close.

But in the back of the car, four women sat on the benches that still had their cushions. They may not have had any firearms, but they weren't about to just sit and wait for the large gang to decide their fate.

Florence Porter said, "At least they didn't molest us."

Mary Ellison snorted then said, "Not yet, but I reckon they'd let me be for a while. You three are all a lot younger and prettier than I am."

"What do you think they're going to do with us and the men?" asked Louise Smith.

Cassie Gray quietly replied, "I don't think that they can let us live. We've seen their faces."

Mary asked, "But why haven't they done it already? They're feeding us and not even threatening us."

"I've been listening to them talking and they're waiting for the railroad to meet their demands. I don't know how much they've asked for, but I'm sure it's a pretty large amount. I don't know if they'll pay, but even if they do, I don't believe that they'll leave anyone alive. We've got to figure out some way to get out of here."

"How?" asked Florence, "They've locked those doors and only open them when they bring us food. They said they'd shoot anyone they see trying to escape."

Cassie pointed to the privy at the front of the car and Louise laughed before saying, "You've got to be kidding! We've been using that all day and I hate to think what's on the ground underneath."

"It's only going to get deeper, but I think that they wouldn't expect anyone to squeeze through that hole and drop into the mess. I'm just not sure if I'd fit."

Mary snickered then said, "I know I couldn't even if I wanted to. But say you did make it out. Where would you go?"

"The tracks are probably just a few hundred yards north. After I reach them, it'll take about two or three hours to reach that town we passed."

"Are you really going to try it?" asked Florence.

"Not tonight because they're still expecting someone to try to get out. I want to listen to them talk and see if they're getting bored."

Mary said, "You'd better hope they don't, Cassie. If they get bored, then there's one thing they can do to have some fun."

"I don't think that their boss is going to let them do any such thing, Mary. He seems very well educated; don't you think?"

"Don't tell me you like him!" exclaimed Louise.

"Of course, not. I'm just saying that he seems to be smart enough to realize our value as hostages until they get their money."

Florence then said, "I know that Louise and I aren't married, and Mary is a widow, but are you married, Cassie?"

"I was until the Fourth of July. My husband died in an explosion. I was on my way to stay with my sister's family in San Francisco."

"Do you miss him terribly?" Louise asked quietly.

Cassie almost slipped into her expected grieving widow role, but quickly stopped the slide.

"I wasn't a very good wife and I'm not going to start behaving like a good widow. He was a good, gentle and kind man. He loved me deeply and would do anything for me."

Florence asked, "Then why don't you miss him?"

"I wanted something different. Ned worshipped me and I didn't want to be a goddess. I wanted to be me. I couldn't behave as I always had until he started courting me. I even cheated on him. As I said, I wasn't a good wife and I'm not a good woman, either."

"I like you, Cassie," Louise said.

"So, do I," echoed Florence.

Mary chuckled then said, "Hell, even an old bag like me thinks you're okay. You just married wrong. At least you didn't have any young'uns."

Cassie quickly changed the topic as she asked, "What was your husband like, Mary?"

"Jasper was a hoot. He was a lousy provider, but he sure was fun. He finally crossed the wrong feller and met his end a year ago. I wasn't surprised when I got the news and stuck around until I got a proposal from an old boyfriend I haven't seen in years. I'm on my way to Silver City to marry him."

"How did that happen?" asked Florence.

"If you must know, I wrote him a letter letting him know that Jasper was gone. I was running kind of low on money and knew where he lived, so I figured I'd suggest that I was available. I suppose you could say that it was me who did the proposing."

The other women laughed, then Florence and Louise told Cassie and Mary why they were on the train. Florence was a teacher and had accepted her first position as a schoolmarm in Salt Lake City. Louise was a nurse who lived in Laramie and was going to Echo to visit her brother's family.

As she listened to their stories, Cassie looked at the privy at the front of the car and wondered if she'd not only be able to fit through the hole but survive long enough to make it to the trees. She absentmindedly ran her hands from her hips to her chest and tried to estimate her widest circumference.

———

Before he mounted Rowdy, Nelson removed a coil of rope from one of Gomer's packs and hung it on his saddle. Then he took out a small canvas tarp and after covering the packs and the Sharps, he tied it down. He would be riding on the road on the north side of the tracks and was sure that they would have moved the train onto their temporary spur on the south side. He was also convinced that they would have lookouts watching the road and tracks for any lawmen, so he wanted to appear as innocent as possible. He wasn't about to don chaps because that would have been going too far. Cowboys traveling with a packhorse didn't wear chaps.

He climbed into the saddle and headed east. It wasn't even one o'clock when he set out and was sure that he wouldn't have to ride all the way to Granger. It was almost a hundred miles away, but there were four small towns along the route. He'd try to locate where they'd swapped out the rails then continue to the next town and send a telegram to William Burns in Omaha. He just had to avoid the appearance of searching for the train which would alert the gang.

He soon left Echo and picked up the pace. The gang wouldn't have set up so close to the big town, but as he rode, he tried to guess where they would most likely have built their personal railroad. It didn't help that none of the workers at the small stations along the way even noticed if the train had passed or not.

He knew the towns and the tracks but wasn't sure of the terrain. The rails followed the contours of the land to minimize having to build tunnels, bridges and switchbacks. He tried to envision those curves and the mountains and hills that made them necessary. It was a good way for him to pass the first hour but knew it was time to start paying more attention to the tracks and the terrain to the south.

The road had been heading northeast since leaving Echo, and the terrain to his right was heavily forested, but too hilly to lay tracks. He began to hum *Seeing Nellie Home*, which was funny because it was about a lady and some of the boys still insisted on calling him Nellie.

He rode for another forty minutes before he spotted indents in a few crossties but didn't stare at them. He stretched then pulled his canteen and took a deep swallow before replacing the cap and hanging it back on his saddle. When he'd brought the canteen up to take his drink, he turned slightly to look at the terrain to his right but didn't let his eyes linger.

Nelson then resumed humming and headed for Castle Rock, the next town on the route. Those dents in the crossties were made by a spike puller and were only in the ones supporting a single rail. The terrain south of the tracks while forested, was reasonably flat. He was sure that he'd found where they'd built their spur.

As he continued riding northeast, he started developing a plan in defiance of the orders he'd received from Mister Burns. He doubted that Jack Rodgers could afford to let the passengers live even if the U.P. paid the ransom. And that assumed that they weren't dead already. Once he'd determined the location of the stolen train, he assumed that they'd stolen the rails, tools and spikes from the large warehouse in Park City. It was at the end of a recently completed spur line and he knew they had a large amount of excess material. How they managed to move the tons of steel rails was another question, but it didn't matter.

But even as he brushed off that issue, another question popped into his head. If they'd inserted their homemade switch at that spot, *where and how did they stop the train?* They would have needed to quickly replace the straight rails with their curved ones after the coal train had passed and they couldn't have just stopped it short of their new sharp curve and waited. They had to subdue the engineer, fireman and control the passengers after it was stopped. The train was well out of Granger and probably moving at a good rate of speed. If the engineer had seen an obstruction ahead, it would take him a good mile to stop the train and he was sure that Jack Rodgers would have taken that into account. He would have planned to stop it well before their switch. His men would be able to take control of the train while other members of his gang swapped out the rails.

He knew how smart Jack was and had to admire the perfection of his scheme. But that didn't mean that the ex-engineer was a good man and would allow the passengers to reach their destinations. He would probably blow up the train anyway even if he got his money.

Nelson decided to continue looking for any signs that might tell him where they'd stopped the train before he sent his telegram. He had plenty of daylight remaining.

———

"Just one man?" Jack asked.

Harry Ent nodded then said, "He was leadin' a pack horse and hummin' a tune, too. He didn't look like a lawman. He didn't slow down or look around, and I watched him for another ten minutes. I figured you'd wanna know."

"Alright. He was probably just heading to Granger. If he comes back, shoot him."

Harry grinned then replied, "It'll be a pleasure."

After Harry left, Jack hoped that he wouldn't shoot the next rider who happened to pass by. Of the three hard men he'd hired, Harry was the most uncontrollable.

————

More than an hour later, Nelson continued to search for signs where they had stopped the train. He knew that Castle Rock was just a few miles down the track and was almost to the long curve that kept him from seeing it. He figured that this was where the gang would have stopped the train. The engineer would have to slow the train when he entered the curve and, at the most, wouldn't be able to see more than a mile ahead.

If they set their obstruction in the right place, the engineer would have barely been able to stop the train in time. But more importantly to the gang, he wouldn't have time to get it moving backwards and escape their trap. Everything that he'd learned about Jack Rodger's plan so far had been meticulously arranged and that meant that he should find evidence of where they'd captured the train soon.

His only concern was the approaching sundown. He hoped to find a lot of hoofprints on the south side of the tracks soon. He believed that even Jack wouldn't have bothered cleaning up the spot where he'd taken control of the train because it didn't matter. Between here and Echo was more than thirty miles and the train had just disappeared.

The concerns about sunset vanished when he soon spotted the large number of prints on the other side of the tracks then slowed Rowdy before tugged on his reins and let his gelding step carefully across the rails.

After crossing the tracks, he dismounted and scanned the ground. He was about to return to his saddle when he spotted footprints heading into the trees. He didn't move for another minute as he studied the tracks and noticed that four sets entered the trees but only two returned to join the mass of horseshoe and footprints near the rail bed.

He let his reins drop but didn't bother pulling his Remington as he followed the footprints and soon entered the pines. He walked another forty yards or so before he spotted Will Hitchens and Jim Kennedy lashed to a tree. Their heads were down, so they were either dead or asleep. He didn't see any blood but did notice that their britches were soaked in urine. He soon picked up more foul smells as he drew closer.

Nelson ignored the stench as he dropped to his heels beside the engineer and as he removed the gag from his mouth, he said, "Will, this is Nelson Cook. Are you okay?"

Will's head jerked up as his eyes popped open.

"Nelson? Is that really you?" he croaked.

"Don't talk. I'll cut you and Jim loose then get you some water. Okay?"

Tears began to roll down Will's cheeks as he nodded.

Nelson removed Jim's gag, then pulled his knife from its sheath and as he began slicing through the heavy rope that bound them, Jim Kennedy looked at him but couldn't speak. He didn't weep, but Nelson was sure that he was just as relieved as Will.

After cutting the rope, he more carefully removed the pigging strings that bound their wrists.

Once the two men were free, he stood, slid his knife home then jogged away to reach Rowdy. He knew the men would need more than water and luckily had two spare pairs of britches in Gomer's packs. He kept them handy because he never knew when the ones he was wearing might be ripped or covered in blood. He was actually pleased to find the two men because he didn't want to believe that Will and Jim had been willing participants in the theft.

After stepping into the saddle, he walked Rowdy into the forest and soon dismounted near Will and Jim. Both were trying to stand but their stiff muscles and joints were making it difficult. He pulled both of his canteens from Rowdy and waited until they were upright and leaning against the pine trunk before handing one to each of them.

He didn't ask them anything yet as they greedily sucked down the water but turned back to Gomer to retrieve his extra britches, a pair of towels and another canteen. After taking them from Gomer, he returned and saw the grateful smiles on their scruffy faces.

"I'll let you boys toss those fouled britches away and I'll dump some water on these towels to let you clean up. Leave them with your britches when you're done. Alright?"

"We thought we were done for, Nelson," Will said as he accepted the pants.

"Did they kill anybody?" Jim asked.

"Not that I know of. They just stole the train. We'll talk after you get changed. I'll get you something to eat while you get rid of those bitchy britches."

Jim and Will both snickered as they began to strip off their horribly smelling clothes but didn't ask about underpants.

Nelson drenched the two towels and waited for them to kick off their boots before yanking off their trousers and hurling them away. When they were naked below the waist, Nelson gave each of them a wet towel before heading back to Gomer to get them some food.

As he rummaged, he was surprised that he'd found them alive and wondered if Jack was going to kill the passengers after all. It hadn't been a question of noise, so he wondered why Will and Jim were still among the living.

He grabbed two large pieces of smoked beef then walked back to Will and Jim. They had just finished pulling on his britches and Will had picked up the half-full canteen.

"Here you go, boys," Nelson said before tossing one chunk of beef to each of them.

Will managed to catch his, but Jim fumbled his but didn't seem to care as he quickly recovered it from the ground and ripped off a piece.

As they chewed, Nelson continued to visit the question of their survival. If they hadn't been gagged, then maybe Jack wanted them to be found so they'd believe he wasn't going to harm the passengers. Even if they had been able to shout, it wouldn't be long before they realized the futility of yelling. The road wasn't used nearly as much as it had been before the tracks were laid nearby and the odds of them being found were remote at best.

He was still thinking about it when Will asked, "Did you say that they stole my train?"

Nelson replied, "The train never made it to Echo, but I think I know how they managed to hide it and where it is."

"Why did they steal it?" Jim asked as Will drank some water.

"They demanded a hundred thousand dollars from U.P. or they'd blow it up and kill all the passengers. They gave them a week to come up with the ransom and told them where to leave it."

Will exclaimed, "They're going to blow up my train! Those bastards!"

"Let's get mounted and we can talk on our way to Castle Rock and where they have the train. We can get there in less than an hour."

Will looked at the two horses and asked, "How do we wanna do this?"

"I'll take you behind me and Jim, you can figure out a way to ride on Gomer."

"Okay."

It took a few minutes but after Will was settled in behind Nelson and Jim had been able to get reasonably comfortable on Gomer's back, Nelson set Rowdy to a walk as they left the forest. After crossing the tracks, he turned onto the road to begin the short ride to Castle Rock.

As soon as they reached the road, Nelson began to explain what had happened and what he'd discovered loudly enough for both of them to hear. He wanted them to learn the aftermath before they told him how the gang had taken control of the train.

It only took him ten minutes, so when he finished, he asked, "How did they make you stop then take over the train, Will?"

Will quickly told him all that had happened before he and Jim were taken into the woods. They had no idea who the men were and were convinced that they would be shot once they were taken into the trees. When they weren't, they were as puzzled as Nelson had been. Because they didn't see anything and only heard muffled sounds, they weren't able to explain how the gang managed to get the passengers under control. But Will did say that he thought that two of the men knew how to operate the locomotive.

"I'm pretty sure I know who set it up and that he hired a lot of ex-railroad men to execute the plan. Do either of you know Jack Rodgers?"

Will replied, "Nope," and Jim shouted the same negative response from behind.

"He used to work for the U.P. as a structural engineer building bridges and trestles among other things. He was unhappy that the bosses didn't recognize his talents and when one of his bridges collapsed and cost them a coal train, they blamed him. He had told them that the beams he'd been provided weren't good, but they ignored him. He left and I'm sure that this was repayment for the way he was treated. I have to admit that it's an impressive plan and an even better execution to pull it off."

"So, do you reckon the U.P. is gonna pay up?" Will asked.

"I have no idea. I was told by my boss back in Omaha to just find the train's location, but not to do anything. When we get to Castle Rock, I'll send him a message to let him know where I think it is and see if I get new directions."

"Do you reckon that they're gonna kill the passengers if they don't get their money?"

"I wouldn't be surprised if they haven't already murdered them all. I was almost shocked to find you both alive and can't figure out why they didn't kill you both right away."

"I guess the only way you're gonna find out is to ask that Jack feller."

"I think you're right, Will."

Will then asked, "What are you gonna do if your boss tells you to back off again?"

"I'll pretend I didn't get the telegram. Tomorrow, I'll head back that way and before I'm close enough to be spotted by a lookout, I'll enter the forest and wind down their way among the trees. I could still be seen, but they won't expect anyone to come from that direction."

"You need some help, Nelson?" Jim asked loudly from his perch on Gomer.

"Not by coming along. The bosses will be expecting to hear from you. So, if Mister Burns tells me to stay put, I'll need you both to tell anyone who asks that I had already left Castle Rock to make sure that I was right. Okay?"

Will snickered then answered, "You do that. I still can't figure the U.P. will risk all those folks. They got a lot of money back in Omaha."

"Most people think that but trying to come up with that much cash even for a big company like the U.P. is really hard. That's another thing about this that has me puzzled. If it had been a regular gang who'd tried this stunt, I wouldn't be surprised by the size of the ransom demand. But Jack knows as well as I do that it's almost impossible for them to collect that much cash within a week."

"Can't the government let 'em borrow it?"

"That's not likely, but they might give them the bills from some of the counterfeit cash they have lying around to buy some time. But I suspect that Jack is expecting they might try that, so it wouldn't work. There are a lot of confusing aspects to this, and how they managed to steal and hide the train aren't the hard ones."

Nelson paused then said, "I just hope I can come up with something before they plant their dynamite around the train.

They threatened to blow it up and I'm sure that Jack meant it. If he hasn't already set the dynamite and fuses, then he will do it pretty soon."

The conversation ended with that horrifying thought, so Nelson began to mentally add more details to his strategy to stop the large gang from killing the passengers.

———

After three more hours with an empty road, Harry Ent was relieved by Boomer Wilson. Boomer climbed the tree to the platform they'd built to give them a decent view of the tracks and road for four miles to the west and two to the east. After he reached their watchtower, Boomer set his Winchester on the crude platform and leaned against the tree trunk. He hoped that cowboy that Harry watched ride past came back. He wasn't very happy with all this sitting around, and it had only been one day.

In the men's passenger car, the frustration ignited a fistfight that grew into a brawl that left more injuries and didn't relieve their exasperation. One of the wives was even hurt when she tried to defend her husband and caught a fist with her nose. Whether it was intentional or not didn't matter, but it fueled a more intense round of fisticuffs.

Most of the women in the other car were either afraid or resigned to their fate. The exceptions were the four women in the back of the car. While there was some fear among three of them, they were far from willing to blindly sit and wait for the gang to dictate everything, including how they died.

"Maybe you could take the entire seat off," Florence suggested.

Cassie shook her head as she replied, "I thought of that, but the only way we could do it is to use a sledgehammer and destroy the entire seat and its support."

"I suppose it's just as well," said Mary, "You'd probably just get stuck and none of us could use it without your permission."

Cassie laughed then said, "I'd charge a fee, but those bastards have all our money."

Louise grew more serious as she looked out the window at the ring of men who'd taken the train.

"Do you think that they'll send a big posse or the army to stop them?"

Cassie replied, "I don't know, Louise. They'd have to find the train and then it'll probably be up to the Union Pacific bosses to decide whether to pay the ransom or act. That might take too long. They asked for a lot of money and even if they decide to pay, I don't know how they could get the money together in time to meet their demands."

"I think they're going to leave us here when they blow up the train," Mary said quietly.

Louise said, "Maybe we should jump them when they bring us breakfast in the morning."

"They'd probably shoot all of us," said Cassie, "The one bringing the food doesn't wear a pistol but the one watching has two in his hands already. They probably hope we'll try something stupid. But let's not give up hope. We'll think of something."

"Did you hear that ruckus from the other car?" asked Mary, "I think they had a first-class brawl over there. I wonder if one of the men tried to escape."

Louise snickered then replied, "No, they didn't. They're beating each other up just for something to do. At least we haven't started pulling each other's hair out yet."

The other three women smiled but knew all they could do now was to hope that the railroad, U.S. Marshals, or the army did something. They may not be as frustrated as the men, but with only one day gone of the seven allowed by the gang leader, they didn't know how much longer they could keep from becoming depressed.

It wasn't just the wait, either. The heat wave had hovered over the area like a plague and even though the tall pines were just a hundred feet away on both sides, they weren't enough to keep the sun from sending its blistering rays onto the tops of the railcars. The women, like the men, had stripped to barely acceptable covering, but even with the windows open, they were drenched in sweat. The gang may have been bringing them water twice a day, but it wasn't enough for bathing. The stench from the car's small privy was just part of the malodorous atmosphere in the cars.

For the women, the final insult was that all of their perfumes and colognes were in the possession of the gang. The one advantage to the women was that their car was almost empty compared to the men's car. A drenching rain or a cold front was fourth on their list of prayers after their freedom, a bath, and a horrific end to the gang.

————

As they approached Castle Rock, Nelson said, "After I send the telegram, I'll splurge for supper at the closest diner, then give you some cash so you can buy what you need. Take the next train no matter the direction. Go to Ogden or Granger and let the bosses in Omaha know where you are. If they ask, tell them I'm out scouting."

Will asked, "You're not gonna stay in town tonight?"

"Nope. I'll take advantage of the full moon and camp out. If I'm lucky, I'll find the train."

"That's a big bunch of bad guys, Nelson. What can you do on your lonesome?"

"I have no idea. It'll depend on what I find and what the gang is doing. It's only been a day, so they'll still be expecting somebody to show up, but the longer they wait with nothing happening, the more complacent they'll become."

"Are you sure you don't want any help?" Jim asked from behind.

"I'll be fine. I'll only take action if it looks as if they're going to hurt the passengers."

"Do you reckon that they're still alive?" asked Will.

"I wondered about that for a while but just figured out why they were kept alive and probably why you weren't killed either."

"We're waitin'," said Will.

"They didn't kill you and Jim because if you were found, they'd believe that the gang wouldn't harm the passengers after the railroad paid the ransom. They didn't kill the passengers yet because that many bodies would attract a lot of attention from scavengers, including vultures. A large flock of circling buzzards would pinpoint the location of the train. Even if they killed them all and stuck the bodies in the stock car, the critters would start arriving at the train in droves."

Will then asked, "But do you still reckon that they'll kill them all even if they get their money?"

"I think that even if they get their money, they'll set their dynamite around the train and blow it up with the passengers still in the cars."

Nelson could hear Will grinding his teeth as they turned off the road and headed into Castle Rock. But as soon as he told Will about blowing up the passenger cars, he had an epiphany. He almost missed stopping at the Western Union office as he began developing a possible way to stop Jack Rodgers' plan.

But after he pulled up next to the telegraph office, he let Will slide off Rowdy's back before dismounting. He tied off his gelding's reins then the three men entered the small office. Nelson was relieved that it was still open this late in the day.

The operator was listening to his key chatter but wasn't writing anything. The message wasn't for anyone in Castle Rock, but it must have been interesting to him. Nelson picked up some of the chatter before the telegrapher noticed them.

As Nelson slid a blank sheet of paper from the stack on the counter and picked up a pencil, he said, "I'm Nelson Cook, the U.P. special agent they're chatting about. Have you heard any more news from Omaha?"

"No, sir. We're all just kind of speculating."

Nelson nodded as he wrote his message then handed it to the operator.

"This should add to the gossip."

The telegrapher quickly read the message, glanced at Will and Jim, then turned and sat at his equipment table and began tapping out the dots and dashes.

"Let's get something to eat," Nelson said, before pulling out a ten-dollar note and handing it to Will.

He hadn't asked if they had any money because even if they did, it wouldn't be much. He knew that he was paid at a much higher rate than even an experienced engineer like Will Hitchens.

They didn't remount, but Nelson just took Rowdy's reins and led them down the street to Mrs. Dempsey's Diner which was just half a block away.

In his message to William Burns, Nelson had reported the safe recovery of Will Hitchens and Jim Kennedy, then given the closest mile marker to the location where he believed the train had been taken from the main line. His ended it by telling his boss that he'd continue to scout for more evidence. He expected that the operator would be shutting his set down soon and any reply wouldn't arrive until the morning. Maybe he'd be able to end the situation before mid-day. A lot depended on the quantity and location of the dynamite that Jack was planning to use to blow up the train. That assumed he wasn't making an empty threat.

———

After they'd filled their stomachs, Nelson shook Will and Jim's hands, mounted a tired Rowdy and left Castle Rock. It was past sunset when he turned right on the railway's parallel road, and that suited him. He didn't intend to stay on the road for very long anyway. There were only eight miles between Castle Rock and the entrance to the gang's improvised spur. He'd walk Rowdy for another hour or so, then cross the tracks and enter the forest. He'd head deeper into the pines until he was about four hundred yards from the rails, then ride parallel as much as possible. With the full moon, he should be able to catch glimpses of the moonlight reflecting off of the shiny steel often enough to maintain the right path.

He didn't want to get too close to the train tonight but would set up a cold camp within walking distance. He'd strip Rowdy and Gomer and let them graze while he walked closer to where the train should be. If he had any measure of luck, he'd be able to spot it and start gathering information.

But it was the dynamite that was key to his plan. When the demand mentioned that they would probably blow up the passengers with the train, he realized just how much explosives they'd need to get the job done. He may not have been an engineer, but he had more than enough working knowledge to have a good idea of the quantity needed.

The problem for Jack Rodgers was that the train was above ground and probably over eight hundred feet long. To destroy the entire train would take two sticks of dynamite per car, so that meant he'd need at least two dozen sticks. A full case of dynamite, which would be easier to steal than individual sticks had forty-eight of the compact explosives. He'd need fuses and blasting caps, too.

Jack was smart enough to store the dynamite away from his camp. And if they had enough time to build the spur, he probably built a shelter for the dangerous explosives as well. He'd locate it a reasonable distance away from their camp to keep his men from becoming nervous, but close enough to be accessed when he needed it. Where that shelter was and what material they'd use to build it was key to his plan. If they'd built it out of cut logs, then his plan had no chance of success.

He soon reached a small clearing that he believed was close enough. There was a small stream that cut across the front that Rowdy and Gomer could use.

He dismounted, then unsaddled both horses before putting on their halters and running long ropes to a nearby pine branch to give them freedom to graze and drink. He pulled his field glasses from his saddlebags, hung them around his neck, then grabbed his Winchester and walked out of the clearing. He continued heading for the train and hoped that it wasn't too far away.

Nelson had only walked for a few minutes when a flash of light popped out between the gaps for just a moment. He slowed his pace and kept his eyes focused where he'd seen the light. When it returned seconds later, he stopped. It was a campfire about two hundred yards away.

He began walking even more slowly and carefully to avoid making noise but soon realized it wasn't necessary. He picked up loud chatter and laughing, so he knew he'd found Jack

Rodgers and his train-stealing boys. He wasn't going to do anything tonight because he'd lose if he tried. He needed to find the dynamite. Hopefully, it wouldn't already be lashed to the train cars.

Each step he took that brought him closer to the train and their camp revealed more valuable information. But even with the bright moonlight, he knew he wouldn't be able to identify Jack Rodgers or anyone else. He would be able to get a more accurate count of the number of men and maybe find the dynamite.

He continued to creep closer as their boisterous talking grew louder. He could have snapped every twig and branch on the ground and not been noticed. He finally stopped behind a large pine when he was just sixty feet from the campfire. He counted ten men sitting around the flames and guessed that no more than two were on guard near the tracks. There were four large tents about ten yards to his right which may have others already inside, but he thought it was unlikely.

The train was another thirty yards away. His current position was opposite the first passenger car. In front of that car was a flatbed car with tarp-covered equipment. The coal car and locomotive were to his left. After the second passenger car, there was the stock car, the express car, two more flatbed cars, then three boxcars and the caboose.

He couldn't see any movement inside the passenger cars but hadn't expected to find anyone enjoying the summer evening with a dance in the aisle. He was still convinced that they were all inside the cars and alive.

After studying the train, he let his eyes arc to the left in front of the locomotive where the tracks ended. The clearing lasted for another hundred yards or so, but just fifty yards in front of the locomotive's cowcatcher, he saw a small log structure. Its isolation alone told him it was the hiding place for their dynamite, but the use of logs instead of boards meant it was protected from a bullet. He was disappointed, but still lifted his field glasses to his eyes to get a better look at the tiny log cabin.

When he focused the glasses on the dynamite's home, his disappointment instantly evaporated. While it had been built of stout logs, Jack had only surrounded the dynamite with three walls. He must have only worried about keeping it dry and out of the sun. He could see a big crate and two small wooden boxes stacked on top of the larger one. If he wanted to kill Jack and all of the other men around the campfire, it would only take one well-placed .45 from his Winchester to set off the dynamite. He would be reasonably well shielded from the blast by the trees. He'd lose his hearing for a while, but the bad boys wouldn't be so lucky. The passengers would feel the train shake and hear the enormous roar, but none would suffer more than a headache. After what they'd already been through, Nelson figured they wouldn't mind.

But so far, all they'd done was to steal the train and bind the engineer and fireman. If he'd found Will and Jim dead, he might have squeezed his trigger. He'd still have to deal with the lookouts, but by the time he or they returned, he'd be waiting.

Now that he had all of the information he needed, Nelson turned and headed back to Rowdy and Gomer. He'd get some sleep and early in the morning, he would return and have a chat with Jack Rodgers.

Once he was a safe distance from the train, he walked more quickly. He hoped that Jack would be reasonable and accept the offer he'd make. Jack was not only smart; he was also logical. But that wasn't enough to convince him to agree. There would have to be both the stick, which the dynamite would provide and a carrot, which would be the contents of the express car's safe. He didn't know how much was in the safe, but it was usually more than five thousand dollars.

When he returned to his clearing, he slid his Winchester into its scabbard, spread out his bedroll, took off his hat and his Remington, then stretched out on his back. He set his pocket watch alarm and laid it under his Stetson next to his head.

As he looked up at the stars, he wondered if the Union Pacific bosses were meeting to discuss paying the ransom but doubted it. He suspected that they'd already made their decision and were probably having a good time at a fancy soiree.

Tomorrow, he hoped to make that decision irrelevant.

CHAPTER 3

Nelson's pocket watch alarm started chiming with the predawn. He hurriedly sat up, grabbed his hat and silenced it before standing. He slid his watch back where it belonged then pulled his hat on.

Rowdy and Gomer were already awake and grazing when he walked to the stream. After relieving his bladder's contents to the ground nearby, he quickly washed and brushed his teeth but bypassed shaving. He had things to do.

After eating three slices of cooked bacon and two biscuits, he washed it down with some water, then hung his canteen over his shoulder and his field glasses around his neck. He buckled on his gunbelt, grabbed his Winchester and took a dozen extra .45-75 Express cartridges from a full box and slipped them into his jacket pockets. He hoped that he didn't have to use one, but if he did, it would be an impressively loud shot.

The sun still hadn't made its appearance when he set out through the trees. He was more confident now but still kept his approach as stealthy as possible. Those boys should still be sleeping, and he wondered if the guards had been posted yet or would only leave the campsite after breakfast. He assumed that Jack was feeding the passengers, but still wasn't completely sure that they were still alive.

He slowed when he knew he was getting close but still didn't hear any voices or anything else from their camp. They must be feeling pretty secure if they were still in their tents.

Nelson soon picked up the scent of smoke from last night's campfire and followed his own footprints to reach the tree that had been so perfectly situated. When he reached his pine protector, he stopped and studied the campsite in the weak light of the predawn. It was still better than what the full moon had provided.

The campfire was just a smoldering black pile and there was no movement anywhere yet. He lifted his field glasses to his eyes to check on the dynamite. He was sure that they hadn't moved it but wanted to verify that it was dynamite and not just a crate of horseshoes.

Even in the predawn light, he could ready the high contrast DANGER DYNAMITE on the crate. From where he stood, it was a shot that was almost impossible for him to miss. He could have brought his Sharps along for its added power, but he was sure that his Winchester could do the job and if Jack didn't accept his offer, then he might need the extra shots.

He was all set and now just had to wait for the train thieves to wake up and start their day. Even after they left their tents, he wanted to wait until they were all gathered around the campfire for breakfast. Then he and Jack would have a pleasant chat…at least pleasant for him. He didn't think that Jack would be pleased at all.

The sun had been up for more than ten minutes before the first tent flap opened and Jack Rodgers stepped out into the morning light. Nelson recognized him immediately and wasn't surprised that he was the first to awaken. He was only surprised that he'd stayed inside for so long.

Jack shouted, "Get up, boys! Let's get some chow!"

After Jack had walked toward the trees to answer nature's call, the others began to emerge from their tents and Nelson hoped that none came too close. None drew closer than thirty feet and soon two of them began building the fire while others collected pans, plates and cups and others grabbed food from one of the tents.

Nelson counted a dozen men, including Jack and hadn't seen any of them leave to take up watch. He guessed that Jack didn't expect any problems for a few days. He'd soon discover that his estimate was inaccurate.

They bustled about preparing their breakfast while Nelson just watched. He'd let them know he was there soon enough. He cocked his Winchester's hammer but waited until they were all sitting around the fire eating.

It was another fifteen minutes before they began walking past the cook with their empty plates and after filling their cups with coffee, sat near the fire. Heat wave or not, the nights were still chilly.

When the last man had dropped to the ground and began shoveling in whatever they'd cooked, Nelson knew it was time.

He leveled his Winchester at Jack's head and shouted, "Everyone stay right there! Jack, this is Nelson Cook. I want to talk to you for a few minutes."

Every one of the men around the campfire was startled when Nelson had shouted, but not one of them reached for his pistol. If Nelson hadn't identified himself and then told their boss that he wanted to talk, they might have.

Jack set his plate and cup down, then stood, brushed off the seat of his pants and headed in the direction of Nelson's shout.

When he saw the Winchester pointed at him, Jack asked, "Are you going to shoot me before we chat, Nelson?"

"Nope. I just wanted to make sure everybody stays put. But before you come closer, I'll take my sights away from you and set them on that box of dynamite. It's an easy target and if anyone starts anything, I'll pull my trigger and, well, you can imagine what will happen."

Jack glanced at the dynamite then quickly evaluated Nelson's protection and understood quite well what the results would be if he fired.

Nelson then shifted his sights to the dynamite and waited for Jack to start walking closer. He didn't need to keep his eyes trained on his target because it was such an easy shot, so after he pointed his repeater at the dynamite, he looked back at Jack.

Jack stopped when he was ten feet away and asked, "Why am I not surprised to see you, Nelson? Anyway, can I assume that you want to bargain?"

"That's the idea."

"Did the boys back in Omaha send you to negotiate?"

"Nope. You know better than that, Jack. When you asked for a hundred thousand dollars, you knew that they couldn't or wouldn't pay. They'd let you blow up the train with the passengers and say that they hadn't even received your demand."

Jack shrugged then asked, "Okay, so if they didn't send you, what kind of deal are you looking for?"

"It's pretty simple. I assume that you've already opened the safe in the express car."

"I have."

"How much was inside?"

"Eleven thousand in U.S. currency."

"Right now, you're only guilty of pulling off the most impressive theft in the country's history. I found the engineer and fireman and had supper with them last night. I assume that the passengers are all still alive?"

"They are. We're feeding them and bringing them water, but the men had a brawl in their car yesterday."

"Boys will be boys. I'll tell you right now that if Will Hitchens or Jim Kennedy had been killed or if you'd murdered any of the passengers, I would have set off that dynamite last night when you were all sitting around the fire."

"Thank you for not blowing us all to kingdom come. So, what's your deal?"

"Take the eleven thousand. Then mount your horses and take your stuff but leave the passengers' things and their horses. I want your men to saddle their horses and leave in pairs or I'll set off the dynamite. If I see a single gun barrel, I'll either kill the man who shows it or shoot that crate."

Jack mulled it over. He didn't doubt that Nelson could outshoot every one of his men, even the three outlaws. The railroad boys would probably just hit the dirt if bullets started flying. He expected that he wouldn't even get a response from the railroad bosses, and now he had no bargaining chips.

"How much time would you give us?"

"I'm going to have to release the passengers and get them to Castle Rock, so it'll take me at least six hours. Besides, there is the chance that the U.S. Marshals or Secret Service will take the matter seriously and show up on their own. You're going to need every minute you can get, Jack."

"Alright. We have a deal. I'll have to explain it to the men. It may take some convincing."

"I think your railroad boys will be more than happy to get out of here, but your hired guns might be unhappy."

"You're right about that."

"Before you go, Jack, I do have one question. I figured out how you got the train here, which was brilliant, by the way. The only mystery still hanging over my head is how you moved those rails out of the Park City warehouse."

Jack smiled then replied, "I'm impressed that it's your only question. I know a lot of my fellow engineers who wouldn't have been able to figure it out. But the rails were easy. One of my boys worked at the warehouse and faked an order for the rails, equipment and other materials, loaded them on the warehouse's maintenance train and brought them here in one night."

Nelson asked, "Can I assume that you'll still try something else to make the Union Pacific pay for the way you were blamed for that bridge collapse?"

"Of course. Can I assume that you'll be trying to stop me?"

"It's my job. Well, time's wasting, Jack. Go ahead and tell your men. I'm going to lower my Winchester, but I can still get off the shot before your boys can pull their pistols."

"I'll make sure they understand that. I'll be seeing you around, Nelson."

"Just don't do anything that makes me have to shoot you, Jack."

Jack replied, "I can't make that promise, Nelson," then turned and walked back the campfire and his curious gang.

After hearing Nelson's loud shout, the passengers in both cars rushed to the windows to see what was happening. They expected to hear gunfire, but when they saw the gang leader talking to the man with the rifle, they were disappointed and thought he was trying to take his cut.

But in the women's car, Cassie knew different.

"That's Nelson Cook!" she exclaimed as she watched.

"Who's he? Do you know him?" asked Florence.

"I know of him and even met him once. My husband used to talk about him even when we lived in Omaha. He's a special agent for Union Pacific and handles any crimes committed by railroad employees or occurring on railroad property. He's almost a legend and I'm sure that he's not out there asking for a bribe."

Louise was staring at the meeting as she asked, "Why are they talking?"

"I don't know what they're saying, but I think we don't have to worry about the army. I'll bet that we'll be free soon. I just don't know how he'll be able to convince them to leave."

"Even if he does, we won't have any of our things," said Mary.

"It doesn't matter; does it? We'll be out of this hell car and we still have our luggage in the baggage car."

Louise muttered, "They probably stole that, too."

Cassie didn't care as long as they no longer needed to fear being killed. Nelson Cook had arrived.

―――――

While a few of the men grumbled, Jack noticed that most of them were relieved that it was already over, and they wouldn't have to depend on the Union Pacific to pay the ransom. The only two who were noticeably angry were Harry Ent and Boomer Wilson. But with Big Bob standing at his side, Jack wasn't concerned. He took Bob with him when he walked to the express car to retrieve the eleven thousand dollars.

Nelson was still watching the men around the campfire closely. He knew that Jack and the railroad men would honor the agreement. After identifying the two outlaws by their scowls, he focused on them. He already decided that if either or both of them drew their pistols, he'd shoot them rather than the dynamite.

When Jack returned with the bundles of cash, Nelson noticed a measurable change in the men's faces, including the two gunmen. Jack was so organized, that as he paid off two men, they'd leave to saddle their horses, but he wouldn't distribute any more of the cash until they'd ridden away. It added time, but it was a smart thing to do. Nelson's only problem was that he wasn't sure what belonged to the passengers and what the gang had brought with them.

That soon proved not to be a problem when some of the men who were waiting to be given their share of the loot began separating packs, bundles and other gear. He wouldn't know if some of the jewelry and cash wasn't already in their saddlebags but suspected that Jack would have kept all of the loot in one spot and only distribute it when they were ready to blow up the train.

When the gang began riding off in pairs, the passengers in both cars realized that somehow, the man with the repeater had convinced them to leave. The frustration, fear and despair that had filled both cars just minutes earlier vanished and was replaced with hope and joy.

The last two to leave before Jack and the big man also saddled two pack horses and loaded them with less than half of the remaining stock. After they'd ridden off, Jack turned and waved at Nelson before walking to their horses.

Nelson hadn't bothered waving back but stayed where he was just in case. He waited until Jack and his giant companion rode out of the campsite before stepping into the clearing. Now he had to act fast.

He kept his eyes on the tracks that they had followed when they departed as he trotted to the first passenger car. He slid his knife from its sheath when he spotted the heavy ropes that kept the door from being opened.

He hadn't seen anyone coming back when he reached the car, so he released his Winchester's hammer before he climbed onto the steel platform. When he began cutting the ropes rather than trying to untie the knots, he saw men's faces appear at the door's window. He wasn't concerned with what they were thinking as he parted the rope. When he pulled it away and threw it aside, the door was yanked open.

"*Who are you?*" one of the men exclaimed.

"My name is Nelson Cook and I'm a special agent for the Union Pacific. I don't have any time to waste in case they return. I want you all to exit in an orderly fashion from the car and those of you who had guns, go to that stack of things they left behind and find yours."

He heard a cacophony of questions behind him as he turned and bounced down the steps then spun to his left and began jogging to the second car. He checked for any incoming riders but didn't see any before he clambered onto the second passenger car's platform.

As he started slicing through the thick rope, he noticed that there were no male faces at the window. They were only women staring at him from the other side of the glass.

Nelson soon ripped the severed rope from the door and when the women pulled the door open, he said, "Please exit the car in good order."

He bounded back to the ground and slid his knife home as he checked for returning shooters again. Finding the path still clear, he headed for the pile that had been left behind where men were already scrounging for their gunbelts. He quickly counted eleven horses then checked to see how many saddles were available. There were eight riding saddles and two pack saddles, which were more than he'd expected to find.

The men were ripping gunbelts from the pile, but there weren't any Winchesters, which wasn't a surprise.

He saw some women and children off to the side watching and assumed that they were related. When he turned back to look at the other women exiting the second car, he didn't see any men, but there were two children. He then realized that when he'd opened the second car, none of the women had even asked his name. It was odd, but unimportant.

He approached the large huddle of men and shouted, "When you're finished finding your things, I need you to saddle all the horses. We need to get out of here quickly in case they return."

Most of them had turned when he started to yell, and they universally nodded. Four of them immediately separated from the crowd and headed for the horses.

The women began arriving, so he said, "When you can get a chance, find anything that you can take with you on horseback. Don't worry about anything in the baggage car. That will be returned to you in Ogden, but it'll probably take two or three days."

One of the women smiled and said, "Thank you, Mister Cook. When you get a chance, can you tell us how you convinced them to leave?"

He returned her smile as he replied, "Yes, ma'am. I'll give you a one-word clue, though. Dynamite."

Cassie laughed then watched him turn and walk toward the locomotive.

Nelson had been surprised that any of them could smile, but even more amazed that the woman seemed to know his name. He assumed she'd heard his first shout to get Jack's attention but was still impressed that she'd remembered it considering how much stress she'd been under.

He'd handle getting things in order later, but right now, he wanted to get the dynamite under his control. While he didn't believe that Jack would change his mind, one of those outlaws might come through the trees as he did and put a bullet into the crate. After all, he'd given them the idea.

Nelson reached the small log shelter and after leaning his Winchester on the log wall, removed the box of fuses and the heavier one with the blasting caps. Both were marked with the same DANGER marking, but they didn't seem as sinister as the warning printed on the big crate.

He then slid the dynamite from its protective home and carried it to the trees as quickly as he could manage. Once he was among the pines, he found a niche between two trees and set it on the pine needle covered ground. He didn't bother trying to hide it under branches because he only wanted it away from where one of the gang members would expect to find it. He trotted back to the small construction and picked up both of the smaller boxes and headed back to the trees. Once he set them on top of the crate of dynamite, he returned to pick up his Winchester.

After grabbing his repeater, he strode back to where the passengers were still sorting through their property. He noticed that more men were saddling horses and hoped that none of them decided to mount and ride away before he had a chance to explain why that would be a bad idea.

Most of them were smiling by the time he reached them. Each of the women had recovered her handbag and were rummaging through them to verify that everything was still there. When each of the women's jewelry had been taken, the thieves had just tossed them into her handbag because it was easy.

When he stopped, most of the passengers turned to look at him, obviously waiting for instructions. Even the men who were busy saddling horses were paying attention.

Nelson obliged when he loudly said, "As I've already told some of you, my name is Nelson Cook and I'm a special agent for the Union Pacific. To answer your next question, I was only sent here to locate the stolen train. When I saw the crate of dynamite, I changed my mission. I threatened to blow it up while they were all around their campfire if they didn't leave. I knew the man who planned and executed the theft because he used to be a Union Pacific engineer. One of the men who designs and builds bridges and other necessary structures.

"I offered him the money from the express car's safe as an added incentive. He accepted the deal and you all saw them leave. That being said, I'm not going to risk any of your lives by following the same path that they used. After the horses are all saddled, we'll load what you need to take with you, then we'll head into the trees. I have to retrieve my horses. But I'll need someone to carry my Winchester and two others to carry the box of fuses and blasting caps. I'll carry the crate of dynamite.

"I told their leader that the U.S. Marshals might be showing up soon, but we both knew that it wasn't likely. But it did give them a good reason to clear out of here as quickly as possible. So, when you have the horses saddled, choose who will ride and who will be the riding partners. I'll have you all in Castle Rock within two hours, then I'll treat you all to a good meal when we arrive. Okay?"

There was a mix of 'okay' and 'alright' replies accompanied with big smiles as there was now an end to their ordeal in sight.

Nelson smiled as he watched them hurriedly return to finding their property.

He then noticed the woman who had remembered his name step away from the others. She was a handsome young woman and he thought that he might have seen her before, but only briefly and not recently.

She stopped in front of him and said, "I'll carry your Winchester, Mister Cook."

"Thank you, ma'am. Excuse me for sounding as if I'm trying to be familiar, but have we ever met? I can't recall having been introduced, but I believe I've seen you before, but it was a while ago."

"You remember me? My husband was a structural engineer and I think you saw me at a Union Pacific get together in Omaha. It must have been four years ago by now."

"That must be it. But we weren't introduced; were we? If we were, then I apologize for my poor memory."

Cassie smiled then replied, "My name is Cassie. But no, we weren't introduced. You didn't stay very long. I had the impression that you hated even being there."

Nelson grinned as he said, "I try to avoid any social gatherings. I was ordered to show up for that one because the bosses wanted to pat me on the back and tell their pals that they were the one who had hired me. Is your husband with the men saddling horses?"

"No. My husband died on the 4th of July in Cheyenne."

"You're Ned Gray's widow? I read about that accident. That must have been horrible for you."

Cassie almost slipped into her grieving widow mode, but quickly stopped herself. She had been trying to divest herself of all of the masks she'd worn since Ned had started courting her and wanted to watch how Nelson Cook reacted to the real Cassie.

"It was shocking to watch, and I was sad for Ned because he was such a good man. But I couldn't deny the relief I felt for being his widow. We weren't a good match."

Nelson's eyebrows peaked as he said, "That's a surprisingly honest thing to say. I've known folks who hated their relatives so much that they would probably have put a .44 into them if they thought they could get away with it. Those same good people wailed, wept and spoke eloquently of the deceased as if he was whisked into heaven on the wings of angels because he was without sin."

Cassie laughed then said, "I've met people like that as well. I know you left Omaha years ago. Where do you live now?"

"I'm stationed in Ogden. I've been there for a couple of years now and I'll probably remain there for a while. It's the hub for a wide area of the U.P.'s operations, so there's always enough work to keep me busy."

"I would have thought that you'd be back in Omaha by now running the whole security office."

"I have no intention of sitting behind a desk. I'd die of boredom."

Nelson looked past Cassie and noticed that folks were pairing off near the saddled horses, so he just watched. Three other women soon headed their way and Cassie waved them over, almost to give them permission as if they might be interrupting.

When they reached Nelson and Cassie, she said, "Nelson, these are my three new friends. Mary Ellison is also a widow, but she's on her way to Silver City to change that. Louise Smith is a nurse from Laramie who was on the way to visit her brother's family in Echo. Florence Porter is a teacher who just graduated from college and is on her way to Salt Lake City."

Nelson smiled and said, "It's a pleasure to meet each of you ladies, I wish it was under more pleasant circumstances," then shook each of the women's hands.

Florence laughed then said, "You have no idea how pleasant these circumstances are compared to what they were just a few hours ago."

"I'm sure that you're all relieved."

Nelson kept glancing at the tracks and the other folks as they readied to leave.

"Have each of you found someone to share a horse before we go? I want to be out of here as soon as possible."

"We have," Mary replied, "that's why we were able to come over to meet you."

"Mary, could you return and ask two men to volunteer to carry a box of fuses and another of blasting caps? They'll only need to walk for about two hundred yards."

"I'll send them over," she said then turned and waited for Louise and Florence to join her before all three of the women walked away.

After they'd gone, Nelson asked, "So, Mary is on her way to Silver City, Louise is going to Echo to meet her brother, and Florence will be the newest schoolmarm in Salt Lake City. What was your destination, Cassie?"

"I was on my way to San Francisco to stay with my sister until I decided what to do. Maybe I'll stay in Ogden instead."

Nelson looked at Cassie and for some reason, wasn't surprised by her answer. He was also pleased that she might be staying in town. She was an honest and bold person yet was still a very attractive woman. It was a delicate balance for women to be confident in manner without being pegged as a shrew.

"Won't your sister be disappointed?" he asked.

"She might be, but her husband wouldn't be upset at all. He's not fond of me because I'm not like my sister. She's a sweet and kind woman and I'm at the other end of the spectrum."

Before Nelson could comment, two men approached.

"I'm Ted Pike and this is Mike Gordon. Mrs. Ellison said you needed a couple of volunteers to carry some explosives, so Mike and I are more than happy to do it."

Nelson shook their hands and said, "I appreciate it. Let's get everybody moving."

Cassie said, "I'll take your Winchester now, Nelson."

He smiled, then handed her his rifle before they walked to the passengers who were now scattered among the horses. Nelson figured some of the animals would be carrying three or even four passengers, but they'd figured out how to make it work.

With the children and women, it was just a question of balancing out the weight. Luckily, they wouldn't have far to ride.

When they were close, Nelson shouted, "We'll be moving into the trees and following the path I used to get here. Go ahead and mount the horses."

As they began stepping into the stirrups on the horses that had saddles while others rode bareback, he and Cassie turned and headed toward the trees while Ted and Mike followed. Nelson wanted to get the dangerous crates moving before the first riding passengers reached the pines.

Five minutes later, he was lugging the heavy case of dynamite while Mike Gordon carried the box of blasting caps and Ted Pike carried the lightest and least dangerous container of fuse.

Cassie walked beside Nelson carrying his Winchester while Mike and Ted followed leading the long line of passenger-packed horses.

It wasn't long before they entered his small clearing and found Rowdy and Gomer staring at the strange parade their human had brought with him.

He turned and loudly said, "Ted, give your box to Mike, then tell the folks to stay on their horses. I'll need to saddle my horses, then load the dynamite on top of the pack saddle."

"Okay," Ted replied, then after setting his small crate of cord onto Mike's box, headed for the other passengers.

Mike and Cassie followed Nelson to his tarp-covered saddles and packs, then after setting the crates down, Mike said, "I'll saddle your horse for you while you set up your packhorse."

"I appreciate your help. Let me get my horses."

Nelson strode quickly toward his tethered horses and wasn't surprised when he found Cassie matching him stride for stride. He didn't say anything but was pleased that she decided to join him.

After untying their leash, he turned and headed back to his campsite and still hadn't said a word to Cassie. She hadn't uttered a sound either.

When they reached Mike, Nelson removed Rowdy's halter and said, "This is Rowdy, he's my primary ride, but be careful. He can be a bit ornery to anyone other than me."

Mike grinned as he picked up a saddle blanket and said, "I get along with horses, but I'll watch for those hooves and teeth."

Nelson nodded then removed Gomer's halter and picked up his second saddle blanket.

Rowdy didn't protest at all and was soon ready to ride, so Mike waved and headed to the line of horses to join his wife on their own horse.

After he'd gone, Nelson said, "Cassie, you can put my Winchester in Rowdy's scabbard now."

"Okay."

While she slid the repeater home, Nelson continued loading his packs of supplies onto Gomer. He planned to cover his normal supplies with one tarp, then load the dynamite and its friends on top before covering them with a second. The second tarp wasn't to protect the crates, but to keep them in place.

Jessie began helping him by handing him packs and his Sharps. She didn't comment until she reached the odd, box-shaped leather pouch.

She didn't open the flap but asked, "What's in here?"

"My crossbow. I made it from a magazine article as an experiment and found it to be an effective weapon. I've never used it against anyone, but initially thought I might have to use it to improve the odds when I found the train."

After giving it to him, Cassie asked, "Have you ever killed anyone?"

"Three. Two were Union Pacific workers who panicked when they knew I was investigating their black-market operation. They figured that their best chance of avoiding prison was to shoot me the first night I was there and snuck into my hotel room after midnight. They fired at my empty bed and I returned fire before they realized I was sitting in a chair in the corner."

95

"What was the other one?" she asked as he threw his first tarp over the packs.

He began tying down the tarp as he replied, "His name was Ralph Woodley. He would board a train, strike up a conversation with a woman passenger who was traveling alone and offer to escort her to her destination. He was a well-spoken, clean-cut man who could charm the wicked witch. After the woman agreed, he'd stay with her and win her confidence. At the next stop, he'd offer to buy her a meal and she'd willingly go with him. Neither of them would board the train again and if the woman's body was found, by the time it was identified, it would be too late to find him.

"I didn't have much information because he didn't use the same route very often. So, I spent a lot of time on the rails. I'd walk through the passenger cars looking for a handsome, well-dressed man chatting with a woman. Most married couples don't talk much when they're traveling, so it was all I had to go on.

"I was on the Pocatello – Shoshone run when it was slowing down for Omani. I'd noticed a man who matched my perception of the man just after leaving Pocatello, but he was alone. I had another possible suspect in the other car, so I spent an hour watching him, but he fell asleep. When I returned to the second car, the man had moved and was sitting beside a young woman. I was sure that I'd found my man but wanted to be sure."

Nelson hefted the crate of dynamite to Gomer's pack saddle and after it was steady, he added the two smaller boxes. He picked up his second tarp before he continued.

"I followed them when they left the passenger car, and they paid no attention to me at all. But they didn't go into the diner as I had expected. I thought I'd made a mistake when the man guided her into an alley, and I realized that he had a pistol pressed against her side. I pulled my Remington, cocked the hammer and as soon as I entered the alley, I aimed at the man who was already making his intentions clear and fired."

He was tying down the second tarp as Cassie asked, "Did it bother you at all?"

"Only that I'd let him get as far as he did. I should have shown him my badge while he was still in the car and kept them from leaving. The lady was terrified after having a man die at her feet, even if he deserved it. She probably had nightmares for a long time."

With Gomer tied to Rowdy, Nelson stepped into the saddle then pulled his left boot out of the stirrup. Without even asking, he reached down and waited for Cassie to take his hand.

There had been no need for a question as she grasped his hand, set her foot into the empty stirrup, then swung her leg over Rowdy's rump and settled in behind him.

Once he was sure that Cassie was in place, he turned to the waiting line of passengers and said, "Let's head to Castle Rock and a late breakfast."

As he nudged Rowdy into a walk, he heard a loud cheer erupt from behind him and felt Cassie's hands on his hips.

———

After they'd received their bounty and ridden away from the train, some of the men followed Jack as he cut cross-country for Park City. Some of the railroaders continued toward Echo but Harry Ent and Boomer Wilson didn't join either group.

Jack had been surprised that he'd retained that many of them but wasn't as disappointed as he'd expected to be when his plan had failed. In fact, the unexpected arrival of Nelson Cook had added a new element to his next scheme. He now had a worthy opponent and was determined to meet the challenge. He just wasn't going to be so logical the next time. Nor was he about to be so humane.

When Jack left the road and the others continued toward Echo, Harry and Boomer slowed until Jack's larger group had melted into the trees.

Harry turned to Boomer and asked, "What do you want to do now? I think we shoulda taken our chances and let a few bullets fly. He wasn't gonna shoot that dynamite. Even if he did, he'd have to hit it and maybe it still wouldn't go off."

Boomer replied, "I ain't so sure, Harry. Jack seemed to believe him, and I wasn't about to find out how big that bang woulda been."

"You didn't answer about what you wanted to do now. We got a lot of cash, but I reckon we might get more if we headed back to that train and checked them mail bags."

"We gotta wait if we do. That railroad agent is gonna be there gettin' the passengers moved and the ones that had pistols will all have 'em back, too."

"I know that. Why don't we head into those trees and wait for 'em to leave? Once they're outta sight, we can go back there and see what we can find."

"Okay. We can wait in the trees about a hundred yards from our tracks."

Harry grinned, then wheeled his horse around to head back down the road toward Castle Rock. He figured that they'd leave the road and enter the trees long before those folks were able to start moving.

———

But the folks had already been moving and were now eight hundred yards past Nelson's small camp.

Nelson followed his own trail as he led the long parade through the trees. He had entered the forest far enough from

99

where any disgruntled outlaws may be waiting, so he wasn't concerned that they'd be spotted when they left the protection of the trees.

He was already thinking about how to get the passengers fed and on the next train to Ogden when the honest and blunt Cassie reminded him that she was there.

She asked, "Are you living alone in Ogden, Nelson?"

"Yes, ma'am. I have a small house on Saint Street."

"Have you ever been married?"

"I was for a while. My wife was a refined young lady who had the mistaken belief that she could smooth out my rough edges."

"You said 'was'. Are you a widower?"

"No, ma'am. After a year of trying, she gave up and just ran off. When she hadn't returned after a year, I filed for divorce and it was granted. I guess it was more my fault in the first place. I was set in my ways and what she had considered a challenge became a frustrating failure."

"That sounds like my marriage, but in a different way. Did you ever meet my husband?"

"I did, but I didn't know him nearly as well as most of the other engineers. I got along with most of them, but your husband was one of the ones who seemed to avoid the company of the regular workers."

"You were hardly a regular worker, Nelson. He actually talked about you fairly often and there were times that I believed that he wished he could be more like you. He knew he'd never change but was still in awe of some of your exploits."

"I just did my job, Cassie. I'm going to need help getting the folks fed and on the next train. Will you be able to organize things for me?"

"I'd love to. I never had the chance to be in charge of anything other than the kitchen until the train was stolen."

"You have the character to lead, Cassie. When we reach town, I'll need to send a telegram right away. Can you take everyone to one of the two diners in Castle Rock? Tell the waitresses that the Union Pacific will pay their bill. It may take an hour to get everyone fed while I arrange for them to board the next train and have someone in Ogden prepare for their arrival. If anyone wants to take a bath, arrange for rooms at the hotel."

"Alright. Are you taking the train with everyone else?"

"No. I need to get back to the stolen train and keep it protected in case any of the thieves return. The word will get out soon enough and other looters will try to find it before the U.P. can send a crew out to modify the tracks again and move the train back onto the main line. I'll want you to go with the other passengers to keep them together. I'll wire the station manager in Ogden and you can tell him everything. Okay?"

Cassie had been ready to tell him that she'd stay with him, but he had preemptively crushed that idea.

"I'll take care of it. How long will it be before you reach Ogden?"

"If none of them return and if the work crew gets there quickly, I should be back in two days. There's a track maintenance crew in Ogden, so that will make it easier."

"I imagine that the bosses in Omaha will be thrilled to hear that they're getting their train back and none of the passengers were harmed."

"We'll see. I did pay the gang eleven thousand dollars to leave. I hope they don't threaten to take it out of my pay."

"They wouldn't dare; would they?"

"Maybe. It all depends on what they were planning to do when they received the ransom telegram and then the one that I'll send when we arrive at Castle Rock."

Cassie found it hard to believe that the company bosses would be anything but ecstatic when they received his telegram. They stood to lose much more than an entire train if Nelson hadn't made the deal. They would have killed more than thirty men, women and children who had paid the railroad to transport them safely to their destinations. She ran the math in her head and came up with a little more than three hundred dollars for each passenger. Cassie thought it was a small price to pay for their freedom and that didn't include the train itself.

Nelson made the turn toward the tracks and soon left the shadows of the pines and entered the bright morning sun.

After walking Rowdy across the tracks, he turned right onto the road and leaned to his right to check on the passengers. He was counting on Mike and Ted who had taken the trail position to make sure that they were all still there. Once he was sure he wasn't leading them into a collision with an oncoming locomotive, he sat straight and continued along the road.

"How close is Castle Rock?" Cassie asked.

"Less than an hour away. You'll see the depot soon and when we get there, I'm going to let you down and wait until the folks start showing up to tell them that I've given you instructions and that you're in charge."

"Some of the men won't like that."

Nelson turned, smiled and said, "I think you can convince them to accept your position."

Cassie grinned then replied, "You have more confidence in me than I do."

"I doubt it. You're just trying to act as if you aren't enjoying the idea of being the boss."

Cassie laughed then just shrugged. She was deeply appreciative of his confidence and was almost stunned that he understood that she was already pleased with her chance to be in charge.

———

Eight miles south of where the passengers had crossed the tracks, Boomer and Harry had entered the trees well south of their temporary tracks to avoid being seen. Once they were hidden, they rode parallel to the rails, just as Nelson had done when he'd been about to execute his daring plan to rescue the passengers and save the railroad's rolling stock.

They wouldn't stop riding for another ninety minutes as they wound their horses around the pine trunks and other obstacles. They figured that if that railroad agent had decided to send the passengers back to Castle Rock on their own, they'd know soon after the next westbound train passed. If it had full passenger cars, the agent would either be on the train or was sitting on one of those flatbed cars on their hidden train. This time, they planned to be the ones to surprise him with their Winchesters. He'd never know how he died.

———

By the time that they spotted the Castle Rock depot in the distance, Nelson had his complex telegram already composed. He'd notify Mister Burns that he'd found the train and because of fortuitous circumstances, was able to take control of the

104

situation. All of the passengers were now safe and would be on their way to Ogden shortly. The gang who had stolen the train had run off and he'd have the work crew from Ogden rebuild the temporary switch to get the train back on the tracks. He wouldn't go into much more detail, including the loss of the eleven thousand dollars, until he returned to Ogden with the stolen train.

Once he did make it back, he'd send a much longer telegram. He still had no idea what their response would be about what he'd done but it really didn't matter. He knew that his actions had probably saved thirty-four lives and that was worth whatever happened, even if someone did make him pay back the missing money. He was also sure that they'd ask him to return immediately to Omaha to answer their questions.

But he knew that the stolen train episode wasn't Jack Rodgers' last scheme. He'd made it clear that he already had other plans growing in his marvelous mind. He'd warn his boss about them but was determined to thwart each of them before they happened. Just a flyer to each Union Pacific office and depot would help. Yet Nelson didn't believe that Jack could be stopped so easily. He would anticipate the company's increased vigilance and had the patience to wait until their guard was down.

The other aspect of their brief talk that was more important to Nelson personally was Jack's refusal to promise not to kill anyone when he put his next devious plan into operation. If that happened, Nelson would have to stop Jack with a slug of lead because no amount of bargaining or threats would suffice.

Cassie was still clutching onto Nelson's jacket as they neared Castle Rock. She could almost hear him thinking and hadn't spoken for ten minutes. She already decided that when she reached Ogden, she'd stay and when he returned, they'd talk much more.

———

Before they reached the depot, Nelson grinned when he spotted Will Hitchens and Jim Kennedy standing on the platform waving. He knew that they'd missed at least two trains since they'd been in town but would have been more surprised if they'd taken either one. He suspected it wasn't just out of curiosity that they'd remained in town. He also wondered if he'd had a reply to his last telegram to William Burns.

Just before he lowered Cassie to the ground, he turned and asked, "Are you ready to exercise your authority, ma'am?"

"I'm more than ready, sir," she replied with a smile.

Before he helped her down, he looked at Will and Jim as they grinned from the edge of the platform and loudly said, "Come on down and I'll tell you both what happened before the folks get here."

As they bounced to the ground, Nelson took Cassie's left hand and waited as she slid from Rowdy. He dismounted and tied Rowdy's reins to the station's hitchrail then stood beside Cassie waiting for the other passengers to start dismounting or sliding off their horses.

Will and Jim were on his right side and Will quickly exclaimed, "We knew you'd do it, Nelson! Did you shoot all of those bastards who took my train?"

"I didn't even have to fire a shot, Will. Your train is still intact and waiting for you. The men who managed to steal it are long gone, but I need to get back there soon in case any of them change their minds or some looters show up. We have to have a work crew get there from Ogden to get it back onto the main tracks, too. I'll need you to return to Ogden with the passengers. When the work crew departs, you need to be with them to drive your train when the temporary switch is replaced."

"How'd you get 'em to leave?" asked Jim.

"They left a full case of dynamite in a spot where I could hit it with my Winchester and set it off. When they were all together around a campfire, I told them that if they didn't leave, I'd take the shot and they'd all die."

"And they just said 'okay' and left?" asked a disbelieving Will Hitchens.

"I negotiated with Jack Rodgers for the money in the express car's safe and he took the deal. He knew that I could have shot most of them before they got away from the campfire anyway. The fact that I hadn't was enough of a convincer. Now I've got to talk to the folks for a minute before I send a telegram. Mrs. Gray will be in charge because I told her what to do and she's a natural leader anyway. If you want to help her, I'm sure she'd appreciate it."

Will replied, "We can do that, but are you gonna stick around long enough to tell us the rest of what happened?"

"I can't, Will. I'll send my telegrams then be on my way. You don't want your train damaged if some of them go back while I'm gone; do you?"

"I reckon not. We owe you for the britches and the ten-spot, too."

Nelson waved the idea away as the dismounted passengers crowded around to hear what would happen now.

Nelson smiled at them and loudly said, "This is Will Hitchens, the engineer of the stolen train, in case you don't recognize him. The fireman, Jim Kennedy, is standing beside him. I've told Mrs. Gray what to do, beginning with getting everyone fed. Mister Hitchens and Mister Kennedy will help her, but she's in charge. After you've eaten, if you want to clean up or even take a bath, she'll arrange for some hotel rooms. The next westbound train with passenger cars isn't due for another three and a half hours, so you don't need to rush. I don't have time to go into any more details."

He then reached into his jacket, slid his wallet from the inner pocket and pulled out sixty dollars and handed the cash to Cassie.

"That should be enough for to feed them and rent some rooms for a couple of hours. The hotel probably won't even charge them to use their bathrooms."

She accepted the bills and slid them into her dress pocket before she looked at her fellow passengers.

"Nelson told me that there are two diners in town, so let's split into two groups. One will go with Mister Hitchens and the second with Mister Kennedy. Leave your horses saddled but take them to the corral so they can be boarded on the train."

Nelson smiled at the forcefulness of her instructions and knew that not one man would object. With the passengers now in her capable hands, he hopped onto the platform and headed for the small Western Union office that was located in the depot building.

Once inside, he didn't have to wait long to learn if he'd received a reply from Omaha.

As he slid a blank sheet from the stack, the operator said, "Mister Cook? I have two messages for you. They're both from a Mister Burns in Omaha."

He held off writing his message in case he had to modify it after reading his boss' two telegrams.

The top one was the earlier reply. He read:

NELSON COOK CASTLE ROCK WYOMING

EXECS UNABLE TO MEET DEMANDS
WILL DECIDE RESPONSE
DO NOT ENGAGE

WILLIAM BURNS UPRR OMAHA NEB

It wasn't a surprise, so he read the second one that had been sent three hours after the first.

NELSON COOK CASTLE ROCK WYOMING

WILL NOTIFY ARMY TO RECOVER TRAIN
REMAIN IN CASTLE ROCK
DIRECT THEM TO LOCATION
LEAVE ANY ACTION TO ARMY

WILLIAM BURNS UPRR OMAHA NEB

"I guess he'll have to send another message to the army now," Nelson said as he folded both telegrams and stuffed them into his jacket pocket.

Neither reply required a single word of his telegram to be altered, so he quickly wrote it down as he'd composed it.

He handed the long message to the operator who wasn't surprised to read what Nelson had written. At least not most of it. He'd seen the passengers arriving and was just curious about the train itself.

He turned then sat behind his key and began transmitting the long telegram.

As the telegrapher tapped away, Nelson took another sheet to write the message to Homer Watson, the station manager who'd interrupted his morning just two days ago…or was it three?

This was an even longer message because he needed to tell Homer about the passengers' arrival, the need to assemble the work crew, what they'd need to bring with them. He also had to have him to talk to Cassie, who had had more details than anyone else.

When he finished writing, the telegrapher was waiting and handed him his first sheet before accepting the second. It didn't contain anything new or exciting, so he quickly returned to his seat and went to work.

Nelson was hungry and briefly thought about joining Cassie for lunch, but he was anxious to return to the train and he had to get the dynamite, blasting caps and fuse off of Gomer.

He waited until the second telegram was on its way to Ogden, then after taking the message from the operator, he quickly left the telegraph office to go to the larger office of the station manager.

When he entered the bigger, but far from prestigious office, he found Al Templeton sitting behind his desk wearing a big smile.

"I was wondering when you'd stop by to tell me what happened, Nelson. I see you got all the passengers out of there, but what about the train?"

"It was untouched when I left, but I'm going to need you to arrange for passage of all of them to Ogden, unless any want to get off earlier. Most of their things are still on the train, but I need to get back there before anyone else does. I also need to unload a full case of dynamite, a box of blasting caps and one with fuses. Can you arrange to have them brought to Ogden as well? You know the rules for transporting explosives."

"You have a whole case of dynamite? Is that what those boys were gonna use to blow up the train?"

"Yup. They didn't get the opportunity, and it turned out to be my biggest ally when I threatened to put a .45 into the crate if they didn't leave. Where do you want me to put it?"

"I'll come with you, but I reckon the best place will be my office. I'll have Pete Filmore help me get it onto the next train."

"Is it on time?"

"Yup."

"Okay, let's get it moved, so I can head back to the stolen train."

Al hopped to his feet and followed Nelson outside.

It only took five minutes to move the three wooden boxes into the office. After shaking Al's hand, Nelson hurried back to Rowdy, untied his reins then mounted.

He waved to Al then glanced down the street and was pleased to see that there were no longer any passengers outside. Cassie had quickly taken over his position as their leader. She was the most impressive woman he'd ever met.

He turned Rowdy back toward the nearby rails and would use the same path return to the train. If any of the outlaws had returned, he didn't want to be seen.

———

"How long before that next train?" asked Harry as he stared east.

"I don't know. Jack was the one who had the schedule. It can't be much longer 'cause the one we took showed up around six in the evenin'. Jack said that we had to time it after the train that used the tracks before us was already over where we had to put in the curved rails."

"That's right. So, it could be showin' up any time now; right?"

"Yup. That agent might show up first, though. So, be ready for just a rider, too."

"I was ready, Boomer. If he shows up first, we kill him then we can go to the train; ain't that the plan?"

"Yup. It'll be better if he's already back there with the train 'cause we won't have to worry about somebody seein' us."

"I just want to get back there and see what we can find."

"It's just noon, Harry. I'll tell you what. If we don't see a train or that agent in a couple of hours, we'll make our way through the trees back to the train and see if he's there."

Harry was still staring down the tracks as he replied, "Does it have to be two hours? Can't we make it one hour instead?"

Boomer didn't see the harm and he was growing anxious to see what treasures they could find in the train, too.

"Okay. One hour and then we move."

Harry grinned and began imagining discovering bundles of cash. He and Boomer each had a thousand dollars already because Jack hadn't taken one for himself, which was much different than what any of the other gang leaders they'd known would have done. They had expected Jack to give each of them five hundred and keep the rest for himself.

———

After crossing the rails and entering the trees yet again, Nelson kept a much faster pace than he'd taken when he'd led the passengers out and even when he'd made his first passage. He knew where he was going now and if he found anyone near the train, he was sure that it would only be four men at the most. He suspected that the three outlaws would be the ones most likely to have returned.

He had no idea who they were or how good they were with their weapons, but he wasn't about to give them a clear shot. He may have warned Jack rather than blow up the dynamite and kill them all, but that was different. He didn't place the railroad men in the same category as hardened criminals and noticed the look of relief on many of their faces as Jack explained the deal he'd made. It was then that he marked two of the outlaws who seemed more than just mildly displeased. He'd have no moral qualms about shooting either of them without warning. He didn't know if there was a third outlaw or not, but he might find out soon.

———

Just as Nelson reached his old campsite, Boomer and Harry decided it was close enough to an hour and mounted their horses. Neither pulled his Winchester from its scabbard yet as they began to move at a slow pace to keep the noise down. They didn't talk for the same reason because they wanted to catch that agent by surprise. If he was still there, then he'd be bored and distracted. Before they'd mounted, they had speculated if the railroad agent hadn't really been ransacking the mail already. He could line his pockets and blame them for any missing cash. They found it hard to imagine that anyone could be honest enough to ignore the chance to enrich himself without the risk of being caught.

Nelson kept Rowdy and Gomer moving until he was close to where he'd stored the dynamite then stepped down. He tied off Rowdy's reins, then slipped his Winchester free and walked to the edge of the train's clearing before he stopped. He hadn't seen any movement, so maybe no one had returned after all. It would have been an unwise thing to do because he'd told Jack that the U.S. Marshals might arrive soon, and he'd heard Jack repeat the warning to his men.

He thought about entering the clearing, but decided he'd wait for another twenty minutes or so. He didn't see any horses, but they could be on the other side of the train. He looked at the four large tents and wondered if there was anyone still inside. He'd been surprised that Jack hadn't bothered to even take anything from the tents. He wished that he'd at least collapsed them before he'd led the passengers away from the campsite. He had been focused on the dynamite and hadn't even looked inside any of them.

Not knowing if someone was in the tents or in any of the train's cars, gave him enough reason to stay put. If someone was still around, they'd probably come into view soon.

Nelson returned to his horses, replaced his Winchester, then walked to Gomer to rummage for his lunch. He wasn't sure what he wanted, but when his fingers touched a glass jar, he smiled. He pulled out the small jar of strawberry preserves, then flipped open his saddlebags and fished out two biscuits from their paper sack. They weren't exactly fresh anymore, but he didn't mind. After splitting them with his big knife, he used the same sharp blade to scoop out some preserves and dump them onto the biscuits. He snickered as he carefully licked the knife clean then jabbed it into the ground. It wasn't exactly what the knife had been designed to do, but it still did a fine job.

After making short work of the sticky biscuits, he took his canteen from Rowdy, washed his hands, then took a few swallows before hanging it back on his horse's saddle. He apologized to his knife before pulling it from the ground. He took one step toward Gomer and took out an old towel. After cleaning the steel, he took out his small vial of gun oil and dripped it on both sides of the blade before using the towel to spread it over the entire knife. Only then did he return it to its sheath. After putting everything away, he pulled out his repeater again then headed back toward the clearing.

He wasn't sure how long he'd taken to enjoy his delightful meal, but still hesitated before entering the clearing. He still didn't see any signs of another human, but rather than go into the clearing near the locomotive, he decided he'd stay in the forest and head toward the caboose. If he still hadn't seen anyone, he'd cross their tracks until he had a good view of the other side of the train. Once he was sure that there wasn't anyone around, he'd leave the protection of the trees and head for the train to inspect it for damage. He might have to return to

Castle Rock to send another telegram for repair parts if Jack had made the locomotive unusable.

As he walked through the trees on the right side of the train, Harry and Boomer rode their horses alongside the other side of the tracks.

They could see caboose's red paint through the trees and before they reached the clearing, they dismounted, tied off their horses and wordlessly pulled their Winchesters.

Nelson had stopped just short of the tracks when he thought he'd heard hoofbeats. But after he came to a halt, he listened but didn't hear the sound again. He wasn't sure what he'd heard but cocked his Winchester's hammer before he began moving, but more slowly and quietly.

After they reached the clearing, both Boomer and Harry cocked their repeaters then left the trees and scanned the clearing for the agent. After seeing no sign of the man or his horse, they relaxed but didn't release their Winchesters' hammers.

"It looks like we got the whole train to ourselves, Boomer," Harry said with a grin.

"Let's check out that express car."

As they began trotting toward the express car, Harry said, "You know, Boomer, we all believed Jack when he said he only found eleven thousand in that safe. What if he found a lot more and that's why he didn't take any for himself?"

Boomer stopped and looked at Harry who had to back up a step.

"I never even thought of that! You're probably right! That bastard musta found twice as much in there."

"What if he was in cahoots with that agent all along? They seemed to know each other pretty good. None of us knew him and he coulda been Jack's old pal. What if the railroad paid off? They coulda grabbed that hundred thousand and already be on their way to Mexico!"

The more Harry talked the more convinced Boomer was of Jack's treachery. Suddenly, even a thousand dollars seemed like a pittance.

Boomer snarled, "Let's take a look in that express car then we'll head out and find Jack."

"Okay."

Nelson had been surprised when he'd seen them emerge from the trees and had used their inattention to get into a good firing position behind them. When they began walking to the express car, he left his protection and walked behind them, leaving just a hundred-foot gap. He'd been listening to their loud conversation and almost continued following them when they'd suddenly stopped and was sure that one of them would see him in his peripheral vision. But even after their round of accusations of Jack's trickery, neither had noticed Nelson just ninety feet away.

But when they began walking again, Nelson knew he couldn't let them reach the express car. If they'd gone into one of the boxcars or the stock car, he'd let them get inside then close the door and lock them inside. But they could do a lot of mischief with the contents of those mail bags and he couldn't let that happen.

His earlier decision to just shoot them if they returned was set aside and replaced with a new one that would make good use of what he'd just heard. He raised his Winchester and set its sights on the smaller man, Harry Ent.

Nelson then shouted, "Drop your rifles!"

Despite being startled, neither man released his grip on his repeater as they both whipped around to see who had shouted.

As soon as he made eye contact, Nelson said, "I said drop your Winchesters! What the hell are you two idiots here for? Did you shoot Jack? He was the only one who was supposed to be showing up."

His theory confirmed, Harry stared down the Winchester's muzzle and snarled, "We didn't kill him. We all split up and me and Boomer came back. You was in it with him; weren't ya?"

Nelson created a pregnant pause as he appeared to be debating about admitting to his involvement.

He finally asked, "Jack kept riding away?"

Harry was relieved to know he wasn't dealing with an honest lawman as he replied, "Yup. He had all those other morons convinced you was honest and gonna blow us up, but not me and Boomer."

"How much did he give you?" Nelson asked as he kept his Winchester leveled at Harry.

"A thousand each. I thought it was kinda queer that he didn't take any for himself. The railroad paid off; didn't they?"

"No, they didn't pay off and never would. We knew that going in. It wasn't about the ransom or the train. It was a way to get our hands on the big transfer of cash that was bound for Salt Lake City."

Harry glanced at Boomer who was just as confused as he was.

Then Harry said, "Eleven thousand is a lot of money, but why didn't he take any?"

Nelson laughed then answered, "You boys may have figured out some of it, but you missed what was most important. I'm a bit surprised Jack gave you each that much, but he was always a bit soft. The cash transfer was eighty thousand dollars."

Boomer exclaimed, "That ain't so! Big Bob was standin' right there when Jack opened the safe and took out the bundles of money! There was only eleven thousand."

Nelson shook his head then said, "Like I said, he's a lot more generous than I am. I would have left five thousand in the safe."

"*What are you talkin' about?*" snapped Harry.

"At the layover in Granger, most of that cash was moved out of the safe. Jack must have jacked up the amount without telling me. That's a pretty good pun; don't you think? Anyway, after I heroically rescued the passengers and Jack got back here, we were going to split up the big money and disappear. It'd take a while to the U.P. boys to figure out, but by then, we'd be in Mexico living like kings."

Harry asked, "So, it's still on the train?"

"It had better be. If Jack took it when you were sleeping, then I'm going to have to track him down and kill him."

Boomer and Harry looked at each other briefly before Harry said, "I reckon you gotta go check to see if it's still there."

Nelson replied, "I was about to do that when you two monkeys showed up. But before I look, I want those Winchesters on the ground. For some reason, I don't trust either of you."

After a few seconds, Harry lowered his repeater to the ground then Boomer followed suit.

"Now unbuckle your gunbelts and let them drop."

There wasn't any pause before they complied with Nelson's order which left each of them disarmed.

"You ain't gonna shoot us; are you?" asked Harry.

"Nope. I might need your services if that money isn't there. Would you be willing to kill your old boss for say, five thousand apiece?"

Harry snickered and Boomer grinned as they both nodded.

"Alright. Now let's head to the caboose."

"He put the money in the caboose?"

"Under the lower bunk. You boys walk in front. In fact, I'll even let you check to see if the big money is under the mattress."

Harry and Boomer walked quickly past Nelson leaving their repeaters and gunbelts in the dirt.

Once they were away from their guns, Nelson lowered his Winchester but didn't release the hammer. The caboose on this train was one of the models that had been configured with added protection against Indian raids. The two windows were small to prevent any marauding Sioux from squeezing in, and they were heavily barred as well. The door opened out rather than in to make it more difficult for someone outside to open. It was not only safe from attack but would make a perfect rolling jail.

The two wanted outlaws walked quickly toward the caboose and soon clambered up the steel steps. Harry swung open the door then entered with Boomer close behind.

As Harry yanked the lower bunk's thin mattress away, he and Boomer found slats of wood but didn't see any cash.

"That son of a bitch took it all!" he exclaimed as he and Boomer continued staring at the barren space.

Nelson then said, "That's because there isn't any and never was. Jack played it straight with you boys. I apologize for my deception. So, you might as well put that mattress back and get comfortable. This will be your home for another day or so. It's a lot nicer than what you gave to the passengers. Of course, I won't be bringing you any food because you might think of jumping me. You've got that big water cask and a small privy that the conductor and brakeman use. So, enjoy your stay at Hotel Caboose. But if either of you try to leave, I will shoot you. You won't know where I am, so if you want to take the risk, go ahead."

He then took one step backward and closed the door. He suspected that they'd make a bull rush soon, so he leaned his Winchester against the caboose wall, took out his knife and placed the point against the door jamb and shoved it into the wood as far as he could. It was only a temporary lock, but it should keep them inside long enough for him to fashion a more secure version.

He grabbed his Winchester then trotted down the caboose's stairs and walked quickly to where they'd dropped their guns. He buckled their gunbelts then hung them over his left shoulder before grabbing both of their Winchester '73 carbines in his left hand.

Nelson then walked to the express car where he'd leave their weapons and find what he needed to secure the caboose. He'd already figured out who Boomer was. He only knew one outlaw who used that moniker, Boomer Wilson. He wasn't a nice man and had a three-hundred-dollar price on his head. He wasn't sure about Harry's identity because there were several bad ones out there who shared his name. But his small stature made it most likely that he was Harry Ent, who was even worse. Nelson was just surprised that he was working this far west or that Jack would hire such a nasty creature.

After finally releasing his Winchester's hammer and leaving their guns in the express car, he found a nice coil of rope that would suit his needs. If he hadn't sliced through the ropes that they'd used to keep the passengers in their cars, he would have used them just for poetic justice. He tossed the heavy coil out the express car's door then hopped to the ground.

125

He strode back to the caboose and expected to hear grousing and cursing echoing off the walls of the red car but there was only silence. For a moment, he thought they might have disregarded his warning and managed to escape. But when he reached the back of the caboose and saw his knife still rammed into the door jamb, he knew they were inside. They might be plotting to escape, but Nelson knew it wouldn't do them any good.

He left his knife in place as tied one end of the rope around the back handle that served as a brace for the conductor when he leaned over the side of the caboose to signal to the engineer. They had one on each side, but the other one was rarely used. Nelson figured they only put it there to make it look right.

With the rope tightly secured to the handle, he carried the rope over the caboose's platform and slid the other end of the rope through the handle and pulled the rest of the rope through as if he was threading a needle. He did it four more times before he tied it off to the first strand in a triple knot. After he'd pulled his knife free and slid it back into his sheath, he was satisfied that Harry and Boomer weren't going anywhere. They might be able to push the door open a fraction of an inch but that was all. He just wished that the heat wave was still there to make them as miserable as the passengers must have been.

Now that the two outlaws were no longer a problem, he needed to take care of their horses. He followed their footsteps back into the trees and soon found their very nice animals tied to pine branches.

As he released them, he said, "Those two thoughtless bastards who didn't even leave you where you could graze won't be doing any grazing of their own for a while. I'll let you join Rowdy and Gomer and then set you all up in a place where you can relax."

He snickered as he mounted Boomer's horse because Harry's stirrups were too short. He took the other horse's reins then walked them out of the trees to retrieve Rowdy and Gomer. It was only when he was passing the caboose that he remembered that Harry had told him that they'd each been given a thousand dollars.

So, when he reached his horses, he dismounted then checked the contents of Boomer's saddlebags. Sure enough, there was a neatly bundled stack of twenty-dollar bills among his other supplies. He pulled it out and then found another in Harry's saddlebags. He moved them to his own saddlebags. Maybe the bosses won't be so angry with him now that he'd only given away nine thousand dollars.

He added their horses to Gomer's trail rope, then mounted Rowdy and led the three animals out of the trees and headed for the tents. He was curious what Jack had left behind. Before he checked the tents, he honored his promise to the outlaws' horses and found a good grazing area near the same stream that he'd found near his campsite. He stripped the outlaws' horses then Gomer and let them graze before he checked on the tents.

There were blanket-covered cots in each of them and one had a large supply of assorted tins of food and other edibles, including six slabs of bacon and eight baskets of eggs.

"You prepared well, Jack. You just didn't count on an honest special agent; did you?"

He snickered, left the food tent and headed for Rowdy. He'd left him saddled because he had one more job to do that wasn't the least bit hazardous.

Nelson mounted his brown gelding and set him walking alongside the track. He evaluated the construction as he passed and was surprised that they'd used so many crossties. They were just split logs, but it was a one-time use track that wouldn't need to suffer the stress from fast-moving, overburdened coal cars. While they were still further apart than standard, Nelson knew that Jack could have used fewer crossties.

He followed the track and after the train disappeared from view, he began looking for the pulled rails and crossties as well as the two curved rails that had allowed them to move the train off the main line.

He soon found where they'd piled everything and smiled when he noticed that they'd even knocked over a pine near the end of the tracks to mask the entrance. He dismounted and examined the large stack. In addition to rails and their split log crossties, there were a lot of the Union Pacific's tools that they'd used for the job. But it was the curved rails that attracted his attention. There weren't just two of them, but four. Jack had impressed Nelson again because bending one pair to the exact arc had been difficult, but two pairs was almost impossible.

He did notice that some of their crossties weren't split but were cut logs of increasing diameter. When he noticed that each of the logs had a different number of gashes in its bark, he understood what Jack had done. He would have had to bring the level of his tracks to meet those of the Union Pacific's main line. He would have put those marks into each one so the men who would have to hurriedly build the last stage of the homemade switch could just roll them in order and finish it quickly.

But even as he admired Jack's thoroughness, he wondered how many men had been left behind to remove the straight tracks, roll the logs into position, then add more of their stolen rails and then the four curved tracks. It would have taken a half a dozen men to get the job done after the last train had passed. But even if they'd built it right to the edge of the tracks and covered their rails with branches to disguise them from the last passing train, he couldn't imagine four men getting it done in just two or three hours.

He walked around to the back of the pile and found his answer when he saw two odd-looking mechanisms that he'd never seen before. They had short forks about eight feet apart and were attached to a lever. He grabbed the lever and when he pulled it, the forks rose then when they were four inches off the ground, a cam roller shifted the forks forward.

"So, that's how you were able to get those rails moved so quickly. The U.P. might want to use these, Jack. You started out trying to hurt the railroad, but you might have just helped them lay tracks faster."

Nelson left the pile and just as he took hold of his saddle horn, he heard the unmistakable sound of a distant train. It had to be the early afternoon run and would hopefully be carrying all of the kidnapped passengers on board.

He quickly mounted then walked Rowdy toward the tracks and after maneuvering past the fallen pine, he turned his gelding to the east and pulled up fifteen feet from the rails.

Louis Charles had seen the rider leave the forest and initially thought he might be another outlaw with more in the trees behind him, so he set his hand on the throttle and was ready to add speed to get past the rider. He also inspected the tracks ahead after hearing the story from Will Hitchens about how they'd stolen his train. They weren't going to pull that stunt with his train.

"I got a rider!" he shouted.

Will, Jim Kennedy and the regular fireman, Zeke Davis, all squeezed closer to the window, but as an engineer, Will took precedence.

He looked past Louis and yelled, "That's Nelson Cook! You gotta slow down, Lou. Those rails ain't been fixed yet."

As his hand was already on the throttle, Louis pulled it back to slow his train. It wasn't going to scrub too much speed off before they passed Nelson, but he didn't want to apply the air brakes and send the passengers flying again.

Will then leaned out of the window and waved wildly.

Nelson had already removed his hat and began waving it over his head as the train barreled down the rails toward him. There had been at least three trains to pass over the replaced rails over the past twelve hours, so he didn't think that they'd have any problems. It would be a tragic ending for what had been a remarkable recovery. He didn't even think about what effect a train derailing just a few feet away would have on him personally.

He kept his hat in his hand as the locomotive passed and he recognized Will Hitchens' grinning face. There was no point in shouting anything as the loud steam engine thundered past.

After the coal car and two boxcars, the passenger cars arrived, and he waved his hat at the faces in the windows. He hoped to see Cassie but wasn't able to pick her out as the cars flashed by.

When the caboose shot past, he watched the train roll down the tracks toward Echo then turned Rowdy around to return to the tents. He passed around the fallen tree and then realized he may as well move it out of the way so the work crew would be able to find the entrance. He dismounted, tied off his rope to one of the heavy branches and after returning to the saddle, nudged Rowdy into motion. The tree wasn't as difficult to move as he'd expected, but once it was out of the way, he dismounted and untied his rope.

―――――

While he may not have seen her, Cassie had been at the window as it approached the spot where the train had been kidnapped. She hadn't been expecting to see Nelson again, so when he suddenly popped into view just a few feet away, she felt her heart skip a beat. Her head turned to keep him in view as long as possible, but she soon lost sight of him. But seeing him again meant that he was safe and should be back in Ogden tomorrow or the next day.

While he had told her that he wasn't married, she hadn't asked if he had any girlfriends. She wasn't sure of his age but knew that he'd been working as a special agent for the Union Pacific for at least six years, so he was probably nearing thirty. She would turn twenty-six in October but because she was barren, she hadn't suffered the aftereffects of childbirth nor the rapid aging that seemed to be part and parcel of raising children.

After six years of being suffocated with almost constant, fawning attention, just those few days of being the woman she always yearned to be were exhilarating. The danger only added to her calmness and determination and then Nelson had given her the chance to continue to grow. She hoped that he wasn't spoken for and had only one real concern, and it wasn't that she was barren. She worried that after he got to know her better, he'd see her as the bitch she really was. A woman who hadn't even wept when her sweet, generous husband had died. Yet when they did talk again, she wasn't about to hide behind another façade. She'd tell him exactly what she was even if he did have a girlfriend. That short ride they'd shared and the conversation that passed between them had given her hope that he'd accept her as she was. She didn't have to make a vow not to try to change him if he did. She thought that he was perfect just as he was.

———

While Nelson may not have had a girlfriend, Tom Richardson, who was now working in Denver, did. After he'd entered into the all-too-brief affair with Cassie Gray, he'd been caught trying to steal a necklace to impress her. When the jeweler noticed it missing before he left the shop, he'd summoned the sheriff. Tom had kept the valuable piece of jewelry but raced to his room at the boarding house and packed everything he owned before leaving Cheyenne. He didn't use his U.P. pass or even take the train because no matter how fast the train sped down the tracks, a telegram was a lot faster. He didn't want to have a badge wearer waiting for him when he disembarked. He suspected that the lawmen in Denver wouldn't care, but he wasn't about to take the risk.

He'd sold the necklace in Denver and gotten a job with the Denver & Pacific Railway. Tom hadn't forgotten about Cassie and relived that one passionate night that they'd shared in his mind many times. His current girlfriend, Anna Jones, was acceptable company, but she wasn't Cassie Gray.

When he read an article about the bizarre death of Ned Gray during a 4th of July celebration that had finally reached *The Rocky Mountain News*, those memories of his time with Cassie exploded. She was now a widow and was available. He no longer cared about Anna if he ever had. He'd spent more than half of the money he'd gotten from the sale of the necklace but hadn't accumulated much more as he'd been spending most of his pay entertaining Anna.

He'd make use of his Union Pacific pass in a few days after his next payday and head up to Cheyenne. He assumed that Cassie would welcome him with open arms and suspected that she had inherited a substantial amount from her husband's death. Ned Gray had come from a well-established family and Tom was sure that he had a healthy bank account before he'd blown himself up. All of that would be Cassie's now, and if he played his cards right, it would soon be his and so would she.

―――

In both Omaha and Ogden, Nelson's telegrams were creating tidal waves.

Homer Watson had begun to prepare the work crew with the equipment necessary to return the stolen train to the main tracks before the passengers even sat down to eat in Castle

Rock. By the time they were boarding the train, he'd arranged for their accommodations at each of the three hotels and the two boarding houses.

When their train arrived, he sought out Cassie because Nelson had identified her as the person in charge in his telegram. With Cassie, Will and Jim all providing help, it still took an hour to take all of the passengers to the large emporium to buy what they needed until their luggage arrived. Homer had the store make up a bill that he billed to the U.P., then it took another hour to get everyone situated.

By then, the Union Pacific executives had met twice. The first time was before they'd received Nelson's telegram from Castle Rock. In the first one, they met to decide whether to send anyone to Ogden. They decided to not make any decision until they had more information. The second meeting was in response to the explosive and very welcome news from their special agent. They first sent a telegram to the army to cancel their earlier request, then sent another longer one to Ogden because Nelson had made it clear that by the time that they received his message, the passengers would be gone from Castle Rock while he guarded their train. Even if Nelson had mentioned the payment of eleven thousand dollars to the gang, it wouldn't have dampened their euphoric mood.

Even William Burns, who was insanely jealous of his special agent, was pleased with how Nelson had handled the dangerous and potentially expensive situation. Mister Burns knew that many, if not the majority of his agents were corrupt and not much better than the outlaws and malcontents that plagued the railroads. Nelson was not only the exception but was also exceptional in every other aspect of being a good lawman. He was easily the highest paid of the U.P.'s agents, and Burns admitted that he was worth every penny. But it was knowing how well-regarded Nelson was by his bosses that made him dislike him. He suspected that it was only a matter of time before Nelson Cook took his job. If he really knew Nelson, he wouldn't have been worried and might not hold such distaste for him.

———

The sun was setting as Nelson sat before the fire and scooped a large fork of scrambled eggs from his plate. He didn't want them to go to waste, so he'd made a very large breakfast.

He may have told his two prisoners that he wasn't going to bring them any food, but before he cracked the first egg, he knew he wouldn't keep that threat. He wasn't about to open the caboose door but knew that the small windows were open because of the heat. So, before he'd cooked his own supper, he'd fried up half of one of the slabs of bacon then scrambled a dozen eggs.

He didn't give them any coffee, but after loading the scrambled eggs and bacon into a set of reasonably clean saddlebags, he'd carried them to the caboose. They must have been sleeping because it took him two shouts to get their attention, then slid the saddlebags through the bars and the open window. They hadn't thanked him for his generosity but hadn't expected to hear an expression of gratitude. He suspected that they knew that when the door was opened in Ogden, it wouldn't be long before they were escorted into another cell with far fewer amenities and a date with the hangman.

He finished his breakfast/supper then cleaned up before returning to one of the tents. He wasn't about to sleep inside because he wanted to be near the caboose just in case the boys managed to figure out a way to make an escape. He figured if he couldn't come up with any way out of the caboose, then they had no chance at all.

But there was still the remote chance that some of the others might return. He remembered that Harry had said that Big Bob had been with Jack when he'd opened the safe and he didn't have to spend any time figuring out who he meant. Big Bob Post wasn't a hardened criminal like the two locked in the caboose. He was just an enormous man who used his size and strength to get his way.

Nelson couldn't recall hearing any occasions when Big Bob had used a pistol. While he may not have been vicious, he wasn't exactly a pleasant giant, either. He was a bully and had killed a store owner with one blow from his massive fist when the man tried to stop him from walking out of his store without paying for a can of peaches. Nelson knew of two other men he'd killed but killing a man over a can of sweet fruit stuck in his mind. If any of them returned, he expected it would be Big Bob.

He also noted that all the time he'd seen the large man, he was always close to Jack. Initially, Nelson thought it was a wise decision to have him act as a bodyguard, but when Jack had been explaining the deal to his men, Nelson noticed that even then, Big Bob stood next to his boss. When Jack had been disbursing the cash, Bob had seemed almost surprised when Jack had given him the last bundle. Nelson wished he'd paid more attention at the time but supposed that it didn't matter.

He dragged one of the cots and two blankets out of the tent and continued walking until he reached the caboose and set it where he could see the back door. After setting his hat on the ground under the cot, he folded one of the blankets into a pillow, then laid down. The heat wave may have left the southwest corner of Wyoming Territory, but it was still too warm for the blanket. That would change in another hour or so, then he'd pull the blanket over him.

He had no idea of what was happening in Omaha or Ogden but expected that Homer would have the work crew on the move shortly after daybreak. He'd be ready to greet them at the end of the Jack's railroad when they arrived.

CHAPTER 4

The twelve-man work crew had assembled before the sun popped over the horizon and boarded the short maintenance train being pulled by an older locomotive that was no longer reliable enough for long runs. The men piled onto the lone flatbed car with their equipment and spare rails and crossties if they were needed. They had been told to expect to meet Nelson where the train had been taken from the main line. Will Hitchens and Jim Kennedy were in the locomotive's cab anxiously awaiting the reunion with their train.

The short train left the Ogden yard heading into the rising sun. They had about forty miles to go before they met Nelson and had to pass through Echo first. The repair job had to be completed quickly to minimize disruption to the scheduled traffic.

Despite a search by the local law, none of Jack Rodgers' men had been found. Homer thought it had been a half-hearted effort at best, but that wasn't his job. Cassie Gray had repeated what Nelson had told her about the gang and the deal he'd made with their leader. She had asked if Nelson would suffer any consequences for giving the money away and Homer had laughed at the notion. When she'd asked if Nelson had a girlfriend, he hadn't been surprised by her question but understood what drove her concern.

139

He'd given her the answer she had hoped to hear and wondered what Nelson thought about her. She was a handsome young woman and quite impressive in her demeanor, but as long as Nelson had been in Ogden, Homer hadn't seen him with any women. He knew that the agent had been married briefly and that his wife had run off with another man. What had caused that split was open to gossip, but Homer didn't place any blame on Nelson. He considered Nelson Cook to be one of the finest men he'd ever met. He wished he could watch what happened when Nelson returned with the train and was reunited with Mrs. Gray.

———

Nelson hadn't given his prisoners any breakfast and only ate the leftover bacon from last night before he saddled Rowdy then mounted and headed for the Union Pacific's rails. With the tree out of the way, he spotted the tracks much sooner and reached the main line just three minutes later. He looked west for the smoke of the work train's locomotive knowing that they'd be holding up traffic until the stolen train was on its way to Ogden.

The early morning eastbound train had already passed, so they'd have at least three hours to do the job without disturbing the railroad's schedule. He didn't think they'd finish that quickly but doubted if the bosses would complain after they got their missing train back undamaged. Then he remembered Jack's ingenious rail lifters and thought they should be able to finish the job without causing any delays at all.

After just a few minutes of waiting, he spotted the work train's smoke cloud on the horizon then saw the locomotive. It wasn't a wood-burner, but it was one of the early coal-fired engines.

When it was about four hundred yards away, he waved his hat over his head and was rewarded with a long blast from the steam whistle.

The train had barely come to a stop when the work crew poured off the flatcar and Will and Jim hopped down from the locomotive's cab as Nelson dismounted.

He shook the engineer's and fireman's hands before saying, "Good to see you again, boys. When the crew gets here, I'll tell Rick where to find everything to get the job done. They won't need any more rails or crossties."

"Good enough. Is the train okay?"

"She's fine. There are a couple of prisoners in the caboose. Two of Jack Rodgers' bad boys came back to loot the place and I managed to disarm them and lock them in the caboose yesterday. When we get to Ogden, we can turn them over to Sheriff Harris."

Before they could ask any more questions, Rick Lovelace reached them leading his work crew. Nelson let Rowdy's reins drop and led them into the trees where he showed Rick the crude crossties with their markings then the rails and Jack's new equipment for lifting the rails. Rick was as impressed with the rail lifters as Nelson had been but didn't waste any time getting his men to work.

As the crossties were laid out in preparation for their rails, Nelson explained the two sets of curved rails and suggested that Rick use the existing holes in the logs as a guide. It was probably unnecessary, but Nelson thought it wouldn't hurt the foreman's feelings.

Now that the work crew was hurriedly rebuilding the temporary spur while others were removing the two rails from the main line, Nelson returned to take Rowdy's reinds then walked with Will and Jim back to their train. They had a lot of work to do and Nelson needed to get Gomer and the other two horses saddled.

After Will and Jim climbed into the locomotive's cab to inspect it and then prepare it to move, Nelson continued to his horses.

He had Harry and Boomer's geldings finished before he saddled Gomer and began attaching the packs, his equipment, the Sharps and his crossbow. He finished adding the three horses to the trail rope then mounted Rowdy and headed for the express car to retrieve their guns.

As he passed the locomotive, he saw both Jim and Will shoveling coal into the firebox. It would take another ten minutes or so to build up enough pressure to move the train, but they'd only be able to roll it to the end of Jack's spur until the curved tracks were in place.

After adding the outlaws' Winchesters to their empty scabbards and their rolled up gunbelts to their respective saddlebags, Nelson headed for the work crew to measure their progress.

He had to pull up before he reached the end of the spur because the workers were blocking the way as they hammered spikes into the homemade crossties. Rather than sit and watch, he turned Rowdy left into the trees and after twenty yards, turned right and soon left the forest.

When he emerged, he dismounted, then led Rowdy to the work train. He'd have to load the four horses onto the real train's stock car when it reached the main tracks, but he had no other functions right now. So, he tied off Rowdy on the flatcar's handle then sat on the steel platform. He knew he could help with the work but didn't want to be a distraction.

The work crew knew what they were doing, even if they had to use the curved rails. He noticed the gap in the tracks where the straight rails had already been removed and was curious how it would look with Jack's modified rails in place. They had already set the log crossties in order and were close to hammering the first of the two sets of curved rails in place. He pulled his pocket watch out and was impressed to find that it was only 8:25. They'd be backing the train out of the woods within twenty minutes. After it was back on the main line, Will would keep it sitting there while they returned the straight rails to where they belonged. He'd board the horses while they waited, but before nine-thirty, he expected they'd be rolling to Echo and then Ogden.

Will and Jim were anxious to get moving, so they prepared to back their train when the main gauge told them that they had enough pressure in the boiler. Before Will pulled back on the throttle, he reached up and pulled the whistle's cord and gave three short blasts to let them know the train was about to move.

The loud sound gave Nelson something to do, so he stood and walked into the trees for just a hundred feet or so then turned left to the tracks. After crossing the spur's rails, he turned to face Will's train. He watched it rolling slowly towards him and grinned when he saw the rope holding his prisoners inside the caboose. Even as he smiled, he pulled off his hat and held it over his head. He could see Will looking back at him from the cab waiting for Nelson to signal when he needed to stop his train.

It was only another thirty seconds before Nelson began waving his hat over his head and Will quickly closed the throttle and applied the air brakes. The train had been moving at walking speed, so it came to a complete stop in less than two hundred feet, well short of the work crew.

As long as the men were still working, Nelson trotted to the locomotive then looked up at Will and said, "I'm going to get my horses into the stock car while you're sitting here. I think they'll have you on the main tracks within twenty minutes."

144

"That's great news!" Will exclaimed before Nelson turned and jogged back down the tracks.

———

He'd barely gotten the horses into the stock car when Rick Lovelace approached him and told him that they were ready. He hopped down as Rick walked back to his men then Nelson trotted to the locomotive again. Will had been anxiously waiting for the word and after Nelson climbed into the cab, he barely had time to say, "They're ready," before Will grinned and put his hand on the throttle.

Will pulled the throttle back slowly until the train began backing down the tracks. He kept it barely moving in case there was a disaster when the caboose first reached those curved tracks. He'd be able to watch the first cars take the turn and once they safely reached the straight tracks, he'd add a bit more power.

Nelson had climbed to the top of the coal pile to get a good look without obstructing Will's view. He was just as anxious as the engineer was as the caboose approached the curved rails. If the caboose derailed and fell over, he wouldn't shed a tear over any injuries his prisoners would suffer, but he knew it would add a lot of time to the final recovery of the train.

As he and Will stared at the caboose, it began to turn and just seconds later, the car in front of the caboose reached the main tracks. Will began to laugh while Nelson just let out a long breath in relief.

The train continued to back out of the trees and Nelson soon waved at Rich Lovelace as he stood with his crew. They were all grinning with the success of their job. Now it was time to do the easy part and restore the tracks then get the two trains back to Ogden.

When Will stopped the train about a hundred yards away, he turned to Nelson and exclaimed, "I can't believe I got my train back! She's just like she was when I left her, too! I really appreciate all you've done, Nelson."

Nelson smiled and replied, "I hope the boys back in Omaha appreciate it and aren't upset that I let the gang go and even paid them to leave."

"I reckon even those big bosses will be grateful, too."

"We'll see."

———

After the tracks had been restored and the spikes that held them to the crossties were hammered into new holes to keep them in place, the work crew boarded their small train and soon began backing toward Ogden.

Will opened the throttle and his much larger train began to pick up speed, but he made sure he wasn't gaining on the work train. He left a four-hundred-yard gap to be sure he had plenty of room to stop even though they only were making about twenty miles an hour.

Nelson had moved to the stock car and had the door open as he watched the landscape roll past. Even though he'd acted as if the executives back in Omaha might be angry with him for losing the money in the safe, he was sure that they'd have just the opposite reaction. Besides not having to pay the ransom and still have to worry if Jack blew up their train with all its passengers, they wouldn't suffer the humiliation of having the story plastered in headlines across the country.

Now they'd be able to brag how one of their own agents had managed to free all the passengers and send the gang packing without any harm coming to their train. And he'd done it on his own…after they'd given him instructions how to do it, of course. He'd send them another telegram when he arrived and let them know about the lost cash and his capture of two of the gang. He'd returned the two thousand dollars to the express car safe, so it wouldn't look so bad.

After he'd turned the two outlaws over to the sheriff, he'd send his telegrams and then take Rowdy, Gomer and his two new horses to his house. Once he was settled and cleaned up, he'd see if Cassie Gray really did remain in Ogden as she said she would. Despite Homer's belief that Nelson didn't spend any time with women, it was far from true. He just hadn't risked being saddled with another Genevieve.

Genevieve, who never could be called by any shorter appellation, was a very handsome young woman from a good family and seemed perfect. In those first two months, she was everything a wife should be. She did all those things that good wives did and did them better than most. But after seven weeks, she began to point out his deficiencies, which he admitted were plentiful. He'd tried to modify his behavior as much to avoid further critiques, but even as he'd change one, she'd identify two more. When he finally decided she may never be satisfied with him even if he walked around their home with a halo suspended over his head, Nelson had ignored her criticisms and strongly worded suggestions.

It was probably not the best tactic to use for a newlywed husband, but Nelson wasn't about to become a fancy gentleman. He wasn't fancy nor was he a gentleman and Genevieve knew that before they'd wed.

When he returned to their house after a job and found it empty, he wasn't surprised but hoped she didn't return. He wasn't angry at her at all but wasn't about to search for her, either. He hoped that she was happy with whomever had whisked her away. He spent more than two years almost in celibacy expecting that she might return, even after the divorce had been granted. He'd ended his frustrating days of sleeping alone, but the concern of having his bedmate turn into another Genevieve kept him single.

But now there was Cassie. Of all the young women he'd met over the past six years, none had come close to being as honest as Cassie Gray. She hadn't flirted or even shown any modesty when she'd mounted Rowdy before she held onto him. During the ride, she hadn't tried to diminish her own faults or blame her dead husband for any inadequacies.

Yet when she described Ned Gray, he fully understood why she would have been unhappy while most women would have been thrilled to have such a sweet and worshipful husband. It was her hidden force of personality that had created her frustration and unhappiness. That same strength of character that would have frightened Ned Gray was very appealing to Nelson. He just hoped that she hadn't continued her journey to San Francisco.

———

He needn't have worried. Two hours after the work train departed from Ogden's yard, Cassie had arrived at the station and took a seat on one of the benches facing east. She'd taken a room at the boarding house then spent a long time in the bath before dressing in her new clothes. She was almost ashamed of herself for primping but didn't think it quite reached the level of flirting. She simply wanted Nelson to see her in a good light. She'd been embarrassed to be so close to him after being locked in that train for two days, but he hadn't commented on her poor hygiene.

Just ten minutes after she'd taken her seat on the bench, she was joined by Florence Porter. Other passengers were also making their way out to the platform as word reached the hotels and boarding houses that their luggage would soon arrive.

After she sat down, Florence smiled and asked, "Fancy another long ride with Nelson Cook, Cassie?"

Cassie smiled back as she replied, "Maybe not a ride, but I intend to spend time with him. He's a fascinating man and the complete opposite of Ned."

"You're not the only one to notice. Or are you unaware that every unmarried woman on that train has set her cap for Nelson, even Mary."

"Does that include you?"

"Well, it doesn't matter about me or Louise. She's already with her sister in Echo and after I get my luggage, I'll be taking the train to Salt Lake City. Maybe he's a Mormon and you can become his second or third wife."

Cassie laughed then said, "I'm reasonably sure that Nelson isn't a Mormon and isn't about to become one just to have many wives. He wasn't happy with the one he had."

"He was married? Why didn't you mention that before?"

"You didn't ask. Can you believe that his wife left him because she couldn't smooth his rough edges quickly enough?"

"Why on God's green earth would you try to change anything about him?"

150

"I have no idea. But the more we talked, the more I realized how similar our marriages were yet completely different at the same time. I couldn't be me and his wife didn't want him to be himself."

"Do you think that he's interested enough to ask you to stay in Ogden?"

"He doesn't have to ask me to stay. I'm not going anywhere. I have quite a large bank account back in Cheyenne and if I want to buy a house in Ogden, I will. But I'll stay at the boarding house until I decide what to do. I'm not going to be coy when I meet him again, either. I think it would disappoint him anyway. I'll be direct and even offer to move in with him. I'm not leaving Utah unless he tells me that he's not interested."

"I'll admit that you seem to have the inside track. He did seem very impressed with you."

Cassie nodded but her attention was drawn by the clanging bell of the approaching work train, but the one with their luggage was nowhere in sight.

"I wonder where our stolen train is?" Florence asked.

"I think they had to stop at Echo to drop off the luggage of the passengers who disembarked there. Maybe they even picked up some other passengers."

"Maybe Louise swept Nelson off the train before you had your chance."

Cassie laughed as she rolled her eyes then exclaimed, "Enough!"

The work crew waved at the passengers clustered on the platform as they passed.

As it was being shunted to the tracks that led to the long maintenance shed, Rick Lovelace shouted, "Your things will be along shortly! They had to stop at Echo!"

"You were right, Cassie," Florence said as they watched the ballet of men throwing switches and doing other tasks necessary to send the maintenance train back into its home.

———

As the train pulled out of Echo, Nelson was composing his next long telegram to his boss. He'd finally admit to paying off the gang but did retrieve two thousand dollars of the money when he'd captured two of them. He hadn't heard a peep from the caboose in all that time and he'd checked on it when he'd loaded the horses and when they'd stopped at Echo. He knew they were still inside, but he'd have Sheriff Don Harris or one of his deputies with him when he removed the rope holding them in their rolling prison.

But after he'd finished mentally writing his telegram, he revisited the conversation he'd had with Jack Rodgers. It was a troubling insight into his next plan. Nelson believed, or hoped, that Jack wasn't really going to blow up the train and the thirty-four people, including some children. That belief existed because Nelson considered Jack an intelligent and rational man. But after Jack had accepted Nelson's offer, he admitted that he'd continue his one-man campaign against the Union Pacific, which didn't surprise Nelson. What made it spine-chilling was when Jack refused to promise that he wouldn't do anything that would make Nelson shoot him. In other words, his next plot might result in the death of innocent people.

Nelson may want to spend time getting to know Cassie, but he had to stop Jack Rodgers before he killed anyone. At least he didn't have two of his hired guns. Big Bob Pope was still with him, but that may prove to be a liability.

There was another impediment which would at least delay being able to spend time with Cassie. He was sure that after he sent his next telegram to Omaha, he'd be summoned to explain all the details in person. He knew it wasn't going to be to place blame or even admonish him. When they read his telegram, they'd want to know more about Jack Rodgers and what he might do next. He wouldn't know what they would do about it until after the meeting.

But that was all speculation. Ogden would come into sight soon and he expected to see the passengers waiting at the depot to pick up their luggage. Even if Cassie decided to return to San Francisco, she'd have to wait until she retrieved her bags.

———

"There it is!" Florence exclaimed as she pointed down the tracks.

"I never would have noticed," Cassie replied as she stood beside her friend.

Cassie may have appeared calm, but her heart was racing as she watched the locomotive's nose growing larger in the distance. When she'd been joking with Florence about Nelson, she may have sounded confident in her belief that Nelson would want to spend more time with her, but she wasn't nearly as convinced as she'd made it appear. He seemed to be comfortable with her on his horse and had even placed her in charge, but that was hardly a suggestion of interest. She hoped to have a better idea when the train pulled into the station. She had a trunk and a large travel bag in the baggage car, so even if he didn't want to take time to talk to her again, she'd still have to wait.

The passengers began to crowd the front of the platform in their anxiety to have their luggage returned to them. It was almost a mob scene that had the potential for disaster if some of the ones closest to the edge were pushed onto the nearby tracks.

Cassie shouted, "Everyone step back! Let's not have someone get killed after surviving that ordeal!"

She wasn't sure if they would listen to her when three of the men turned and glowered at her, but they all began to slowly move back until the potential for tragedy was averted.

Florence looked at her new friend and said, "They did what you told them to do, Cassie."

"It's because Nelson put me in charge before he left."

"I don't think so. I think it's because it's how you are."

Cassie shrugged as she watched the train slowing as it approached the station. She was at the back of the crowd now and wouldn't be able to see Nelson disembark. She hoped she didn't miss him altogether because she knew he'd have a lot to do when he stepped off the train.

When he saw the passengers queued up on the platform, Nelson smiled. He couldn't see Cassie, but that was understandable as the larger men were in front. But the stock car was closer to the caboose, and the porters at the station would distribute their luggage from the baggage car which was a couple of hundred feet away. He'd have to find Sheriff Harris and deliver his prisoners first. Jurisdiction wouldn't matter in this case because both men were wanted dead or alive and the theft of the train would probably be a minor offense for both outlaws. It was just a question of which town or county wanted them the most.

Just before the train lurched to a stop, Nelson hopped out of the stock car and trotted alongside the train on the left side as he knew that they'd be unloading the baggage to the anxious passengers.

He soon passed the locomotive, hopped over one rail, bounced off a crosstie and then landed on the other side of the tracks before continuing his fast pace into Ogden. Crossing tracks was second nature to him, and he didn't even need to watch where his boots landed anymore.

Nelson soon reached the county courthouse and after passing the main entrance, reached the sheriff's office next door. He'd worked with Sheriff Harris often since he'd arrived in Ogden and regarded him as a friend as well. He had four deputies and Nelson believed them to be basically good men with varying degrees of skill and integrity.

When he entered the large jail, he found the sheriff himself at the desk, so all of his deputies must be out and about.

Sheriff Harris looked up from one of his deputies' reports and exclaimed, "Good Lord, Nelson, you've been one busy feller! I'm hearing all sorts of stories about that vanishing train of yours. It's back at the station, I assume."

"Yes, sir. But I'll need you to help me with my two prisoners. Two of the gang returned after I made a deal with them and I got the drop on them. I've got them locked in the caboose. The good news for you is that you don't have to do a lot of paperwork on the train theft on either of them. One of the bad boys is Boomer Wilson and the other is Harry Ent. I'm sure you've got wanted posters on both of them."

The sheriff shot to his feet as he excitedly replied, "*You got both of those bastards in the caboose?* You're damned straight I've got posters on both of them. Let's get them out of your cell and into mine."

Sheriff Harris grabbed his hat and followed Nelson out of the jail then got in step when they headed for the train.

As they walked, Nelson gave him a quick rundown of everything, knowing that the stories that the sheriff had already heard were probably wildly inaccurate, either good or bad.

He hadn't finished when they approached the back of the caboose and while the sheriff stood back with his Colt drawn and cocked, Nelson started to undo his knots. He was surprised that they weren't tighter, which indicated that the caged outlaws hadn't made much of an effort to escape. If he wasn't sure of the caboose's construction, he would have worried that they might have found another way out.

After the knot was removed, Nelson just began pulling on the rope and letting it fall to the ground at his feet as it buzzed over the steel handles. When the entire rope was lying in a heap near his boots, he pulled his Remington and stepped onto the platform.

Before he opened the door, he glanced at the sheriff who nodded, then he yanked it open. He almost laughed when he found the outlaws bolt upright from the two bunks when the loud noise had interrupted their peaceful sleep.

"Let's go, boys. Sheriff Harris had new accommodations for you."

Neither said anything that was worth hearing as they slid their feet to the floor while grumbling under their breaths. They grabbed their hats and as they walked to the door, Nelson stepped back to the ride side of the platform and pointed to the left side where Sheriff Harris stood.

They squinted in the bright sunlight as they slowly stepped to the ground and Nelson followed a few seconds later.

Neither of them made any attempt to break away, even though both would probably have a date with the hangman in the near future. They knew that they wouldn't make it twenty feet before they were shot and there was always a chance to make an escape before they even reached Cheyenne or Laramie, the two towns that wanted to see them hang.

After locking them in separate cells, Sheriff Harris said, "I reckon you still have a lot to do, Nelson. I'll notify the jurisdictions that are looking for Boomer and Harry, but I hope you can stop by when you get a chance to tell me all of the story."

"I appreciate your help, Don. I do have a lot to do and I think I'll be summoned to Omaha pretty soon. But I'll still fit you in before I head east. Oh, one more thing. I have their horses, tack and their guns, too. I'll keep the horses, at least for a while, but would you like their two Winchester '73 carbines and Colts?"

"I wouldn't mind the extra firepower. The county is a bit cheap when it comes to expensive things like Winchesters."

Nelson grinned then said, "I imagine you aren't worth twenty-two dollars then."

Sheriff Harris snickered, popped Nelson on the shoulder then watched him wheel around and leave the jail. If he didn't know that Nelson earned more than twice what he was being paid as the county sheriff, he would have offered him a job as a deputy years ago. His deputies were acceptable and didn't cause him too much grief, but they had their moments when he wished they worked elsewhere.

Nelson knew Rowdy, Gomer and their new corral-mates would be waiting for him in the stockyard, so he'd send the long telegram to William Burns and then see if he could find Cassie. The crowd of passengers should be thinned out by now as they collected their luggage and headed back to their hotels. Almost all of them would board another train, but some would stay. He hoped that Cassie was one of those remaining in Ogden.

He didn't even reach the large Western Union office before he had his answer when he spotted Cassie waiting near the telegraph office door. He noticed her new dress and even though he'd been impressed with her strength of character, he couldn't deny that he found her very attractive.

Nelson hopped onto the platform and strode to where she stood wearing a big smile. He was grinning himself when he reached her and almost didn't notice Florence standing nearby.

"I thought you'd need to send a telegram to Omaha," she said when he stopped.

"It's going to be a long one, but I've already composed it, so it won't take me long to get it on the wire. Do you want to come inside with me?"

"I need to send a telegram myself, so I'll be happy to join you."

He then offered her his arm which she happily took before they walked through the open doorway.

Florence's luggage had already been sent to her hotel room and she had to catch the morning train to Salt Lake City tomorrow, so she headed back to the Utah Arms Hotel.

Nelson and Cassie each took a blank sheet and a pencil from the cup then began to write.

As she wrote, Cassie said, "I'm letting my sister know that I'm safe but won't be coming to San Francisco. I'm going to stay in Ogden."

Nelson continued printing his message as he asked, "How long will you be staying?"

Cassie set the pencil back in the cup as she answered, "That depends on you, Nelson."

Nelson paused, then looked at her and said, "I don't think so, Cassie. From what I've already learned about you, I believe that you will decide whether to stay or leave without any suggestions from me."

She smiled as she replied, "Maybe."

Nelson chuckled as he shook his head then continued writing his very long message.

When he finished, he and Cassie approached the operator and he let her be the first to hand her message to the telegrapher.

He dutifully counted the words, then looked at her before glancing at Nelson. He didn't ask for payment but reached for Nelson's message.

Cassie didn't know why he hadn't told her how much she owed but thought he was just waiting until he'd finished counting the words in Nelson's message. But he didn't even look at Nelson's sheet before he turned around and began tapping his key as he sent her news across the wire to her sister.

When he set it aside and began transmitting Nelson's message, Cassie looked at Nelson who didn't seem to be confused at all.

After the receiving station's operator sent his acknowledgement, Nelson said, "Thanks, John. Let me know when they reply. I think they'll want to talk to me in person pretty soon."

John Hipper grinned as he said, "I reckon so, Nelson. I've been hearing a lot of chatter about what happened since you left. You really outdid yourself this time."

"It was interesting. I'll give you that."

He waved to John, then took Cassie's arm again and left the office.

Once outside, Cassie asked, "Why didn't he charge me for the telegram?"

"Western Union and the Union Pacific have a gentleman's agreement. I never pay for telegrams, even if they aren't official."

"But I'm not a Union Pacific employee. I may be the widow of one, but I don't recall that Ned had that privilege."

"He did, but you probably never saw him exercise it. John just assumed that you were with me and extended you the same courtesy."

162

"Oh. What are you going to do next?"

"I need to get my horses from the stock corral, then take them home and put everything away. Did they already move your luggage?"

"They're bringing it to my room at the boarding house. Do you mind if I come along with you?"

"I'll be honest with you and tell you that I'd be more disappointed if you didn't, Cassie."

"And I'll be just as frank and say that if you'd declined my offer, I would have walked beside you anyway, even if you mounted your horse."

Nelson laughed, then with Cassie on his arm, stepped across the almost empty platform and soon reached the corral where Rowdy and Gomer stood near the fence.

When they approached the corral, Charlie Nix asked, "What about these other two, Nelson?"

"They're mine now, Charlie. They belonged to two of the gang who stole the train. The bad boys who sat in their saddles are in Sheriff Harris' jail right now and will probably be standing before their Maker soon enough."

"I reckoned as such. They're fine-lookin' animals."

"That's why I decided to keep them for a while anyway."

163

Charlie opened the gate and Nelson took Rowdy's reins and wasn't surprised when Cassie took the reins of the black Morgan. Charlie didn't comment but tied the other gelding's reins to the Morgan's saddle before Nelson and Cassie led the horses away from the corral.

Carrie asked, "How far do we have to walk before we reach your house?"

"Not far. Just three blocks. It's not a big house, but it suits my needs."

"What happened after you left us in Castle Rock?"

He smiled and replied, "More negotiations with criminals."

She laughed before asking, "Seriously, what happened?"

As they led the four horses toward Saint Street, he began more of an overview of events rather than a detailed narrative as they'd reach his house in just a few minutes. He still wasn't sure what she would expect of him when they reached his small barn to unsaddle the horses, but just having her walking beside him was a good start.

Cassie wasn't quite sure what she would do when they reached his house either. Asking him if she could come along had been an instant decision and she was pleased about it. But while she may not want to seem like the sweet woman Ned believed her to be, she didn't want to appear shrewish either.

But even as she listened to Nelson, she hated the very thought of trying to be anything other than herself.

As they turned onto Saint Street, Cassie resolved to pay no attention whatsoever to wearing even a semi-transparent mask. She'd just be herself. It was what she'd promised herself after Ned's death and if Nelson found it offensive, then maybe he wasn't the man she believed him to be. It wasn't a pleasant thought, but Cassie wasn't about to change her mind or her behavior to please anyone.

When Nelson turned down the drive beside his house, Cassie was surprised that it wasn't nearly as small as she'd anticipated. Granted, it wasn't nearly as large as the homes she'd shared with Ned, but it appeared well built and meticulously maintained.

"You have a nice house, Nelson," she said as they passed the north side enroute to his small barn.

"Do you want to see the inside after I unsaddle the horses?"

"I was going to help you bring your things inside anyway, sir."

"Well, thank you for your consideration, ma'am."

They led the horses into the barn and Nelson began unsaddling Rowdy while Cassie began stripping the tack off of the Morgan.

"What are you going to do with the two outlaws' horses?" she asked.

"I don't know yet. Do you want the Morgan you're unsaddling?"

"Could I? He's a handsome horse. How old do you think he is?"

"Around six or seven years old. He seems to have a pleasant personality, too. Most Morgans do. Now Rowdy here is a different story. He can be ill-tempered at times which is what earned him his name. Gomer is much nicer but not as smart, so I use him as a packhorse most of the time."

"Thank you, Nelson. Can I leave him in your barn?"

"I don't think the folks at the boarding house would be happy if you kept him in your room."

Cassie laughed as she slid the saddle from her new horse then said, "I might buy a house in Ogden. If I do, I'll look for one with a barn like this one."

Nelson had Rowdy's harness in his hand as he said, "Why don't you wait for a while before you start looking?"

She understood why he had made the suggestion and wasn't about to coyly ask, "What do you mean, Nelson?"

Instead, she said, "I wasn't going to rush down to the bank and ask them to show me what they had available. I thought we could spend time getting to know each other first. You might

166

want me to buy a house in San Francisco once you understood me better."

Nelson looked at Cassie as she kept her hazel eyes locked onto his grays. He knew she was honest and not about to mince words, but even he'd been startled by her blunt reply.

But as he stared into those expressive eyes, a smile slowly began to form on his lips.

"I don't think any man ever born understands women, even the one who gave him life. I'll admit that you're a complex woman, Cassie, but I believe I've got a pretty good handle on what drives you and makes you such a remarkable person."

"Don't be so sure. Let's finish with the horses and get your things inside and we can talk while I cook you something. You probably haven't eaten much today; have you?"

"No, ma'am. Just a few strips of cold bacon."

"I haven't had lunch yet either. I may have been a terrible wife, but I was a good cook."

Nelson didn't comment because he knew she wanted to talk about why she believed that once he got to know her better, he'd want to move on.

———

Sixty-seven miles northeast of Ogden, in the town of Leroy, just two stops north of Castle Rock, Jack Rodgers sat with Big

Bob nearby as he talked with the five other ex-railroad men who'd stayed with him.

"That was a good operation, boys. I screwed up by not taking Nelson Cook into account. That won't happen again. The problem was that we had to wait for the Union Pacific bosses to try to come to a decision after we stole the train. That gave Cook enough time to find us and make us leave. Our next job won't give him or anyone else that opportunity. We'll make our money and get our payback at the same time. And if we time it right, we'll eliminate Nelson Cook at the same time."

"How long is it gonna take to plan this one, Jack?" asked Audie Scott.

"That's the beauty of the next one, Audie. When I had my little chat with Nelson Cook, I got the impression that he expects me to sit tight for a month or two while I developed another complex plan to hurt the U.P. But we're not going to do that. We'll do something that Cook wouldn't expect us to do."

"What are we gonna do, boss?" asked Mick Gifford.

"We're going to derail a train just south of here. There's a bridge across a big creek that'll serve our purpose. We don't need any dynamite or even have to pull a single spike. All we need to do is chop through a few of the critical supports and that bridge will collapse and take the train with it. We'll strip everything we want before it's even overdue at McCammon.

The small stops won't matter just like they didn't with the first job."

While the railroaders had been disturbed about blowing up a train with passengers inside, none of them seemed to be bothered with derailing one and probably killing a dozen or two people in the process.

Carl Brown asked, "When do we do it, Jack?"

"I'm pretty sure that Cook will be summoned back to Omaha to meet with his boss pretty soon. Carl, you'll set up your set and listen to the traffic. Once he's gone, we'll start setting up. He won't stay long, but he'll send a telegram back to Ogden letting them know when he's leaving and maybe even tell them which train that he'll be taking. We'll track the train and as soon as it leaves Granger, we damage those supports and we get to watch the train collapse into the creek. We still need to pick up another packhorse and some more tools and supplies first."

"We all have that thousand dollars you gave us, boss," Big Bob replied, "You can have all of mine, except maybe twenty dollars, so I can have some fun."

Jack smiled at his large bodyguard as he said, "Thanks, Bob. You're a good man. We'll talk about that later. Okay?"

Bob grinned as he nodded. Jack was the best man he'd ever met and if anyone even looked cross-eyed at him, he'd be sorry.

But to Jack, the only man who could block his path was going to be returning from Omaha in a few days. After the train carrying Nelson Cook exploded in a fiery disaster, he'd unleash hell on the Union Pacific without restraint.

———

All of his gear had been moved into his house and Cassie was preparing their lunch while Nelson began putting everything where it belonged. He set aside the two Winchesters and gunbelts for Sheriff Harris but kept their boxes of ammunition. His Remington was chambered for the same cartridge.

Before he left his spare bedroom, he glanced at the bed he'd left in place when he'd bought the house. He debated about asking Cassie if she wanted to use the room after he left for Omaha. He was certain that if he'd asked any other woman, he'd probably feel the palm of her hand across his face, but not Cassie. She may decline his offer, but she wouldn't be offended.

When he returned to the kitchen, he walked past her without saying anything and began setting the table.

She turned and watched as he placed the plates, cups and silverware before two adjacent chairs and smiled. She was impressed when he took two surprisingly fancy napkins from a drawer and placed them under the fork and knife.

"Did you buy the napkins?" she asked.

He turned and smiled as he replied, "No, ma'am. They were here when I bought the place. So was all of the cookware, china and flatware. All I did was add some food to the pantry and move my horses into the barn."

"Have you lived alone since your wife left you?"

"After she ran off, I avoided women for two years, but I've had a few ladies spend a night or two with me since then. I haven't had any stay with me since I moved to Ogden, though."

"Why not?"

"I've been too busy."

He sat down as she asked, "Why did you avoid women for two years? Were you worried that she might turn into another version of your wife?"

"That was it. That was also why you impressed me so quickly. You're an honest person, Cassie."

She continued her lunch preparation as she said, "I'm not as honest as you seem to believe, Nelson. For more than five years, I lived with Ned and pretended to be someone I wasn't. I told you that he treated me like a porcelain doll, and that was true. But I was never honest enough to make him stop behaving that way. I was a phony and then I did something that showed just what a horrible person I am. It was more than just bad; it was shameful."

Nelson didn't say anything because he suspected that Cassie was about to confess the horrible thing she'd done and already had a good idea of what it was.

When he didn't ask what she'd done, Cassie said, "Just three weeks before the accident that took his life, I committed adultery. I spent a night in our own bed with another man while he was out of town. I may have regretted it before Tom Richardson even rolled over and fell asleep, but that doesn't diminish my immoral behavior. Tom had to suddenly leave town just a week later, so I could have gotten away with it. I wrestled with it for three weeks, but my guilt began to consume me. I was so ashamed that I was going to tell Ned when we returned to the house after the fireworks display, but I never got the chance."

Nelson waited to make sure she'd finished talking before he asked, "Didn't Ned, um, exercise his husbandly duty properly?"

Despite the difficulty in making her confession, Cassie smiled at Nelson's abstract question.

"He tried. Lord knows, he tried. He was so gentle and considerate that he always asked if I was in the mood before we did anything. I'm ashamed to admit that I often told him I wasn't even if I was. It was just one more indication of what a horrible woman I am."

Nelson let twenty seconds of silence own the room before he said, "I don't believe you're nearly as terrible as you claim to be,

172

Cassie. I'm not just telling you that because I want you to feel better, either. I can understand how frustrated you must have been when you had to hide your true character. And I can understand why you might seek the attention of another man who may not be as gentle as your husband. I won't condone your adultery, but I do understand why you did it."

"Did you ever cheat on your wife?" Cassie asked quietly.

"No. But don't forget, I wasn't even married to Genevieve for a year before she ran away. Maybe I would have if I had been married to her as long as you'd been married to Ned."

"I doubt it. I'm not as good a person as you are, Nelson."

"No, you're probably a better person than I am. I know my faults, and so far, nothing that you've said has lessened my opinion of you."

Cassie turned and glared at Nelson as she exclaimed, "You have got to be kidding! I lived a lie for more than five years and then ignored my marital vows. *How can you not see what a bitch I am?*"

He wasn't surprised by the harshness of her reaction, so he calmly replied, "For the very simple reason that you aren't what you claim to be. Let me ask you this. Why didn't you try to dominate Ned? It sounds as if he didn't have the strength of character to defy you."

She thought about it for just a few seconds before she quietly answered, "I didn't want to hurt him. Sometimes when I even objected mildly, he would weep. I knew that if I pushed him even a little bit, it would destroy him. He was too gentle and too good for me to do that to him."

"If you'd been the bitch you just called yourself, you wouldn't have cared one bit about how Ned felt. You would have been the boss of the house and he'd become your obedient puppy. Genevieve didn't have your drive, but she still tried her utmost to mold me into a gentleman. If she'd been married to Ned, even though he already was a gentleman, she would have tried to change him into something else.

"You didn't try to hurt or change him because you're a warm-hearted, good woman who happens to have a strong character. I noticed your inner strength immediately, which is why I put you in charge. You took control of those people, including some rough-looking men and never backed down. I think you're a remarkable person, Cassie."

Forgetting about the food on the cookstove, Cassie slowly walked to the table and sat down near Nelson.

"Do you really believe what you just said, Nelson?" she asked softly.

"Every word. As we're being so honest with each other; I have another question for you. Do you want to stay in my house after I've gone to Omaha?"

"You're leaving?"

"I assume so. Obviously, I haven't received a reply to my telegram yet, but I'd be surprised if they didn't want me to explain everything face-to-face, so they could ask questions."

Cassie took his hands and asked, "Do I have to wait until you leave?"

Nelson smiled because he hadn't quite reached that level yet but should have expected it from Cassie, especially after all she'd just revealed.

"No, you don't. But will you be disappointed if I ask you to use the spare bedroom?"

She smiled then replied, "Yes, I will be disappointed, but I understand. We need to talk a lot more; don't we?"

"Maybe not that much more. But you might want to pay attention to the cookstove, I think you're about to burn my house down."

Cassie glanced to her smoking skillet. then leapt from her chair and grabbed a towel before sliding the skillet off of the hotplate while Nelson laughed.

Seeing that their lunch had been ruined, Nelson stood and stepped closer to Cassie and took the towel from her hand.

"Let's go to Jenny's Café and I'll buy us lunch. I'll clean this up later while you arrange to have your things brought to the house. I imagine I'll receive my summons to the inner sanctum of the Union Pacific headquarters by the time we're finished eating."

Cassie smiled and took his hand before saying, "I'll gratefully accept your offer, kind sir."

Nelson and Cassie left his house then walked down Saint Street heading to the diner. He wasn't about to release her hand and Cassie wasn't going to let him go, either. From their first conversation, each of them knew that they were a perfect match.

Now that her concerns were more than simply swept aside, Cassie's greatest hope was that Nelson didn't have to leave so soon.

If he did go to Omaha, she knew that she couldn't go with him. Ned's family still lived there and after his funeral, she knew that she wouldn't be comfortable seeing them again. It was only a possibility, but she didn't want to take the risk of meeting them. She knew that his parents and sisters didn't like her at all. Even when they'd been courting, her parents had thought her unworthy of their only son. If they realized her true nature, they probably would have locked him in their home.

By the time they entered the diner, Nelson was sure that half the town already realized that he and Cassie were now a couple, even if they had no idea who she was.

After they took a seat at one of the tables, the waitress didn't take long to arrive, even though the place was almost full.

She smiled and said, "I hear you had an exciting couple of days, Nelson."

Nelson returned her smile as he replied, "Not as exciting as it could have been, Betty. I never even fired a shot. I'd like you to meet Cassie. She was one of the passengers on the train and was instrumental in getting them all safely back to Ogden."

Betty's smile remained in place as she said, "It's a pleasure to meet you, Cassie."

"I'm glad to meet you as well, Betty."

Nelson said, "I need something fast and filling, Betty."

"I'll bring you your favorite," she replied then looked at Cassie.

Cassie said, "Whatever Nelson's having will suit me fine, but I don't believe I'll need it in the same quantity."

"I wouldn't think so. I'll be back shortly."

After she'd gone, Nelson said, "Betty is a recent widow herself. Her husband, Willis, was a butcher and cut his hand. It became infected and he refused to even see the doctor. I guess he didn't see a future as a one-armed butcher. I think she won't be a widow or a waitress much longer, though."

"I was curious. She seemed to like you but wasn't annoyed that I was with you either."

"Would you believe that there are rumors in Ogden that I don't even like women? Most of the folks who know me don't believe them for a moment, But the fact that I was married for less than a year before my wife left me and that I haven't been seen with a woman since I arrived adds fuel to the gossip."

She smiled as she said, "So, I'm proof that the whispers are all nonsense."

Nelson grinned while he replied, "That's an unexpected bonus, Cassie."

Cassie laughed at both his reply and the notion that anyone would believe such rumors.

"I'll drop you off at the boarding house after we leave, then I'll swing by the station and have a porter stop by to move your things. Okay?"

"That's perfect. I was wondering how to get the trunk moved. Will you check to see if you've received your reply from your boss while you're there?"

"I will, but I'd be surprised if they decided what to do so quickly. The bigger the organization, the slower it operates. They have to have meetings and discuss each suggestion and usually form committees to study the ideas. At least this isn't a hard decision to make. All they'll need to do is get the bosses together and the president says, 'Let's get him back here to tell us what happened and then we'll decide what to do about it'."

Cassie smiled as she said, "I noticed that myself, and I was just a wife of an engineer. As you're probably going to be going back to Omaha, you might want to know that Ned's uncle, John M. Fitzpatrick, is one of those executives. He's the brother of Ned's mother. You might want to avoid mentioning my name if he's in the room."

"Thanks for the warning. Does the rest of his family live in Omaha?"

"Yes, but they don't work for the railroad."

Before Nelson could ask another question, Betty arrived with their order.

When Cassie saw the amount of food on Nelson's plate, she was surprised that it wasn't as much as she'd expected. Of course, she'd anticipated that his standard order would require at least two loaded plates.

After Betty had gone, she said, "I expected your plate to be almost too heavy for Betty to carry. That's only a little more than what I have."

"Betty just doesn't want me to get a tummy ache."

———

Forty minutes later, after he'd escorted Cassie to the boarding house so she could pack her things, Nelson headed for the station. He knew it had just been wishful thinking that there would be a delay before he received the reply with his marching orders. It wouldn't take a board meeting for the president of the Union Pacific to tell William Burns to have Nelson return to Omaha post haste.

He stepped onto the platform, then asked Joe Nobel to move Cassie's luggage from the boarding house to his. Joe didn't even bat an eye before he said that he'd take care of it.

When he entered the Western Union office, John Hipper waved him over then pulled a sheet from the table next to his set and held it out to him.

"This showed up a little more than an hour after I sent yours. That's about the fastest I've ever gotten a reply from Omaha."

Nelson didn't read the message before he replied, "I'm not surprised. I assume they want me to get my carcass back there to answer their questions."

"Yup. But they sure seem mighty pleased with what you did. Maybe they'll make you the new president of the Union Pacific when you get there."

Nelson laughed as he nodded then read the telegram.

NELSON COOK OGDEN UT

EXCELLENT JOB
RETURN TO OMAHA
USE 246
BRING HITCHENS AND KENNEDY
CONCERNS ABOUT RODGERS

WILLIAM BURNS UPRR OMAHA NEB

"Now that's odd. I can't believe that my boss actually said I did a good job. He's been worried about the possibility of my taking his job for some time now. I suppose I could just tell him that they couldn't pay me enough to sit behind a desk, but I enjoy watching him squirm. He's used his connections to earn his promotions and hasn't got a clue about what's going on out here. He probably knows that a lot of his agents are as bent as the crooks they're supposed to stop, but he doesn't do anything about it."

"If you're a crook, Nelson, you sure do a good job of hiding it."

Nelson grinned then said, "That's why I'm the best crook of them all."

John chuckled before he had to turn to receive an incoming telegram.

Nelson left the telegraph office mildly annoyed that he had been directed to use engine 246 so he could get to Omaha

181

more quickly. The locomotive had been stranded in Ogden for almost a month after suffering a boiler leak. It had been repaired and was awaiting its return to the main yard in Omaha for a complete overhaul. He was sure that its condition was good enough to make the trip, and the main office would clear the track once they got underway. He'd need a second crew to relieve them as well. The good news was that a new crew had already taken the stolen train out of Ogden, so Will and Jim were rested and available. He would use a less-well-rested crew to relieve them. He'd have Gill Small and Leo Bench join him in the caboose when they left.

He stopped at the station manager's office to tell him what he needed and wasn't surprised that Homer had already begun the process of having 246 prepared and had even notified Gill and Leo as well as Will and Jim. He'd received his own telegram from the bosses while he and Cassie were enjoying their lunch.

"I'm just waiting on track clearance, Nelson. The coal car is topped off and I'm having the caboose stocked. I reckon you'll be rolling in about an hour or so."

"Thanks, Homer. You're a good man," Nelson said before leaving the office to find Cassie.

Nelson walked briskly to Spruell's Boarding House knowing that Cassie probably hadn't finished packing. After her confession of infidelity, he had been curious about the man who made up the other half of their adulterous relationship. It sounded as if Cassie wasn't overly fond of Tom Richardson and wasn't sure if she knew what he'd done that forced him to leave Cheyenne. It would be a touchy subject for most women, but he believed that Cassie could handle it. But Nelson also believed that if the man discovered that she was now a widow, he might try to find her to renew their acquaintance.

When he approached the boarding house, he found Joe Nobel already lifting Cassie's trunk onto his baggage cart near the entrance while Cassie stood nearby with her two travel bags. Before she could hand either bag to Joe, she spotted Nelson and could only smile as both her hands were in use.

Nelson smiled back and waved as his hands were free then just before reached her, Joe took her heavier bag then set it atop the trunk.

Joe turned and said, "Just in time, Nelson. You can take the lady's bag."

"I was going to offer, Joe, but it's up to the lady if she wants me to carry it for her."

Cassie laughed and handed Nelson the bag before taking his arm then stepping beside him as they headed for Saint Street. Joe was grinning as he began rolling the cart behind them. Nelson was very popular with everyone at the station because he wasn't full of himself, despite his achievements. He treated each of them as if they were as important as he was.

Nelson didn't tell Cassie about his almost immediate departure and Joe didn't mention it, so either Homer hadn't told Joe, or he was being courteous.

———

After helping Joe lug her trunk into his house and giving him a silver dollar for his efforts, Nelson and Cassie moved her things into the spare bedroom.

When they were alone and Cassie prepared to unpack, Nelson said, "I received the telegram from my boss. They want to see me as soon as possible."

She stopped unloading her trunk and asked, "When is the next train going east?"

"It doesn't matter. They're really worried about what Jack Rodgers might do, so they want me to use a locomotive in the yard, so I can leave right away. They're preparing it now and the station manager told me it'll be ready to roll in ninety minutes or so. The good news is that I'll arrive in Omaha a lot sooner than if I'd taken a scheduled train. With two crews, we should be able to get there in about thirty-six hours. I should be back in four days."

Cassie was disappointed, but knowing he'd return sooner balanced his rushed exit somewhat.

"I wish we had more time," she said as she resumed unpacking her things.

"So, do I."

"Do you need help packing?" she asked.

"No. I have a travel bag ready for these kinds of trips. Sometimes I have to be ready to board a train on a moment's notice. You won't have to worry about the horses. I'll move them to the stock corral before I leave. Will you be all right until I return?"

"Of course, I will."

"You can explore the wonders of Ogden, Utah while I'm gone."

"I intend to do that, but why were you concerned?"

"I wasn't worried about anyone in Ogden, but when I was leaving the station, I wondered about Tom Richardson."

"I'm surprised you even remembered his name."

"Well, I did. Cassie, do you know why Tom Richardson had to leave Cheyenne so quickly? Was he worried about Ned finding out?"

Cassie placed her folded nightdress into the top drawer, then turned and replied, "No, he wasn't the least bit concerned about that. I don't know exactly what happened, but I heard that the sheriff was looking for him. I would have asked someone, but I had other things on my mind at the time."

"Do you know where he went or what he's doing?"

"I heard he headed to Denver, but I don't know more than that. He worked as a foreman for the Union Pacific, so he might have gotten a job with another railroad. Why are you interested in him at all? Surely, you don't think I'm about to go looking for him."

"No, but he might come looking for you now that he knows you're a widow."

Carrie slowly turned to her open trunk and pulled out a light jacket as she thought about that possibility. She'd never even thought about Tom Richardson after leaving Cheyenne until she told Florence, Louise and Mary about him.

"Maybe he will, but if he returns to Cheyenne to find me, then he'll probably be arrested if the sheriff sees him. Even if he asks anyone who knows where I went, they'd tell him I was in San Francisco with my sister and he'd probably just return to Denver."

"I know it wouldn't be difficult for him to find out that you'd been on the famous disappearing train and head this way. I'll admit that it's only a remote possibility, but I didn't want him to show up while I was in Omaha."

"It was a very brief affair, Nelson. I'm sure he's moved on and found another willing woman in Denver."

"Don't underestimate your attraction, Cassie."

She smiled and asked, "Would you go all the way to California to find me, sir?"

"I'd go to China if you'd decided to become a missionary."

Cassie laughed then continued to unpack.

Nelson said, "When I was out with my two pals waiting for the repair crew, I was thinking about you a lot, Cassie. I decided that if you were really going to stay in Ogden, that I'd ask to court you. I guess that we already began our courtship when I found you waiting at the telegraph office."

"No. It started when I took your Winchester. At least that's when it started for me. And that was before I even knew that you were unmarried."

"We don't need a long courtship; do we?"

She set her folded dress on her bed, stepped close to him and softly replied, "No, we don't."

He took her in his arms and asked, "Will you marry me when I return, Cassie?"

"I'll have the minister or justice of the peace waiting with me on the platform," she replied as she locked her fingers behind his neck.

Nelson smiled as he said, "I wouldn't be surprised if you did."

"Are you going to kiss your fiancée before you leave me for your other engagement in Omaha?"

Nelson was about to do just that before she asked, but the play on words in her question made him chuckle instead. He couldn't imagine any other woman who would react that way. He knew that for the rest of his life, Cassie would keep him on his toes.

But after his brief period of appreciative merriment, he slid his right hand behind her neck and kissed her.

Cassie had been kissed often but never like this. She felt her knees about to buckle and held onto him for support even though Nelson held her tightly against him.

While his knees weren't about to fail, Nelson felt Cassie's incredible passion which overwhelmed him. He had expected the kiss to be powerful, but not anything close to what he was experiencing.

If there had been any doubt that each had been born to be with the other, it evaporated with that first kiss.

But as their lips parted, they also knew that circumstances prevented any further expression of their newfound and explosive love.

After they had enough air in their lungs to speak, Nelson said, "I wish I didn't have to leave, Cassie. Our timing is horrible."

"As much as I want to pull you to my new bed, I know that I'll have to set aside my own very intense needs and desires and let you go. Even if I can't have a minister with me when you return, I don't intend to keep them in check a second time."

"Nor do I, ma'am."

She quickly kissed him again, but knew it had to be a one of farewell and nothing more.

Nelson then asked, "Why don't you finish unpacking while I get my things?"

"Alright. Just don't try to sneak off without me."

He grinned as he said, "I wouldn't dream of it," then quickly left the room to prepare for his departure.

———

An hour later, they shared one last kiss before Nelson hopped onto the caboose's steps and Will Hitchens opened 246's throttle.

Cassie waved as the short train accelerated quickly down the tracks and Nelson waved his Stetson high over his head. She stayed on the platform and watched until the train passed over the horizon. She sighed, then turned and headed back to the house.

Once inside the caboose with Gill and Leo, Nelson sat at the small, bolted desk across from the double bunks to begin writing a detailed report. Gill and Leo didn't bother him knowing that he needed to concentrate.

Nelson found it difficult to concentrate as he sat staring at the blank sheet with an unmoving pen in his hand. Cassie was so dominant in his mind that he was unable to even recall how the whole thing started.

With concerted effort, he finally remembered Homer pounding on his door to tell him about the missing train and began to write.

The fast-moving train passed through Echo as he continued to put pen to paper. Once the mental dam had collapsed, the events flowed more smoothly. He took six pages to finish the report before he set down his pen to let the ink dry.

As he'd written the report, he had taken more time and written more words about the critical conversation he'd had with Jack Rodgers. Now that he'd stopped writing, he spent more time reviewing each word they'd shared. Jack would already be planning for another attack on the Union Pacific and Nelson had to stop him before he hurt anyone.

He didn't even hear the steady clicking of the steel wheels as they passed over the gaps between the rails. Nor was he trying to ignore Gill and Leo who were now chatting behind him. He wanted desperately to try to anticipate Jack's next move. The scheme to take control and then hide an entire train was brilliant and had taken a long time to execute. It had also required the assistance of a large crew of railroad workers to make it work. According to Boomer Wilson and Harry Ent, only six men rode away with Jack, and one of them was Big Bob Pope. He wouldn't be able to pull off another elaborate crime again unless he recruited more workers and that would take time. But Jack was a patient man, so maybe time didn't matter.

Nelson closed his eyes and pictured Jack in his mind as they'd talked. It was the look in his eyes when he's said that he'd be willing to do something that would make Nelson shoot him that was different. Until then, he'd been cool and calculating, if not downright pleasant. When he'd said that one sentence, his eyes changed, and Nelson had seen the devil inside. It wasn't long and Jack had quickly smiled, but for just those two or three seconds, Jack's demons had escaped.

———

But Jack's demons had already taken control when he'd seen the short train pass. He smiled knowing that in another two days at the most, Nelson Cook would be returning. He'd have everything ready for the bridge to collapse under his train on his return trip.

Then he could inflict whatever damage he saw fit and not have to worry about being stopped. The rest of their agents or anyone else who might try to stop him were either crooked, idiots or both.

———

The train was almost to Granger when Nelson began to believe that Jack wasn't going to wait very long before he launched his next salvo. The short delay meant it would probably be much more direct and deadly. Nelson now shifted his thoughts to the most likely method he would use and the target he would probably choose.

The most obvious would be a derailment, but Jack wouldn't bother just removing spikes. After the train theft, he'd know that the engineers on those locomotives would be watching for any signs of tampering with the tracks. He'd use his engineering skill to make a train fall from the rails. The most obvious second choice was to weaken a bridge or trestle. It wouldn't be spotted by the engineer until his locomotive dropped beneath his feet.

If he was right, then that posed another problem. Just on the Union Pacific line between Granger and Ogden and the second branch between Granger and Pocatello, there were at least sixty bridges or trestles that Jack could weaken. In addition to their number, Nelson was sure that Jack could do his damage and mask the cuts to make them difficult to spot.

When the train slowed to add water in Granger, Nelson finally stood and smiled at Gill and Leo.

"Thanks for letting me write my report and brood."

"We figgered you'd need some kinda privacy," Gill said.

Leo grinned and said, "I reckon you were thinkin' about your lady."

"I was at first, but after I finished scribbling, I spent some time thinking about Jack Rodgers and what he's planning to do."

"You reckon he's gonna try to steal another train?" asked Gill.

"No. He doesn't have the manpower anymore and I don't think he wants to waste the time to set it up. I think he's going to try to weaken a bridge or trestle to destroy a train."

Leo exclaimed, "*You reckon he's really gonna do that?*"

"It's just a guess, Leo. I could be wrong, but after talking to him for those few minutes, I got a good read on him. But even if he derails one, I don't think it will be the end of it."

Leo then asked, "Why's he so damned mad at the Union Pacific?"

"A few years ago, he was given substandard materials to build a large bridge and told his boss that he wasn't going to use it. His boss, who no longer works for the U.P. by the way, told him to go ahead anyway. He built it and it collapsed under the weight of a loaded coal train. His boss blamed him but didn't fire him. Jack quit and went to work for some other line. I knew him and thought he was one of the best engineers they had, and so did he. He was frustrated and angry when less talented engineers were getting the plum jobs and promotions that he felt he deserved. Even if it was true, and I'm not sure that it was, he let it eat him inside.

"The bridge incident was just the last straw for Jack and I'm sure that the same day he quit; he began plotting his revenge. I'm not even sure if he really expected his stolen train scheme to work. I'm sure he knew that the U.P. couldn't come up with the hundred-thousand-dollar ransom in a week even if they decided to pay it. I don't know if he was going to really blow up the train and the passengers. But now, I think the gloves are off. He won't care if folks die this time."

Gill asked, "Are you gonna tell the bosses in Omaha that?"

"Yes, sir. I don't know if they'll believe me, but I'm sure that they'll order me to find Jack Rodgers and kill him this time. They'll probably be a bit miffed that I didn't blow them all up when I had the chance."

"I heard about that," Leo said then asked, "Why didn't you set off the dynamite? The train and the passengers weren't gonna get hurt."

"I know. But most of those boys were just railroad men like you and Gill. I imagine not all of them were Union Pacific men either. They were probably out of a job and down on their luck. When Jack approached them with his offer, the thought of making a lot of money must have been impossible to refuse. I couldn't kill men like that. That's why I didn't pull my trigger and made the deal instead. If they'd all been outlaws like the two that I captured later, I wouldn't have hesitated."

Gill asked, "Do you reckon the bosses will see it your way?"

Nelson grinned as he replied, "If they don't; they can always fire me and send my boss out here to find Jack and his boys."

Leo snickered but didn't comment as the train came to a stop to quickly fill its water tanks.

The sun was gone as 246 tugged the two cars east along the Union Pacific rails. Homer had thoughtfully left a cot in the corner near the water barrel, so while Will and Jim slept in the bunks, Nelson was able to rest on the cot. They'd tried to convince him to take one of the more comfortable bunks, but Nelson insisted he preferred the cot so he could have easier access to the small privy that was really just a seat with a lid covering a hole.

When they'd stopped at Cheyenne to fill the water tank and top the coal bin, Gill and Leo had taken over the locomotive. As the two crews switched jobs, Nelson had stood on the caboose's platform and looked into the town. This was where Cassie had lived with Ned Gray, had her one-night affair with Tom Richardson and where her husband blew himself up.

He thought that maybe on his return, he'd visit the sheriff and ask about Tom. He wasn't sure if he was really concerned about the man looking for Cassie or if he just wanted to know more about him. But that was for the return trip and he still had to reach Omaha and tell the collected bosses what had happened and what he believed Jack might do next.

As Will guided the small train across the Dakota plains, Nelson slept on his cot. Tomorrow evening, he'd arrive in Omaha and probably meet with the bosses the next morning. Before he let the rocking motion take effect, he allowed himself a few private moments to spend with Cassie.

———

Cassie thought she'd be busy cleaning the house after Nelson's train left, but she found it remarkably clean for a bachelor's home. She almost began to believe he did have a woman before she arrived but maybe he'd hired a housekeeper.

After she realized that the house didn't need cleaning, she left the house to find Florence to tell her the exciting news.

She had planned to go the bank to open an account earlier that day. She still had almost half of the cash that Nelson had given her as well as her own money that had been returned after the gang left. But now she no longer needed to open a bank account but would wait until Nelson returned and told her which bank he used. Then she could deposit what she had and have the money from her account in Cheyenne transferred to their new account.

She hadn't told him about the Cheyenne account because she knew that he really didn't care. After she'd sold their house, she had a balance of just over eight thousand dollars. She knew that Nelson was well-paid but wasn't sure how much he had saved. He didn't seem to have many expenses and hadn't even mentioned the rewards he would receive for capturing the two outlaws.

As she stepped along the boardwalk, she was surprised that so many townsfolk smiled at her and even greeted her by name. She didn't know any of them and suspected that the gossip express had roared through Ogden. She smiled when she remembered when Nelson had told her about the rumors about his lack of interest in women. She really was his bonus by dispelling those whispers.

She entered the hotel where Florence been staying and found that she'd already taken the train to Salt Lake City. She now had no one she knew in town.

CHAPTER 5

Nelson sat at the large table with his notes spread out before him. He had prepared the notes before the train arrived in Omaha because he'd give his full report to whomever met him at the station. He didn't recognize the secretary who greeted him and taken the report but thanked him for arranging for his room at a nearby hotel. He was impressed that both Will and Jim were also given a room, but they had to share.

After he'd arrived at the headquarters early that morning, he had expected to report to Mister Burns, but the receptionist had escorted to the conference room. When he entered, he found that most of the executives were already waiting for him. If he'd been a less confident man, he would have been uncomfortable in the presence of so many powerful men. He also noticed that neither Will nor Jim was present. He suspected that they'd be interviewed only if they might know something that Nelson didn't.

He had just smiled and taken his seat at the end of the table with the president of the Union Pacific, Mister Sullivan, seated at the other far end. He noticed William Burns sitting two seats on his right but acting as if he didn't even know his special agent. Nelson assumed he was waiting for Edgar T. Sullivan's reaction.

He'd just finished giving his oral report and was now waitng for the questions.

Mister Sullivan said, "We're all very impressed and pleased with the way you were able to avoid any harm to the passengers and recover the train without damage. I doubt if another man in the country could have managed that."

"Thank you, sir."

"My first question is the most obvious one. Why didn't you shoot the dynamite knowing you could eliminate the entire gang without harming the passengers or the train?"

"As I noted in my report, sir, if they'd all been outlaws, I would have. But only three were criminals, and I captured two of them later that day. I've been told that only five of the ex-railroaders and one outlaw stayed with Jack Rodgers."

"I haven't had a chance to read your full report yet, so excuse my ignorance. I can understand your reasoning. Do you know what I find even more astonishing than the recovery of the train and rescue of the passengers?"

"No, sir."

"That you returned the two thousand dollars you recovered from the two killers you captured. When I read that telegram, I found it unbelievable. Most men in that situation would have shot them both and taken the money. No one would know and, frankly, we wouldn't have cared."

"I cared, sir. The Union Pacific pays me well to do my job and if I can minimize the loss to the railroad, I will."

The president laughed then said, "I wish we had more agents like you, Nelson. Now, what can you tell me about Jack Rodgers?"

"It's difficult to express on paper, sir. When I first learned of the train's disappearance, it didn't take me long to determine who was behind it. When I had my Winchester aimed at the dynamite and we talked…"

What he found difficult to convey with the written word was much easier when he could use his hands and his own expressive face. He explained what he believed was motivating Jack and then what he expected him to do next.

When he finished, he waited to hear the president's reaction. He wasn't surprised when the heavyset man just leaned back in his chair and looked at him as he evaluated Nelson's suspicions.

After almost a minute, he turned to William Burns and asked, "What do you think, Bill?"

Nelson looked at his boss and wondered if he'd risk offering a different opinion. He would have been stunned if he did. If he did, then he could be proven wrong, but if Nelson was wrong, it would be on his head.

As expected, William Burns replied, "I agree with Nelson, Mister Sullivan. I also agree that it'll be very difficult to find which bridge or trestle he plans to destroy."

The president nodded then looked back at Nelson and asked, "Can you think of any way we can stop him?"

"The one advantage we have is that the last outlaw, a man named Big Bob Pope, seems to be devoted to him. I'm sure that wherever Big Bob is, Jack will be nearby. Big Bob, as you can imagine, is an enormous man. He's about six feet and four or five inches and probably weighs almost three hundred pounds. That makes him easily identified."

"I can have telegrams sent to all stations to have them watch for him," Mister Burns said.

Nelson shook his head as he replied, "No, sir. I wouldn't do that. I'd send a system-wide telegram warning engineers and other crew members of the potential for damage to bridges, trestles and tracks, but don't mention Big Bob or even Jack Rodgers. That ransom telegram was sent by someone with a practiced hand using a portable set. Even if he wasn't able to intercept the telegram, Jack probably has contacts in many of those stations who would warn him that we're looking for Big Bob."

"Isn't he wanted?" asked Charles Whitcomb, the vice president of operations.

"Yes, sir. But unlike the other two, who were bona fide killers, Big Bob was more like a giant bully who took what he wanted. He may have killed a couple of men, but on the ladder of men who are wanted, he's pretty far down the list. I'm not sure of the price on his head, but I'd be surprised if it was more than a hundred dollars. No bounty hunter and few lawmen would take the risk of confronting an angry Big Bob after putting a .44 into him."

"Are you serious?" Mister Whitcomb asked with raised eyebrows.

"Yes, sir. If you'd seen him, you'd understand. I carry a Winchester '76 that uses a powerful .45 caliber cartridge that can stop a charging black bear. But I'm not sure that two of those slugs would put him down."

"How could you stop Jack if you have to deal with him?" asked Mister Sullivan.

"I've been thinking about that. I didn't mention that Big Bob was really like a giant child. He's not very bright and I'm sure that Jack has treated him better than anyone else ever had in his entire life. He probably befriended him, so he'd have protection against the other smarter and nastier outlaws he planned to hire. If I do find them, I may need to come up with a way to let Big Bob discover that Jack really is only using him. I won't be able to figure out how to do it until I find them."

"How many agents do you want to join you in your search?" Mister Burns asked.

Nelson knew that his boss was only making the offer to impress Mister Sullivan. There were only six special agents west of Cheyenne and none were very trustworthy and might even warn Jack for a price. It was one of the reasons he was so highly paid and given so many assignments.

"I'd rather handle it myself, sir. The more men who are on the search, the more likely that Jack will know I'm onto him."

Mister Sullivan then asked, "Won't he know that after he told you he was going to continue to plague the U.P.?"

"I don't believe so. As I mentioned in my report, he probably thinks that I believe that there will be a month or two delay before his next action because of the need for complex planning. He won't expect me to know he might act much sooner. Besides, I'll even give him another reason for believing that I'm not focusing on him. When I return to Ogden, I'm going to get married. I'll make sure it's in the newspapers, so Jack will believe that he's the last thing on my mind."

"You're getting married? Who's the lucky lady?" asked William Burns, as if he really cared.

Nelson smiled and replied, "One of the passengers. I'd met her before, and it didn't take long for either of us to realize that she wouldn't be boarding another train for a while."

He'd avoiding saying her name because he wasn't sure that her uncle wasn't sitting at the table. He wished they'd at least had nameplates sitting in front of them, but they all knew each other, so it wasn't necessary.

Before anyone could ask her name, he said, "Mister Sullivan, as I don't want to keep her waiting, I'd like to catch the afternoon's westbound freight train."

"Nonsense. The least I can do is to let you take my executive train on your return trip. I can have it ready in three hours and you'll arrive much sooner. When we're finished, come with me to my office and I'll tell my secretary to make the arrangements."

"I appreciate the offer, sir, but it really won't save much time and it won't be conspicuous. If I take your train, they'll clear the tracks, and everyone will know it's coming. It'll be a perfect target for Jack."

"I can see your logic, Nelson. If you need anything, just let me know."

"Thank you, sir. I'll do that."

The president then scanned the other executives' faces as he asked, "Do any of you have any more questions for Nelson?"

There were head shakes and a few 'no, sirs,' before Mister Sullivan rose and like trained dogs the other dark suited men popped to their feet.

Nelson managed to avoid smiling as he stood and was the first to leave the conference room. He needed to send a telegram to Cassie letting her know of his pending departure on the freight train and when it was scheduled to arrive in Ogden.

———

Before he boarded the freight train's caboose, Nelson sent the telegram to Cassie. The train would depart Omaha just after one o'clock, and he expected to be in Ogden in less than forty hours. While the freight might be slower, it wouldn't be stopping to pick up passengers. It would only pause for water, coal and crew changes.

While most freights still made stops to drop off and add cargo, this one consisted of only seven cars, including the caboose. There was one boxcar, but the other five were all flatcars with large steam engines and pumps bound for mines around Pocatello.

For Nelson, it was much better than the executive train that the company president had offered. He'd share the caboose with the conductor and a brakeman because the freight wasn't equipped with air brakes. He thought that the job of brakeman was much more dangerous than his. One false step during a rainstorm or blizzard and they'd have to hire a new brakeman.

———

Jack had to move his men out of Leroy because there had been too many questions. Rather than choosing another town as their new base, Jack had them build a nice camp with new tents north of town. It was just a mile from his chosen bridge. They had enough supplies for at least two weeks and had the tools necessary to bring down the bridge.

It was late that afternoon when Carl rode into the camp with a big grin on his face.

As he stepped down, he looked at Jack and said, "He's on a freight that should be leaving Granger in two days."

Jack smiled as he nodded then replied, "That's good news. You'll only have to set up once more to get me an exact time for that train's arrival in Granger and then we'll go to work."

"I'll do that, boss. Do you know what was funny about that message? It wasn't sent to the station manager in Ogden. It was sent to some lady named Cassie Gray. It sounds like he's planning to marry her."

"Cassie Gray was on that train? How did I miss that? She was married to this worm of an engineer whose uncle was on the U.P. board. He wasn't nearly good enough for her, either. Nelson is more her type, but I guess she'll never get a chance to be a two-time widow. I wonder if she'll cry when she hears the news about the destruction of his train."

The other men snickered and chuckled before they returned to the campfire.

———

When the freight pulled into Grand Island to change crews and top off the coal bunker and water tank, Nelson took a few minutes to stand on the caboose's steel platform and look across the Plains. He'd spent too much time trying to outguess Jack Rodgers, so when he returned to the caboose, he'd let his mind dwell on the exciting reunion with Cassie.

He hadn't met either the brakeman or the conductor before, so the first part of the journey was spent answering their questions about what the Union Pacific workers were now calling the ghost train incident. He was pleased that it helped pass the time but wanted to spend more time thinking about what Jack Rodgers would do next.

Nelson decided that other than when he had to get some sleep, he'd spend his time out here on the platform. It was hot and stuffy in the caboose during the daytime and he'd be more comfortable outside. He didn't think the brakeman and conductor would mind as they were busier than he was.

He was pleased when he calculated that the train would pass through Cheyenne mid-morning tomorrow and he might have a chance to talk to the sheriff about Tom Richardson. It probably didn't matter if he didn't get to meet him, but it would satisfy his curiosity. He wondered if it was Harry Ent or Boomer Wilson who would hang in Cheyenne. The two outlaws should be on their way east out of Ogden even as he traveled west.

———

207

After Cassie had made herself some lunch, she headed for the Western Union office. She hoped that she'd have a telegram from Nelson letting her know what was happening in Omaha. She wondered if he'd remembered the name of Ned's uncle or if he'd mentioned that he was going to marry his nephew's evil widow even before a proper mourning period.

She'd taken just one step into the telegraph office when John Hipper pulled a sheet of paper from his box and said, "I was just going to have my boy take this to you, ma'am. It's from Nelson."

Cassie trotted quickly to the counter and avoided snatching it violently from John's fingers in her anxiety. He still smiled when he saw her greedily scan the page knowing that she'd have an impressive reaction to its contents.

Cassie's eyed expanded and a big smile grew on her lips as she read:

CASSIE GRAY 23 SAINT ST OGDEN UT

EVERYTHING WENT WELL
REMEMBERED NAME OF UNCLE
LEAVING SOON ON FREIGHT
WILL RETURN IN TWO DAYS
NEXT DAY FOR WEDDING

NELSON COOK OMAHA NEB

She didn't say a word but smiled at John then whirled around and exited the office in a flash.

John laughed as he shook his head then turned back to his key to continue sending the long message from the Utah State Bank. It was a weekly statement that was transmitted to its parent bank in Salt Lake City, so he could afford to interrupt sending it to watch Cassie as she read Nelson's very interesting telegram.

Cassie knew that there was no real reason to rush because Nelson wouldn't be back for another two days, but she was so excited that she couldn't help herself.

When she entered the house, she took off her hat and hung it on the coat rack. Then she stood in place as she decided what she wanted to do next. The house was certainly clean enough and she had taken a bath that morning. She finally remembered that Nelson had said he was going to give the two Winchesters and gunbelts to Sheriff Harris. She smiled and headed for Nelson's room, which would soon become their bedroom. He'd moved all of his guns out of her bedroom and knew which one of the Winchesters was his. His was the '76 with the brass plate on the butt. The two gunbelts were on the top shelf in his closet.

After she slid the gunbelts from the shelf, she hung one over each shoulder before taking a Winchester in each hand. It was a bit awkward for her, but she was determined to take them to the sheriff's office.

She must have looked a sight to the folks she passed as she strode along the boardwalks with her armory. They continued to smile and greet her by name, which was still surprising.

When she entered the jail, she found one deputy at the desk but didn't see the sheriff.

The deputy smiled then stood and stepped around the desk as he said, "Those must be the guns that Nelson said he'd donate to the office and you must be Cassie."

She smiled as she handed him the repeaters then shrugged the gunbelts from her shoulders.

"I am. Is the sheriff in?"

"No. He'll be back shortly. He had to talk to the county prosecutor. I'm John Phillips and I'm pleased to meet you, ma'am. You're getting a good man."

"I know I am," she replied, "I've got to get back to prepare for Nelson's return. He'll be arriving in three days."

"I'll let my boss know you stopped by with the guns. Tell him we really appreciate it and that he's a lucky feller, too."

"I will," she replied before turning and leaving the jail.

When she returned to the house, she decided to move her things from what would become a spare bedroom again to the room she'd share with her new husband.

Cassie had finished moving her things to their bedroom and returned Nelson's weapons to the spare room. Luckily, she knew where each of them belonged, including the crossbow. He'd shown it to her and explained how it worked. She may have been strong for a woman, but she was still unable to pull back the lever to bring the bowstring taut. Nelson promised to show her how it worked when he returned.

But it was his pending return that was important to her. When that freight train arrived, she wanted everything to be perfect. The house was ready and so was she.

———

Nelson sat at the small table with a cup of coffee. As much as he wanted to spend some imaginary time with Cassie, he needed to return to the issue of Jack Rodgers and his next attack. But as he continued to dig deeper into Jack's mind, he found it becoming even harder to predict what he might do.

Then he backed out of Jack's mind and entered the simpler world of common criminals. If another gang had taken the train and lost the big payday the gang leader would be furious and sought revenge against the man who'd ruined his scheme. *Would Jack follow a similar path?* While Nelson didn't believe that he'd act simply out of revenge, he might decide to kill him just to prevent any further interference.

Once Nelson recognized that possibility, he remembered what he'd told the president of the railroad. Jack probably was intercepting telegrams using that portable set that he'd used to send his ransom demand. It would be his best source of intelligence and that meant that Jack would know that his nemesis had just left Omaha and was returning to Ogden.

While he still believed it was unlikely that Jack would try to shoot him, he could imagine that the engineer would use the opportunity to kill two birds with one stone. He'd be able to destroy a bridge and train at the same time he killed their best agent.

As the train rolled westward in the night, Nelson finally blew out the lamp and headed for one of the bunks.

He tried to spend his last waking moments thinking about Cassie, but the long day and the rhythmic clacking quickly pushed him into sleep.

CHAPTER 6

Cassie had slept in Nelson's bed and was in a cheerful mood when she'd awakened. She stayed that way as she began her day by taking another bath before making herself breakfast. By nine o'clock, she was already bored.

With no one to talk to, Cassie thought she'd spend the time looking at Nelson's weapons. She'd never fired a gun before and wasn't about to learn but was curious about them. When she'd carried the Winchesters to the sheriff's office, she was surprised that they weren't as heavy as she'd expected.

So, when she entered what used to be the spare room, she picked up his '76 and realized it was heavier. She had noticed that its barrel was longer, so that was probably why it weighed more. But his other rifle was even longer. She picked up his Sharps and lifted it into a firing position before setting it back down. She found it difficult to keep the sights from moving and wondered how Nelson could even fire the thing with accuracy. It was one more thing she could ask him when he returned.

After examining his Remington pistol, she left the room and returned to the kitchen. She was disappointed that her gun inspection had only wasted thirty minutes. She then remembered seeing a small bookcase in the corner of the front room, so she walked down the hallway to see what selections Nelson had available.

When she dropped to her heels and read the titles, she was surprised. She'd expected to find adventure and action-filled novels but found one shelf with all of Dickens' works and the other two stuffed with other examples of serious literature.

Cassie selected Hawthorne's *The Scarlet Letter* and sat down on the couch. As she opened the cover, she knew that there was much more for her to learn about the man she was about to marry. While she had told him that she'd explore the town, the discovery of the wealth of reading material proved a better way to spend the next day and a half.

She'd gotten an updated schedule for Nelson's arrival from Homer and was pleased to find that he would be arriving tomorrow evening around seven o'clock.

———

As Cassie read about Hester Prynne's sin, Jack and his boys were setting up for their own much more egregious crime.

The bridge was a hundred and thirty feet long with a forty-foot drop to the wide creek. The creek wasn't very deep at this time of year, so his boys wouldn't have to wade in deep water. The supports they would damage were on both sides of the rocky shore.

Their saws and axes were in place under the bridge, so when Carl had confirmation of the train's departure from Granger, it would only take them forty minutes to make the supports unstable.

Jack had already marked the spots that needed to be cut, but the first axe wouldn't strike the wood until Carl returned with his report.

———

As the sun set that first night, the train was still in Nebraska and would still be in the long state for until well after midnight. When Nelson returned to the still toasty caboose interior, he took off his hat, jacket and shoulder holster then stretched out on the lower bunk. Phil Anderson, the brakeman, had convinced Nelson that it was available because he didn't stay put for very long, which was true. A brakeman's job, even on a freight, was hectic as well as dangerous. He'd be needed to apply the manual brakes and release them whenever the train began a downslope as well as when it needed to stop for water and coal.

He didn't fall asleep very quickly as he anticipated having Cassie in his arms again tomorrow night. They may not be getting married until the next day, but that didn't mean they'd sleep in separate beds. And they wouldn't be getting much sleep, either.

———

Cassie was just excited as she slipped beneath the sheets in what would be their marital bed tomorrow night. For a woman who'd been married for almost six years and sinned with another man, it was a surprising sensation. It wasn't hard to understand why she felt this way, but the level of her excitement still took her by surprise.

Her marriage to Ned had been more like a duty. Even as she walked down the aisle in her silk gown with her face hidden behind the gauze-like veil, she didn't feel a rush of anticipation. She knew that Ned was one of the most highly regarded bachelors in Omaha and he loved her. But she felt as if she was just doing what was expected of her. Her parents were more thrilled than she was, even though Ned's whole family had daggers in their eyes as they watched her step past.

The following years with Ned had been more like an army enlistment than a marriage. She counted the time and waited until her time of service ended. It was what had resulted in that despicable affair with Tom Richardson. The violation of her vows was bad enough, but she could have chosen a better partner to help her commit adultery.

Tom was as far removed from Ned as she could imagine and that was probably why she caved in to his advances. But even after she discovered just how crude Tom was, it hadn't made her appreciate Ned. It was as big a reason for her guilt as the act itself.

But when Nelson returned, Cassie knew that there was no possibility that she would be disappointed. She may have known that she was falling in love with Nelson even before she climbed onto Rowdy behind him, but it didn't take long for her to realize just how perfect they were for each other. There was no doubt in her mind that Nelson loved her just as much and this time, she would give herself completely to her husband.

———

Nelson was sitting on the caboose steps watching the sun poke into the sky above the Great Plains as the train continued heading west. They'd changed the crew in North Platte and would soon enter Wyoming Territory. In about three hours, he'd hope to find Sheriff Peters and ask about Tom Richardson. He'd only met the sheriff twice before but not in the last year. He hadn't heard of a change, so he assumed that Sheriff Peters was still in charge.

It was a cool morning for early August, especially out on the Great Plains. The higher altitude and mountains that started between Cheyenne and Laramie kept the summer temperatures more moderate. He may have appreciated the topography of western Wyoming and Utah, but he knew how troublesome it had been for the engineers and laborers who had built the railroad. The Chinese laborers who worked for the Central Pacific had it much worse when their railroad had to fight its way through the Sierra Nevada Mountains, but no one could ever tell that to the Irishmen who constructed the Union Pacific once it left the plains and entered the Rockies.

The freight was still climbing the long slope to the mountains, but it was so gradual, it was only noticed by the laboring locomotive that had to move the heavily loaded flatcars. It was burning a lot of coal as it worked its way to higher elevations, but once they crossed the Continental Divide, it would be mostly on a downslope. The number of bridges, trestles and tunnels would skyrocket after they reached the mountainous terrain, too. The tracks that could follow a reasonably straight line across the open plains would have to follow valleys and passes as it snaked around mountains and hills. Those same mountains held the winter snow that still sparkled in the hot summer sun on the taller peaks. When it melted, the flowing water created a web of streams, creeks and rivers that would eventually find their way to the oceans.

As Nelson watched the landscape pass, he was convinced that one of those bridges was going to be Jack Rodgers' next target. While he'd recognized that Jack might want to eliminate him at the same time, he still believed that Jack would need to reorganize after the ghost train disaster. Still, he'd mentioned that possibility to the replacement crew in North Platte. The engineer told him that they'd gotten a telegram from U.P. warning them about that possibility, so he'd be watching for any damage.

Even as he saw the tail end of Nebraska rolling by, Nelson knew that no engineer, regardless of his eyesight or perseverance, would be able to spot Jack's damage before it was too late.

―――

While Jack hadn't received any updates from Carl since Nelson's train left Grand Island, he expected to get word that it had departed Cheyenne within a couple of hours. He and the boys were enjoying a big breakfast of fresh venison as they sat around their campfire. Big Bob had taken down a doe with his Winchester and was unashamedly bragging about the shot.

He had already begun to think about his next target as the freight train carrying Nelson Cook was as good as destroyed in his mind. He was surprised that he felt such a rush of pleasure knowing that the agent would soon be crushed beneath the falling cars and locomotive. He'd enjoy watching that freight train follow the collapsing bridge into the creek.

―――

Cassie knew that she should at least spend some time in Ogden, but after having breakfast, she wanted to finish reading the book before she left the house. By then, she could go to the station and ask about Nelson's arrival time. He might even be earlier than she hoped.

She was still reading when the freight pulled into Cheyenne to take on water and coal.

―――

Nelson stepped down from the caboose and walked into Cheyenne. The train would be in the station for almost an hour because the engineer and fireman needed to do some routine maintenance while it took on water and fuel.

He strode quickly along the street until he reached the end of a boardwalk and popped onto the wooden walkway. He passed the stores and shops and headed for the county courthouse. He hadn't asked Cassie where she'd lived because he had no intention of seeing the house and didn't want to dredge up her memories of Ned or Tom Richardson.

He soon passed the courthouse entrance and passed through the open door of the neighboring sheriff's office.

The deputy at the desk looked at him with a measure of indifference and asked, "Can I help you, mister?"

"I'm Nelson Cook, a special agent of the Union Pacific. Is Sheriff Peters in?"

The deputy's attitude changed, and he quickly replied, "Yes, sir. I'm sure he'd like to talk to you."

"Thank you, Deputy. I can find his office," Nelson said before he walked past the front desk and then the four cells before he reached the sheriff's private office.

He rapped on the doorjamb then said, "Howdy, John," before he entered.

Sheriff Peters grinned and replied, "You've been pretty busy, Nelson. You're even sending me a present."

Nelson removed his hat and took a seat as he asked, "Which one is yours, Harry or Boomer?"

"We want Harry Ent. Did you come here to tell me the true story about that ghost train caper?"

Nelson snickered then shook his head. He'd only heard it called that in Omaha and now he heard it again in Cheyenne.

"No, sir. I have to catch a train shortly. I'm going to get married when I return to Ogden."

"Well, it's about time, too. Who's the lucky lady?"

"Cassie Gray. I'm sure you know her."

Sheriff Peters' eyebrows popped up as he answered, "I do. I knew her better than her husband. You heard about how he blew himself up, of course."

"I read about it the next day. What I came to ask you about was a man named Tom Richardson?"

The sheriff grimaced and shifted in his chair before he asked, "Why do you want to know about him?"

"Cassie told me about her affair with him and I'm concerned that he might come looking for her now that she's a widow."

John exhaled sharply in relief. He thought that Nelson had only heard rumors and would change his mind about marrying Cassie. Just like Nelson, he'd been impressed with Mrs. Gray and thought that Ned was a poor match. While he could understand why she wasn't happy, he was stunned when he'd learned of her liaison with Tom Richardson, which wasn't the well-kept secret Cassie believed it to be. Tom was a talker.

The sheriff said, "I'm not sure if he'd dare to show his face in Cheyenne, Nelson. But those ghost train stories are being printed in all the newspapers in the West. Some even have a list of the passengers who were saved."

"Is that where this ghost train name came from?"

"I reckon so. I saw it in the *Cheyenne Republic*, so I imagine they got it from other ones. Anyway, what do you want to know about Tom Richardson?"

"What did he do?"

"He stole a necklace from Rudolph Wheeler's jewelry store. By the time Rudolph found me, Tom was already gone. I heard he went to Denver and picked up another job with a different railroad."

"That's what Cassie told me. What does he look like?"

"Average height and build with black hair and brown eyes. He's not a bad looking feller, but he's not very fastidious, if you know what I mean."

"That description doesn't help much. Does he have any identifying marks?"

"Just one that I know about. He has a notch in his left ear. It's pretty easy to spot unless he grows his hair long. I don't know how he got it, but it looks almost like a .44 buzzed a bit too close."

"Does he wear a pistol?"

"Yup. He's got a Winchester too, but that's not unusual. But if you're expecting him to show up, the easiest way to spot him might be by finding his horse. When he was here, he rode a pinto gelding. He had a mostly black head with two white ears and a white muzzle. He might have another horse by now, but if he doesn't, that pinto is pretty easy to spot."

"Thanks, John. I'd love to stay and tell you about the stolen train, but I don't want to miss my train or my wedding."

"Tell your bride that I reckon she's probably the only woman in the territory who could keep you from doing something stupid."

Nelson grinned as he rose, shook the sheriff's hand and replied, "I'm not sure that even she could prevent that, John."

"Congratulations, Nelson, and not for saving the ghost train."

Nelson was still grinning as he left the sheriff's office and waved at the deputy when he passed by the desk. He knew he wasn't in danger of missing the train because they would delay their departure until he returned. But he did want them to move as soon as possible. It was another six hours to Granger, then just three more to Ogden and Jessie.

As he quickly walked to the train, he thought about what the sheriff had told him about Tom Richardson. Even though Cassie had freely admitted to the man's crudeness, he was a bit surprised that even the sheriff had noticed. His notched ear and his pinto were valuable things to know. Even though no one, including the sheriff, seemed to believe he'd bother to find Cassie, Nelson felt better knowing how to spot him.

He hopped onto the caboose's steel steps, opened the door and stepped inside.

"We're almost ready to roll, Nelson," said Joe Hillman, the conductor.

"That's faster than I expected."

"They got the greasing done faster than they figured. I'll let them know you're back."

Nelson sat at the desk and watched Joe leave. He took off his hat and set it on the desk. The train would have to stop once more for coal and water at Rawlins, then the next stop would be Granger. They'd top off the water and coal there, then be on their way to Ogden.

He felt the train jerk before it began to slowly accelerate. Getting those heavy cars moving put the greatest strain on the locomotive. Once they reached Granger and started down that long downslope, the engine could almost coast once it had the cars up to speed.

By the time Joe returned to the caboose with Phil, Nelson was already sitting on the caboose steps. He hadn't seen much of a change in the landscape yet but knew that would soon change.

———

"His train just left Cheyenne, Jack," Carl said as he trotted into their camp.

Jack nodded then replied, "Okay. Six more hours to Granger and then another ninety minutes before he reaches us. The next scheduled train will pass in two hours heading to Granger and the last one heading to Ogden will cross our bridge three hours later. Then we can go to work."

"Are we going to stay and watch the bridge take that train down?" asked Pooch McGregor.

Jack answered, "We have to make sure nobody survives, Pooch. It'll be pretty impressive when that locomotive hits the bottom, too."

Joe Smith asked, "Have you ever seen one go down like that, boss?"

"Nope, but I know what will happen. The cars go down first. Now that bridge is only a little over a hundred feet long and the freight train must be a good eight or nine hundred feet. So, when the bridge goes, the locomotive and coal car will almost be on the other end. They'll be yanked backwards while the cars right behind it go straight down. The cars on the other side of the bridge that haven't reached it yet will be pulled down as the other cars fall.

"When the locomotive's coal car hits the bottom, it'll make an enormous cloud of coal dust. Then the firebox flames will ignite it like a giant bomb. It'll send pieces of bridge, locomotive and cars hundreds of yards away. We'll be watching from a safe distance in the trees for safety, but it'll still be spectacular."

The thought of watching the incredible disaster squashed any remaining sense of guilt that the railroad men still harbored. Big Bob didn't have any guilt to quash, so he just grinned.

———

When she'd arrived at the station, Homer told Cassie that the freight would be arriving just before seven o'clock. It was about what she'd expected, but hearing Homer confirm the time still made her smile.

She'd returned to the house to have her lunch and decided to prepare a big meal so she wouldn't have to cook when Nelson arrived. She'd have plenty of leftovers that they could share after they shared each other.

Cassie set to work with an almost uncontrollable enthusiasm. In just seven more hours, she'd be reunited with Nelson. She realized how silly it would seem to anyone else because he'd only been gone four days, yet she was acting as if he was returning from a four-year voyage of exploration. She didn't care how silly it might have been, she just wanted Nelson back.

––––––

The freight had just rolled out of Granger and Nelson stepped back out of the caboose to let Phil and Joe get some rest. Just before he left the caboose, he'd removed his shoulder holster in anticipation of Cassie's welcome. He didn't want to damage her ribs with the pistol knowing how tightly they would be embracing. He'd rolled it up and stored it in his travel bag.

So, when he took his now accustomed seat on the caboose's steps, he was unarmed for the first time in years, except when he slept. He wasn't even without a pistol for much of the times that he'd been resting away from his house, for that matter. But this was a special time for him. He only had Jessie on his mind and had set Jack Rodgers aside for a while.

––––––

Sixty-two miles away, Jack hadn't forgotten about Nelson. He had joined his men and he swung his axe at one of the designated supports. Big Bob had already finished with two of them while the others were still sawing or chopping at their first. It was important to leave enough structural strength so that the bridge didn't collapse on their heads, so just forty-five minutes after they started, Jack was satisfied that they'd done sufficient damage.

After collecting all their tools, they climbed out of the creek's small canyon using the ramps that the workers who built the bridge had created. After the four on the northern side crossed the bridge to join Jack, Big Bob and Mick Gifford, they walked to their horses and returned their tools to the pack saddle.

"We'll watch from over there," Jack said as he pointed to the nearby trees.

Audie Scott swallowed the water from his canteen then asked, "Is that far enough away, boss?"

"The trees will block all of the falling debris. The force of the explosion will be directed into the sky by the walls along the creek. We'll be fine."

"Okay, boss. Let's go," Carl said with a grin before he mounted his horse.

Jack was smiling as well when he stepped into his saddle then glanced north toward Granger. He knew that the freight wouldn't arrive for another two hours or so, but he was already envisioning the explosive calamity in his mind. He already decided that it wouldn't be the last Union Pacific train to meet its end this way. He'd have to make sure that the next one had an express car so his boys would be rewarded.

They soon reached the trees and dismounted. Some of the men lit cigarettes, while others chewed jerky or tobacco. Jack just checked his pocket watch. Soon…it would be soon.

———

Now that the locomotive had the assistance of gravity, the same throttle setting that had it moving at thirty miles per hour, would now have it moving at more than forty. But even using a lower position still had the train heading for Ogden at thirty-five miles per hour.

It may not have been a noticeable difference, but it unwittingly altered Jack's calculations for the bridge collapse. Another factor he'd failed to take into account was the nature of the train itself. Most freight trains had at least fifteen cars, with a mixture of boxcars, flat cars and stock cars. The train that was heading for disaster may have been just as heavy as a normal freight, but it was much shorter.

When he first spotted the smoke in the distance, Jack didn't have to tell the men that the train was coming. They were all pointing and excitedly chattering about the imminent crash.

———

Nelson was still sitting on the steel steps and watching the more interesting scenery pass by. The next time Joe and Phil had to leave the caboose to do their jobs was when the train approached Ogden. They'd just passed Bridger and the next small station was Leroy. Then it would roll past tiny Piedmont, the larger town of Castle Rock and finally Echo. An hour after leaving Echo, he'd see Cassie again.

He was still picturing Jessie waiting at the platform when he heard a loud crack, almost like a giant bullwhip, then the train shook, and he immediately knew what had happened.

He shot to his feet and was about to grab the caboose door to yank it open so Phil and Joe could escape, but he never got the chance.

Just three seconds after hearing the sound of timbers snapping, the caboose was yanked forward, sending him flying off the steel platform. He hit the railbed but missed the tracks and crossties as he tumbled and rolled across the ground while the bridge collapsed under the massive weight of the train.

None of the men who were responsible for the disaster noticed Nelson but were watching their handiwork.

It was Jack who first realized the mistake he'd made when the locomotive and coal car successfully crossed the bridge before it began to fail. As the cars tumbled with the rails and supports, they began tugging the locomotive back from the solid ground. Just when it appeared that the locomotive would join the rest of the train, the coupling between the coal car and the first flat car snapped.

While the locomotive didn't rocket away, it did stop sliding backwards. As soon as he'd felt his locomotive being pulled back toward the collapsing bridge, Al Brewster had shoved his throttle to the wall while his fireman leapt out of the cab.

Charlie Tubbs slammed hard into the ground after leaving the cab, but after he regained his feet, he sprinted away to find safety from the explosion he knew was imminent. As he ran, he kept glancing back watching the locomotive continue to slide backwards. Just before the coupling snapped, saving the engine and coal car, he entered the safety of the trees and found himself facing seven armed men.

When Al felt his locomotive stop after the coupling snapped, he quickly yanked back on the throttle to a more normal setting. He wanted to get about a hundred yards away from the bridge before he left his cab to check on the disaster behind him.

Nelson had stopped rolling but didn't get up. He expected that the locomotive would soon add its explosive force to the collapse, and he was close enough to the bridge that the blast would be devastating.

When he looked across the fallen bridge, because of the enormous dust cloud, it took him a few seconds to find the locomotive still on the tracks. It may have been a horrendous accident, but he believed that it was Jack Rodgers' work. With no imminent explosion, Nelson stood and walked to the edge of the creek to see if Phil or Joe had survived. It wasn't likely, but he still had to check. The dust cloud was denser down in the creek, but he could make out the remains of the caboose under one of the steam engines and knew that they were both dead.

He dusted himself off and looked back at the locomotive. It was still difficult to make out, but he did notice that it was slowly moving away from the creek. He assumed that the engineer was leaving because he had realized the collapse had been caused by Jack Rodgers' gang. He'd been warned about that possibility by the U.P. telegram and by Nelson himself.

He knew that the engineer couldn't come back to pick him up, so he began looking for the best way to cross the creek. He knew that the bridge and rail cars would make it impossible to cross here, so he walked away from the tracks to reach the road that usually ran parallel to the railroad but would usually cross a river or creek at a ford that was out of the railroad's surveyed path.

He'd only walked about fifty feet when he heard two gunshots and whipped around. He still couldn't see very well and wasn't sure where the shots had originated. So, he froze in place and just waited.

Big Bob holstered his pistol and didn't say anything. Charlie Tubbs lay dead just twelve feet in front of him with two bullet holes in his chest.

The railroad men were stunned by Bob's reaction when he'd seen the fireman.

Jack's attention was already on the slowly moving locomotive. He felt cheated when the steam engine hadn't been ripped off the tracks. Like Nelson, he believed that the engineer would simply push his throttles forward and head for Castle Rock to tell them of the disaster, but he soon smiled when he saw Al Brewster stop his locomotive then hop to the ground.

"Let's get that engineer," Jack quickly said before he pulled his pistol and left the trees.

Bob was the first to follow and the others trailed their boss and the big man.

Al had heard the gunshot, but thought it was another timber cracking or one of the flat cars shifting, so he didn't even look at the trees as he trotted toward the downed bridge.

Nelson was surprised when he saw the locomotive stop and wanted to shout, but immediately realized that if he did, it wouldn't save Al. It would, however, let Jack know that he was alive. If he even had his Webley, he would have still shouted to let Jack come after him, but he had nothing.

He continued to walk away from the tracks but still watched the drama unfolding a few hundred feet away. He hoped that he was wrong about the gunshots and Al would be able to return to his locomotive with Charlie and let the railroad know of the damage. When he spotted motion just behind Al, he knew that he hadn't been mistaken.

Al never heard anyone behind him before Bob and Jack each put a .44 into his back.

After Al collapsed to the ground, Jack turned to Mick Gifford and said, "Get into the cab and move the locomotive another four or five hundred yards down the track. Then open that throttle all the way and get it moving in reverse. Bail out of there and head for the trees once it starts rolling."

Mick grinned then exclaimed, "You got it, boss!" before he trotted back to the locomotive.

Jack turned to the others and said, "We'd better get back in those trees, boys. The show isn't over yet."

He turned and began walking quickly toward the pines leading the others.

Nelson had seen Jack and Big Bob shoot Al in the back and cursed himself for not being able to put a .45 into each of them before they pulled those triggers. He still may not have set off the box of dynamite but was no longer convinced it had been the right thing to do. He may have saved some disgruntled railroaders, but he'd just cost the lives of four innocent men.

Before he resumed walking, he noticed one of them heading for the locomotive while the others walked in the other direction. It didn't take a genius to figure out what they were planning to do, so Nelson began jogging away before that locomotive exploded.

Mick Gifford climbed into the cab and without bothering to even glance at any of the gauges, pushed the throttle until it began moving forward. He glanced out of the cab's window to gauge the distance before he pulled the throttle to its back stop, then hurried back to the ground as the locomotive's drive wheels quickly reversed and slowed the locomotive.

The steam engine was pouring smoke out of its stack as it gained speed and Mick raced for the closest trees.

He wanted to reach their protection and still be able to watch the show.

Nelson could hear the locomotive's drive wheels as they squealed to change its direction and knew he didn't have much time. He didn't look behind him as he picked up the pace and just before he spotted the roadway, he turned right and ducked into the trees.

He didn't need to watch the locomotive tumble over the edge but covered his ears as he waited for the blast.

Jack hadn't warned anyone about the shock wave, but when he placed his hands over his ears, the others who were with him did the same. Only Mick Gifford watched with his hands by his side.

The coal car tipped and angled over just seconds before the locomotive followed. It seemed to be instantaneous to the men watching, but the process of the coal car smashing into one of the fallen flat cars, sending its tons of coal and accompanying clouds of dust into the air took more than a second. The locomotive's firebox's ignition took only a tiny fraction of the next second. As powerful as that explosion was, it was almost immediately enhanced by the powerful eruption of steam when the locomotive's boiler ruptured. It seemed like one massive blast, but it was really two.

The knowledge of physics and chemistry necessary to understand what had happened didn't matter to any of the men who had created it. They were just in awe of the power they'd unleashed.

Nelson may not have understood it either, but even as debris began raining down nearby, he knew that unless he killed them all, they'd do it again.

With the giant cloud of dust and water vapor still hanging over the creek, Jack turned and said, "Let's get out of here before anybody shows up."

After they were joined by a temporarily deaf Mick Gifford, they mounted their horses and headed back to their camp. They'd be out of the area within an hour. The only evidence they'd left behind that would let the investigators know it hadn't been an accident were the two bodies with bullet holes in their backs.

Jack didn't care if they knew he was behind it. He'd eliminated Nelson Cook and there was no one else who would be able to predict what he might do next.

———

Nelson was still fuming as he walked along the road heading toward Piedmont. He also felt incredibly guilty knowing that four men had died because of his generosity to those ex-railroaders. If he'd pulled his trigger and set off that dynamite, they'd still be alive. He didn't care as much about the bridge or train. They were just things. And derailments and bridge collapses were an expected cost of the railroad business. But he'd have to set aside that heavy weight of guilt until after he ended this. He couldn't afford wasting any emotions or thought until Jack Rodgers was dead.

He was sure that the bosses who had praised him just two days ago would demand his head. But it didn't matter if he still had the badge or not. He'd track down Jack Rodgers no matter how long it took.

But now Jack had unwittingly given Nelson an advantage. Jack probably knew he was on the train, so as far as Jack was concerned, Nelson was now dead. It wasn't much of an advantage, but it was something.

After crossing the ford, he started thinking about how he could use that advantage. He had to avoid using the telegraph to let Cassie or anyone else know he was alive because he suspected that Jack would find out. He could have walked to nearby Leroy but thought Jack's gang might be in down.

Nelson still had almost eighty dollars in his wallet, so when he arrived in Piedmont, he'd see if he could buy a horse or a mule.

If he had to ride bareback, he could handle it for the remaining ninety miles to Ogden.

He knew it was only about ten miles to Piedmont, so he should be able to reach the town long before sunset. Trying to find a cheap horse might be difficult. He knew that he'd be able to borrow one if he showed his badge or identified himself but may as well send a telegram telling Jack that he was still breathing.

He was still five or six miles out of the town when he saw a ranch house and barn in the distance. More importantly, he saw a corral with at least a dozen horses. He picked up the pace in anticipation of making a deal.

––––––

In Echo and Ogden, the first signs that there was trouble was when a message coming from Granger stopped in mid-word. The operators in both towns began sending test messages to determine where the line was broken. It didn't take long to determine that it had to be between Piedmont and Leroy.

As Echo was the closest big town to the break, they would dispatch a two-man crew to repair the line. It wasn't uncommon, so there was no rush. Telegraph traffic would just have to be rerouted around the break until it was fixed. The same was true for railroad traffic, but it was a lot more troublesome and would add much more time and cost for the trains to reach their destinations.

———

Nelson approached the ranch house but stopped a hundred feet away.

He shouted, "Hello, the house!" then waited for someone to step outside.

He was still waiting when a voice came from his right.

"What can I do for you, mister?"

Nelson turned and smiled at the middle-aged man who was wiping his hands with a red towel.

"I just saw the railroad bridge collapse and the freight train that was crossing crashed into the creek."

"I thought that mighta been thunder. Anybody killed?"

Nelson nodded and said, "The engineer, fireman, conductor and brakeman. None of them escaped."

"Who are you? How come you know who was on the train?"

Nelson realized he had to trust the man because things could get touchy if he didn't.

"My name is Nelson Cook and I'm a special agent for the Union Pacific. I was on sitting on the caboose's platform when the bridge collapsed and was thrown to the ground."

"You're that feller that found the ghost train; ain't ya?"

"Yes, sir. The same men who stole the train are the ones who made the bridge collapse. I think that the man who organized it was trying to kill me as well as damage the railroad. I don't want him to know I'm still alive because I intend to kill them all."

The rancher studied Nelson for a few seconds before he asked, "Do you need to get to town?"

"I need to get to Ogden without anyone knowing that I'm still breathing. I was going to buy a horse in Piedmont."

"There ain't no need for that. You can borrow one of mine and a saddle, too. I can spare 'em. You hungry?"

Nelson replied, "Not yet, but I will be later. It's a long ride to Ogden."

"About eight hours if you push it, I reckon. I'll tell you what. I'll have the missus make up somethin' to take with ya while you pick out a horse from the corral."

Nelson smiled then asked, "Don't you want to at least see my badge?"

"Nope. You seem like an honest young feller."

"Thank you."

The rancher waved and headed for his house while Nelson walked to the corral. He was surprised and grateful for the man's trust and hadn't even asked his name. He'd remedy that when he returned. He'd need a strong horse for the hurried journey because he would need its endurance. When he returned the horse, he'd send along Boomer Wilson's horse as well as a form of payment.

––––––

Twenty minutes later, Nelson waved to Elmer Tincher as he rode down his access road to reach the road to Piedmont. He'd stop at the small office to have them send a telegram from an onlooker who had seen the collapse. It would spur Homer into action. He wasn't worried about another train falling on top of the first because the missing rails were easily spotted and would give the engineer plenty of time to pull his train to a stop.

He had to word it carefully to make it sound as if it was sent by a cowhand rather than a railroad man. He wished he could send a message to Cassie to let her know he was alive and well but was still concerned that Jack might be listening to the traffic.

––––––

Cassie was blissfully unaware of the tragedy or even the broken telegraph connection as she prepared for Nelson's return. She had plenty of food ready and had even folded back the sheet to their bed as if he needed the incentive.

She was reading Dickens' *David Copperfield* to fill the rest of the empty time before Nelson's train arrived. She still planned to be on the platform by six o'clock.

––––––

Nelson was lucky to find Piedmont's only telegrapher still in his office, but not surprised. The break in the telegraph line would create a lot of traffic between Piedmont and the bigger towns of Ogden and Echo as they worked to repair the damage.

He quickly wrote out his message and almost left without paying the eighty cents in order to maintain his anonymity. But his message did explain to the operator the reason for the downed line and its location. He almost used his own name as the sender, but quickly created a fictional name that might give Cassie a clue that he wasn't dead.

After he returned to the road to Castle Rock, he set the nice gelding to a fast trot. He wanted to reach his house as soon as possible. He expected that once Cassie heard the news of the derailment, she would be more than just upset unless she was able to decrypt the sender's true identity. Hurting Cassie was one more reason for his burning desire to stop Jack and his men. He no longer cared what they had done for a living before joining Jack. They were all killers now, and he wasn't about to let them harm anyone else.

———

Cassie set her book down and even though it wasn't six o'clock yet, she stood and walked to the door. She pulled her hat from the coat rack hook and put it on before leaving the house. It was a pleasant summer evening, and she was looking forward to a much more pleasant summer night.

At the Western Union office, John Hipper just finished sending his acknowledgement to the Piedmont operator and wished he hadn't written the message he'd received. He'd give it to Homer Watson and was relieved that Homer would be the one to have to tell Cassie. When John had given her the last message from Nelson, he'd almost giggled. This new one was beyond tragic and hoped she talked to Homer before she came into his office because he knew he couldn't hide his distress.

He handed it to Billy Emerson and told him to bring it next door to Mister Watson when his key began chattering again. When it finished, he'd send a telegram to the Union Pacific in Omaha using the southern line to notify them of the collapsed bridge and the loss of their freight train with Nelson Cook on board.

Billy knew better than to open the telegram and after seeing Mister Hipper's face, he wasn't going to stick around after he gave it to Mister Watson. It must be horrible news.

Homer was only in the office because he, like many of the other local Union Pacific employees, wanted to be there when Nelson's freight arrived. It wasn't just to ask him what the bosses said, either. The news that he and Cassie were going to be married tomorrow had been the source of much gossip and ribald humor among the railroad men.

Billy entered, handed Homer the telegram and wordlessly hurried away.

243

Homer was surprised that Billy hadn't patiently waited for a penny, even though he knew such generosity would be a rarity. He hadn't even smiled at him, which was even stranger.

He quickly opened the page and felt his stomach drop as he read:

UNION PACIFIC OFFICE OGDEN UT

BRIDGE COLLAPSED NEAR HOMER
FREIGHT TRAIN GONE
NO SURVIVORS
NOT ACCIDENT
SAW ENGINEER SHOT
SEVEN RIDERS
AFTER ENGINEER SHOT
MEN DROVE ENGINE INTO CREEK
COULD NOT HELP
SORRY

H GRAY PIEDMONT WY

Homer read it again and despite his crushing sense of loss, knew he had a lot of work to do. He wasn't even thinking of Cassie as he stood and walked slowly out of his office. He needed to get a repair crew ready to assist the bigger team that would come from Cheyenne to repair the bridge. He was depending on John Hipper to notify headquarters but would ask him once he got things moving.

Cassie was almost gliding across the boardwalk as she made her way to the station. Nothing seemed amiss as she crossed the main street to reach the platform. It was only when she was about to place her left foot on the platform and saw Homer talking to another man that she began to suspect that something was wrong. Homer's face was taut, and the other man seemed agitated by what Homer was telling him. She still didn't believe that it had anything to do with her or Nelson but stepped onto the platform and walked slowly toward Homer.

Homer's back was to Cassie, but when Gary Newton saw her over Homer's shoulder, he quickly shushed Homer as he nodded towards her.

Homer turned and didn't try to mask his anguish as he quickly asked, "Will you come into my office, Cassie?"

"What's wrong, Homer?" she asked sharply.

He took her arm and simply replied, "Please."

As she stepped beside Homer, Cassie suddenly understood that whatever was creating the tension must involve Nelson. She was imagining all manners of evil as they entered his big office. When he closed the door, she almost collapsed into the chair.

Homer didn't sit behind his desk, but half-sat on the front of the desktop as he looked down at Cassie.

"Cassie, I just received this telegram," he said as he handed her the message.

He had planned to tell her, but he found it almost impossible and was surprised that he could even tell her about the telegram.

Cassie took the sheet from his trembling fingers and expected the worst. If she wasn't so worried about the message, she might have been proud of herself because her own hand was steady.

She took a deep breath and read the block letters. After she finished, she closed her eyes and felt tears begin to slide across her cheeks. *This wasn't possible! How could this happen before they spent even a single night together?*

Homer watched her quietly weep and wished there was something he could do. His wife could probably help but he didn't want to leave Cassie alone.

Cassie continued to cry without sobbing as she tried to absorb the reality in those ten short sentences. Nelson was gone and she had to learn to live without him. He'd already given her so much by letting her be herself and now it was all she had. She had many decisions ahead of her but was determined to do nothing that would have disappointed Nelson.

She opened her eyes and wiped the moisture from her cheeks as she looked up at Homer.

"I'll be all right now, Homer. I'm going to go home and rest. May I keep the telegram?"

Homer nodded because he knew that there was another copy in the Western Union office.

Cassie rose, walked to the door and after opening it, left the office and soon stepped back onto Jackson Street to make the lonely walk back to Nelson's house.

Homer still had work to do but decided to run home and tell Edith so she could visit Cassie tomorrow.

Cassie didn't even hear the greetings from the folks she passed as she walked along the boardwalks then turned onto Saint Street.

After she'd entered the house, she closed the door and walked to the couch. After lighting a lamp, she slowly sat down to let her mind adjust to a world without Nelson Cook. She was certain that it had been Jack Rodgers who had collapsed the bridge and killed Nelson. The man who'd sent the telegram had reported that he'd seen seven riders.

As she recalled reading about those seven men, she snapped, "*What kind of man watches them shoot someone and does nothing?*"

She opened the telegram again to see the name of the coward who had sent the message. She was sure that she wouldn't know him, but when she had the chance, she'd find him and give him a tongue lashing that he'd never forget.

When she read the name, she was startled. *What were the odds of the stranger having the same name as her dead husband? Why didn't he include his Christian name?* All he'd written was H. Gray. If it had been a short telegram, she could understand his need to save a few pennies, especially if he had a long name. But it had been a long telegram and Western Union probably hadn't even charged him for it. *So, why did he just use the letter H?*

Maybe he was embarrassed by his first name. That made more sense, so she began running down the list of Christian names beginning with H. Hank, Harry, Henry...

Then she stopped and stared at the message again. When she'd asked Nelson about his Christian name, he said that is father was a distant relative of the famous English sailor and explorer, Admiral James Cook. He'd named his firstborn son after another British naval hero, Admiral Nelson. She'd never asked him his middle name because it hadn't come up. Suddenly, it loomed as incredibly important.

She stood quickly and walked to the bookcase and on the bottom shelf, found a worn copy of Robert Southey's *The Life of Nelson*. She slipped it free and opened it to the title page.

There was an inscription from Nelson's father that read:

248

To my new son, Nelson Horatio Cook,

I know that I reversed the order of the greatest seaman who ever commanded a ship of the Royal Navy, but I'm sure that when you start your schooling, you will be grateful.

I don't expect you to find your way to the ocean to honor his memory or mine. You will be your own man and make your own mark on this world, as Admiral Nelson did. You don't have to achieve fame to be a great man. If you become an honest and good man who treats all men and women with respect and courtesy, then I will be even prouder of you than if you had accomplished great feats yet become an overbearing elitist.

With a father's love,

Henry James Cook

April 11, 1865

She read it once more for the value the short message his father had given to his newborn son. After reading it again, she slowly closed the book and returned it to the bookshelf.

Cassie knew that the telegram had claimed that there were no survivors, but the sender's name gave her a glimmer of hope that it had been sent, not by H. Gray, but by Nelson Horatio Cook. It was just that, a tiny spark, and little more. But it was hope and even a drop of hope was worth more than an ocean of despair.

She sat back on the couch and tried to think of the reason why he would have used a false name to send the telegram. After some thought, she understood why he would prefer not to use either his first name or its initial. Then she laughed in relief and rose from the couch and walked to the kitchen to have some coffee. She could only wait but hoped she just wasn't clutching at straws and that there wasn't really a Hank Gray living in Piedmont.

After starting a fire in the cookstove and filling the coffeepot with water, she sat down and used the time to estimate how long it would take to ride from Piedmont to Ogden. She didn't even know where the town was, but assumed it was somewhere between Granger and Ogden. Even if it was halfway, Nelson could be back before dawn.

By the time that her coffee was ready, Cassie hadn't given a thought of attending his funeral. They couldn't be married tomorrow because it was Sunday, which he'd failed to notice in his telegram, but she'd be attending her marriage ceremony with Nelson on Monday.

————

Nelson passed through Castle Rock around seven o'clock and after giving the horse a short break, set out for Echo. He'd reach the bigger town in two hours and then have another forty miles to go before he entered Ogden. He didn't expect to see any rail traffic until he passed Echo. The spur south to Park City was still open but unless a work crew left the warehouse at Park

City with supplies to rebuild the bridge, the rails should remain empty. He didn't appreciate the irony that they'd be using the same maintenance locomotive and flat cars that Jack Rodgers had used to move his stolen rail to his spur for the ghost train. As much as he didn't think the term was appropriate, it was shorter than hijacked or stolen. It also had a ring to it.

As he rode into the summer sunset, he was sure that Union Pacific folks on both ends of the lost bridge would be burning the midnight candle getting a large crew ready to be dispatched to the gap in the line. They'd recover as much as they could from the fallen train even as they began the repair work. The yard in Ogden was one of the largest west of Omaha and with the other in Cheyenne, he expected that work would begin tomorrow.

He didn't think that Jack and his gang would remain near the devastated bridge long but would be preparing for his next strike. If he was planning on doing it soon, then he'd hit one of the longer bridges close to Ogden.

Nelson wasn't about to make the mistake of giving him that opportunity again.

———

Jack's men had set up a new camp well south of Piedmont to take a short break. Jack had been pleased with the end result, but not with the execution. If that engineer had realized why the bridge had collapsed, he could have slammed that throttle to the wall and escaped. That could have had severe consequences as it would have removed the expected delay before the disaster was discovered.

It wouldn't happen again. But what irritated him was that he knew it was his fault. He'd misjudged the train's speed and its length. He'd need better intelligence before their next job and that included his own.

They'd probably expect him to sabotage another, longer bridge, but after he'd seen the massive explosion, he quickly had a very different plan in mind that would be even more spectacular.

———

His abused mount was tiring, and Nelson hadn't even reached the halfway point between Echo and Ogden. He'd rested the horse three times and let him graze while he ate Mrs. Tincher's very tasty bacon sandwich but knew that he was still pushing the animal too hard.

He checked his pocket watch and knew that as much as both he and the horse needed to stop for a few hours, he didn't want to enter Ogden after sunrise. He only had another two and a half hours left and almost begged the horse to stay healthy. He wasn't even worried about his own lack of sleep. Getting by with just short amounts of rest were part of the job.

He reduced the horse's speed to a slow trot even though it would add another twenty minutes or so. Aside from his growing concern about Jack's next attack, he was even more worried about Cassie. He was sure that she'd been told about the bridge collapse and the loss of his train but didn't know if she'd seen the telegram. Even if she had, he would be surprised but impressed if she was able to make sense of the sender's name. He just wished her husband had been named Henry rather than Ned. If he'd been able to use N. Gray, she might have had an easier time realizing who had sent it. Hopefully, she'd still be at the house when he snuck in, assuming the horse survived to finish the journey.

————

Jessie was not only still in the house but was still awake. After she'd estimated the earliest that Nelson could return, she had taken a nap. She found that the clock on his mantle had an alarm then wound it to make sure the spring would have enough stored energy to ring the bell long enough to wake her. She had napped for more than two hours and after struggling to wake, slid from under the quilts. She took a cold bath and then heated the coffee. She'd make a new pot around two o'clock for Nelson. She was sure he'd be close to exhaustion but would have to stay awake for a little while to tell her what happened and to ask for her help.

————

Nelson knew that the horse was close to the point of collapse, but there was only another mile in front of them. As much as he wanted to find Cassie to let her know he was alive, he owed it to the horse to take care of him first. He couldn't squeeze another one into his small barn, so he'd leave the gelding in the stock yard after unsaddling him. There was a large trough and a long box full of hay in the corral to calm horses that were awaiting loading. He may be tired himself, but he could survive the three-block journey on foot.

He soon walked the horse to the stock corral gate, dismounted and pulled it open. After leading him to the hay box, he stripped him and left his tack on the closest fence railing. He wished he had a pencil so he could leave a note, but he'd worry about that later.

After closed the corral gate, he strode quickly along quiet, dark Jackson Street heading for Saint Street. He thought that the work crew that would be heading out to the collapsed bridge might already be loading their flatbed, but the station had been quiet. He guessed it was close to three o'clock in the morning, so it wouldn't be quiet much longer.

When he made the turn onto Saint Street, he expected to find it as dark as the rest of the town, but he saw one house with dim light coming from its windows. He knew it was his house and suspected that Homer's wife, Edith, was still with Cassie trying to comfort her. The Watsons were good people.

———

Cassie was curled up on the couch still reading *David Copperfield.* It was difficult to keep track of the plot or remember the characters as she kept glancing at the door, hoping to see it open at any moment.

It was 2:48 a.m. when she heard someone step onto the porch. If it was an evil man who had decided to take advantage of the news of Nelson's death, she didn't care. Before the door handle turned, she dropped the heavy book onto the couch and sprang to her feet.

Nelson expected to find Edith and Cassie talking on the couch but discovered his error as soon as he entered and was happy that he was wrong.

He didn't have a chance to take off his hat or even close the door before Cassie was in his arms with her head buried against his chest. She wasn't crying, but he could feel her shuddering.

Cassie may have convinced herself that Nelson hadn't died but holding him was still a monumental relief. She thought that she was going to be able to restrain herself and just kiss him. Then she would tell him that everyone else believed that he was dead, but she figured out why he used H. Gray as the telegram's sender. But seeing him alive was too overwhelming and restraint wasn't possible.

Nelson finally kicked the door closed with his heel as he continued to hold Cassie.

The sound of the door slamming shut acted as an exclamation point ending Cassie's silence.

She didn't move her head as she said, "They all thought you were dead, Nelson. I did too, until I looked at the name on the bottom of the telegram. Then I knew it was you who had sent it. Why didn't you use your own name?"

"I couldn't use N. Gray for obvious reasons. And I didn't want Jack Rodgers to know that I was alive. I wanted desperately to send one to you, but I'm convinced that Jack has a man listening to the telegraph traffic."

"Well, I don't care about Jack Rodgers or anyone else now. I already had a nap, but you must be exhausted. Do you want to get some sleep or have some coffee and something to eat?"

"Coffee and some food sound good. I'll tell you what happened and what I need you to do after sunrise."

"Alright."

Before they separated, they shared a long, intense kiss. Then Nelson finally removed his hat and jacket, took Cassie's hand and walked with her to the kitchen.

He sat down at the table while she filled two cups of coffee. After setting the coffee and his plate of leftovers before him, she sat down and waited to hear what had happened.

Nelson took a long sip of the very welcome coffee before saying, "I was sitting on the steps of the caboose's platform when I heard a loud crack. Before I even had a chance to open the door to let the conductor and brakeman out…"

As he spoke, Cassie tried to visualize the horrific scene in her mind but knew it was much worse than she could ever imagine. She could see the frustration and anger that was embedded in each word. Cassie understood why he was so upset and probably felt guilty for the accident because he'd let Jack Rodgers go. She also knew that there was nothing she could do to drive that guilt from him. She wasn't even sure that he'd feel better if he was able to put an end to the gang. It made her guilt over her infidelity seem almost petty.

"After I sent that telegram, I just rode that poor horse until he was ready to crash beneath my feet. I left him at the stock corral, but I still have to get him back to his owner. Then I walked here."

As soon as he finished, he began to eat his food while he waited for Cassie's questions.

Cassie had many questions but just smiled at him as he rapidly emptied the plate. For a young woman who had been anxiously expecting to greet her man in a very different fashion just hours ago, she was now simply grateful that she was able to welcome him at all. She understood that all of their other plans had to be set aside until Nelson could deal with Jack Rodgers.

When he popped the last bite of buttered biscuit into his mouth, she asked, "What do you need me to do, Nelson?"

Nelson swallowed then replied, "After sunrise, I want you to go to the station and find Homer. Tell him that I'm alive but not to let anyone else know. At least not yet. Tell him I left the horse in the corral and to just take care of him for now. Then have him come to the house as soon as he can."

"Alright. What else?"

Nelson hung his head and quietly said, "I really messed up, Cassie. I should have shot that case of dynamite and none of this would have happened. Four men are dead, a bridge collapsed, and a train lost because I was so full of myself. I thought it was a game that I was playing with Jack Rodgers, but it's not a game. Jack knew it wasn't, but I was too damned conceited to recognize what it really is. It's nothing less than a war for Jack. He doesn't care about casualties. He wants to do as much damage as possible to the Union Pacific.

"When I talked to him, I thought I understood him. I thought he was logical and would avoid hurting people. After we made the deal, it was only when he refused to promise not to do anything that would make me shoot him that I realized he might not be so reasonable after all. But I didn't realize my mistake until it was too late. Now I have to stop him before he does something worse."

Cassie quietly asked, "Do you have any idea what he might do?"

Nelson slowly shook his head. He knew he wasn't thinking straight and even when he'd been alert and pondering that same question, nothing had seemed obvious or even likely.

"I guess the most obvious guess is that he'd pick an even longer bridge over a much deeper chasm, but I don't think so. I just have no idea what he'll do."

"You're too tired, Nelson. Why don't you get some sleep? Even a couple of hours will help. You have a busy day ahead of you. I'll wake you before I go to talk to Homer."

Nelson looked at her and said, "You're right, Cassie. As much as I want to do something, I'm already too foggy to concentrate on anything. I'll just take off my boots and lay down."

"Let's get you to bed," she said as she stood and took his hand.

Nelson didn't even toss a witticism about getting to bed as he stood and walked with her to their bedroom.

When they reached the bed, Nelson sat down, yanked off his boots and then just stretched out on the quilts with his head on the pillow.

He smiled at Cassie then just before he closed his eyes, she leaned down and kissed him softly before turning and quietly leaving the room. She left the door open before she returned to the kitchen to clean up. She was tired, but nowhere near Nelson's level of exhaustion.

The predawn would arrive in less than two hours and then when the sun first peeked over the horizon, she'd leave the house to find Homer. Cassie knew that Nelson would be leaving her again soon and hoped that their second reunion would be more like the one she'd been expecting when he'd taken that short train to Omaha.

———

When the operations chief in Omaha had received the delayed telegram from Ogden about the disaster, he'd awakened Mister Sullivan and received his marching orders. While Nelson may have blamed himself for the calamity, the president of the railroad had nothing but admiration for the special agent. He'd warned them all about Jack Rodgers and even suggested that it was likely that he'd do something like this. He still believed that Nelson's solution to the release of the train and passenger was not only the correct one, but brilliant as well. But the loss of Nelson Cook meant that he'd have to depend on less competent men to put a stop to Jack Rodgers. It would require the intervention of the U.S. Marshals and maybe the army. The man had to be stopped.

———

That man was sleeping in his big tent with his large outlaw protector snoring on the other side. But before he'd fallen asleep, Jack had begun to outline the first steps of his next costly act of revenge against the Union Pacific. It would take three or four days to execute but would be even more

260

spectacular and damaging than the last. It would take many more lives as well, but as Nelson had finally realized, this was war.

CHAPTER 7

Cassie looked at Nelson who hadn't moved since falling asleep and decided to let him stay that way rather than waking him before she left. She thought that even another twenty minutes of sleep would valuable.

She pulled on her hat and left the house as the sun sent its morning rays across Ogden creating long shadows.

She expected that there would be a beehive of activity at the station because of the repairs and salvage work necessary outside of Homer. She had just stepped onto Jackson Street when that belief was confirmed. There were men shouting and others carrying all sorts of things as they prepared a nearby train that already had flatbed cars full of material.

When she reached the station, she didn't bother going to Homer's office but stopped on the platform and searched among the workers. When she saw him pointing and giving orders to one of them, she wasn't sure that Homer would be able to leave the yard at all but stepped quickly towards him.

Homer had just finished telling Dan Karnowski where to find a large pulley and rope when he spotted Cassie heading his way. He hadn't expected her to be out of bed yet because she'd probably wept for hours before falling asleep. He'd told Edith to visit her around nine o'clock, but now he was going to talk to her much earlier. He just had no idea what she wanted.

He met her just before she stepped off the platform, so he hopped onto the broad floor instead.

"What's wrong, Cassie?" he asked.

She glanced at the madhouse behind him then asked, "Can you leave for thirty minutes or so, Homer?"

He shook his head as he replied, "I wish I could, but we need to get that train out of here as soon as we can. We loaded most of the stuff last night, but I knew the men needed to rest before they left, but they're just about done now. Why would you need me to leave?"

"It's about Nelson. He's not dead and arrived at the house early this morning. He was the one who sent that telegram but didn't want Jack Rodgers to know he was alive."

Homer exclaimed, "*He wasn't killed in that crash?*" then realized he'd been too loud and hoped no one had heard him.

Cassie cringed at his almost shout then said, "He asked me to come and find you so he could explain everything. He was still sleeping when I left. That horse in the corral is the one he borrowed to get here. He said to just take care of it for now."

Homer looked back at the corral then said, "Give me five minutes. I'll tell Charlie to take care of the horse but won't

263

mention how he got there. The work train is almost ready to roll, but I need to make sure we haven't missed anything."

"Thank you, Homer," Cassie said before she turned and quickly walked away.

Homer hadn't quite recovered from her revelation and almost forgot he had a train ready to depart.

He soon recovered and headed for the corral to talk to Charlie. There weren't many animals in the stock corral because of the drop in Union Pacific traffic through Ogden.

Cassie quietly entered the house and after closing the door and hanging her hat, she tiptoed to the bedroom. When she stepped through the threshold, she found Nelson still soundly asleep. If she hadn't seen his chest rising and falling, she might have thought he'd succumbed to some unknown injury.

She smiled at his peaceful face and wished she could let him sleep, but with Homer's imminent arrival, she knew she had to end his short rest. But she wasn't going to shake him into the world of the living.

She slowly stepped closer to the bed and sat on the edge. She touched his stubbled cheek with her fingertips before she leaned forward and kissed him.

Nelson hadn't been dreaming since he crashed onto the bed, but when he felt her touch and then her lips, he believed he'd entered the most wonderful dream possible. He didn't open his eyes, but as he added his own emotions to the kiss, he placed his left hand behind her head.

When she felt his hand, Cassie knew that he was awake and wished she could join him rather than force him to leave the bed.

Nelson knew he had to end the very real dream, so when the kiss ended, he opened his eyes and smiled at Cassie.

"I hope Homer's not watching," he said quietly.

"He'll be here in a few minutes, so I suppose we have to be on our feet when he knocks on the door."

"I guess so."

Cassie stood and waited for Nelson to slide his legs from the bed then stretch his arms once he was sitting upright.

He rose and took her hand before they left the bedroom, but once in the hallway, he said, "I'll be right back," then hurried to the kitchen and left the house to use the privy.

Nelson soon returned then took a few minutes to wash but still wore a heavy coat of stubble on his face. Cassie had just emptied and refilled the coffeepot and was waiting for the hotplate to earn its name when Homer knocked on the front door.

Nelson quickly strode down the short hallway, crossed the front room and opened the door.

Homer grinned and grabbed Nelson's hand free hand as he closed the door with the other.

Homer exclaimed, "I couldn't believe it when Cassie told me you were alive! *What happened?*"

"Let's head to the kitchen and sit down. I know you're probably busier than all get out, but I need to find out what the U.P. is doing."

They were already walking when Homer replied, "You probably can guess most of it. They dispatched a crew from Cheyenne last night and I just sent our crew out."

They sat at the table with Cassie as Homer continued.

"They contacted the army and they're sending a whole company of soldiers to guard the bridge while they fix it."

Nelson wasn't surprised but said, "I don't think Jack's boys are anywhere near that place anymore. I'm just having a devil of a time trying to guess what he's planning."

"I saw that warning from headquarters about bridges, but I guess it didn't help much."

Cassie could see the pain Homer's reminder had caused Nelson, but Nelson didn't mention the guilt he felt for what he perceived as his failure.

Nelson said, "It doesn't hurt to have the army there, but even before that bridge collapsed, I began to wonder if Jack wouldn't

266

want to get me out of the way so it would be easier to continue his reign of terror against the Union Pacific. I even told the crew of my suspicions and felt like an idiot for believing that Jack considered me important enough to destroy a bridge and the train. Now that he believes that I'd dead, I want to use that to try to stop his next attack. The problem is trying to figure out what it will be."

"Do you reckon he's gonna take down another bridge or maybe blow up a tunnel?"

"I don't think so. I don't believe he has any more dynamite, and I don't think he wants to do the most obvious thing and collapse an even longer bridge. He probably expects that the Union Pacific will send crews to inspect them and he'd run the risk of being caught in the act."

"What else can he do?"

Nelson was thinking about it when Cassie said, "Couldn't he burn down a station like Echo or even Ogden?"

Nelson looked at her and replied, "He could, but it wouldn't be nearly as destructive as taking down a bridge and he'd risk being seen. He'll want something at least as dramatic as the last one."

"What are you going to do, Nelson?" Homer asked.

"I need to stay in the house and think about it, but there is one more thing you could do for me."

"I'll do anything you need, Nelson."

Nelson smiled at Cassie then said, "Can you and Edith come here later today and bring Judge Bye? Have him bring the paperwork so Cassie and I can be married."

Homer stared at Nelson for a few seconds, then shifted his eyes to a smiling Cassie as he began to smile himself.

Cassie didn't say anything but squeezed Nelson's hand.

Homer said, "Edith is going to stop by around nine o'clock anyway. I asked her to come and comfort Cassie, but I reckon she'd rather be a witness for a wedding."

Cassie still had Nelson's hand tightly in hers as she laughed. Nelson just smiled and nodded as Homer stood to leave.

"I'll show myself out. I reckon you two have some serious talking to do."

"I'm afraid that's all we can do, Homer," Nelson said before Homer turned and left the kitchen.

After they heard the front door open and close, Cassie said, "You know that it's Sunday; don't you?"

"I wasn't sure, but that doesn't matter. Homer will drag the judge out of his house if he has to, but I don't think it'll be necessary. I just don't want to leave here again before I make you my wife, Cassie."

"If you're worried about leaving me destitute, you shouldn't be. I'm well situated."

"I hadn't even thought of it. I promised you in the telegram I sent from Omaha that we'd be married the day after I returned, and I'll honor that promise."

Cassie smiled as she replied, "It was well after midnight when you returned, Nelson. Tomorrow is the next day."

Nelson laughed and asked, "So, does that mean you want to delay the ceremony? Just to warn you, it's more than likely that I won't be here tomorrow."

"No, I don't want to push it off another day, even if you weren't leaving. We were meant to find each other; weren't we?"

"I felt the same way from the start."

"Do you realize that even if you consider our courtship to have begun when I took your Winchester, that it's only been a week? And most of that time, we've been apart."

"I know. I courted Genevieve for more than six months and still had doubts the day we were married. I'm sure that even if you and I courted for another year, I'd be just as sure on the last day as I am now."

"I had more than just a few of those doubts even before Ned asked to court me. I've known that you were the one man I wanted to share my life from that first day."

"I guess that it's the only good thing to come out of this whole Jack Rodgers disaster."

Cassie grew serious as she asked, "How can you stop him?"

"I don't think that I'll be able to track him down in time because he could be anywhere in Wyoming, Utah or Idaho. I have to try to come up with at least an inkling of what he might be planning."

"You said it had to be more impressive than collapsing a bridge under a train. What could be more spectacular than that if it wasn't just finding a longer bridge to destroy?"

Nelson closed his eyes as he tried to imagine something incredibly destructive when Cassie provided what had to be the only likely possibility.

"What if he figured out how to crash two trains?"

Nelson's eyes popped open and then stared at her.

Cassie saw the flash of insight in his eyes and waited for him to respond but suspected it might be a while.

As soon as she'd said two trains, Nelson's mind had started to churn. Damaging or changing switches to keep two trains traveling in opposite directions on the same track wouldn't work. They'd have to have a train of their own that wasn't supposed to be on the tracks at all to create a head-on collision. They'd already stolen one train and maybe that had been Jack's plan all along. If it hadn't been for the dynamite and the ransom telegram, he would have believed it. But if Jack was going to arrange for a massive collision, it was a new plan and would require that he steal another train.

He finally said, "I think you may be right, Cassie. It's different enough from what he'd done before and would be even more disastrous. I have a lot of details to figure out, but the more I think about it, the more I'm convinced that's exactly what Jack will do."

Cassie was pleased that her idea had been willingly accepted. It was another example of how Nelson saw her as a partner and not a servant.

She smiled and asked, "If we're going to be married in a couple of hours, don't you think you should at least shave for the occasion?"

Nelson grinned as he stood and replied, "I'll even take a bath, ma'am. I'm sure that I smell to high heaven. I'll draw another bath after I'm done because you won't want to use the muddy water I leave behind."

"Thank you, sir," she said before he left the kitchen and headed for their room to get some fresh clothes.

She remained sitting at the table after he'd entered the bathroom but soon realized that the water in the coffeepot had almost boiled completely away.

———

Even as he scrubbed away the accumulated filth, Nelson tried to think of how Jack could manage to steal another train. He couldn't use the line to Granger because it was going to be closed for at least a week while they rebuilt the bridge. If Jack hadn't been so focused on the Union Pacific, it would be much more difficult to try to determine where he'd strike next. The Central Pacific and the Denver & Pacific each used Ogden as a central hub. Nelson didn't believe that Jack would steal a train from either of them to ram into a Union Pacific train. He'd want to limit the damage to the U.P.

By the time he was scraping the whiskers from his face, he'd at least decided to take a few steps that would make that possibility less likely. He was still convinced that Jack was able to pick up the messages that passed over the Western Union wires, so he had to be careful not to tip his hand.

After he'd cleaned the tub of its dark ring and refilled it for Cassie, he left the bathroom in his clean clothes and headed for the kitchen.

Cassie bounced to her feet when she heard the door open, grabbed her nicest dress from the table and hurried to the bathroom but was intercepted and kissed before she was allowed to continue.

Nelson poured himself a cup of coffee and began to compose a telegram he'd have Homer send to the bosses in Omaha. He didn't want them to know he was alive yet and wasn't sure if they didn't want his head as badly as Jack did. He was sure that William Burns was already telling Mister Sullivan that he wasn't to blame for his agent's blunder.

He hadn't finished his coffee when he walked to his room and took out some paper and a pencil from his desk drawer then returned to the kitchen.

He wrote his carefully worded telegram and set it aside and sketched a crude map of the Union Pacific lines that ran out of Ogden. It was just a method to help him focus.

———

Even as Nelson studied his hand drawn map, Jack Rodgers had his men on the move from their camp south of Castle Rock. They didn't go anywhere near the tracks as he was sure they'd be crowded with repair crews by now. They were riding through the same forest that Nelson had used to find the ghost train and to bring the passengers to safety at Castle Rock. They were further south than where they'd built their small spur, but still following the contour of the landscape.

Jack would have them set up camp just east of Park City and then he'd explain the details of their next job. Jack was reasonably confident that if Nelson Cook still lived, even he wouldn't be able to figure out what that plan would be. But now that the agent was dead, he wasn't concerned at all. They'd all be expecting another bridge collapse and would send dozens of workers to inspect the beams supporting every one of them. He smiled at the thought of their wasted effort. Idiots…they were all idiots.

———

By the time Cassie joined him at the table, Nelson still hadn't figured out how Jack could manage to steal another train, especially after Homer sent the warning telegram.

"No luck, yet?" she asked.

He smiled and replied, "Not yet. You look very nice, Cassie. Have I ever told you how pretty you are?"

"No, sir. You haven't commented about my appearance a single time. I suppose I should be offended, but I'm actually very pleased that you hadn't. I'm grateful that you seem to value my character more than my packaging. But I hope that you'll still appreciate my wrapping enough to make me cry out in ecstasy."

Nelson laughed then said, "I am very fond of your packaging, ma'am. It's not that I haven't noticed, it's just that I've never had the chance to tell you just how much I do appreciate everything about you. I love you, Cassie. I love everything about you."

"I love you too, Nelson. Will we have time to consummate our marriage before you leave?"

"I haven't even figured out what to do yet, so you'll be the sole focus of my attention after the judge and our witnesses leave the house."

"Even in the middle of the afternoon in broad daylight? What of my modesty?"

Nelson laughed before replying, "I'll close my eyes before I rip off your dress and throw you to our marital bed. Is that sufficient?"

"Don't you dare close your eyes, Mister Cook! You'll spoil half of the fun."

"I was going to suggest that we wait until after sunset, but I imagine that's even worse than closing my eyes."

"I don't expect us to wait that long, but I don't plan to let our first night together go to waste either. I want to make the most of every minute we can spend together."

He was still smiling as he took her hands and said, "I wish I didn't have to leave at all, Cassie."

"I know. But you don't have a choice, Nelson. It's not about what your bosses tell you to do, either. It's what you need to do now."

"Thank you for understanding me, Cassie. Hopefully, this will be finished in less than a week. Whatever the Union Pacific chooses to do with me later doesn't matter."

"I don't think they'll blame you for what happened, Nelson. You even warned them that it might happen."

"That warning wouldn't have been necessary if I had put a .45 into that case of dynamite. If they knew I was alive, my boss would be loudly reminding the president of the railroad that he'd ordered me to just scout and not interfere with his much better plan which probably didn't even exist."

"I still don't think you're going to be fired. But you're right. It doesn't matter. I have plenty of savings so you can do whatever you want."

"I'm not about to make the expected manly response by telling you that it's your money and I won't be a money grubber. We can share our money because it's just part of sharing our lives. I don't want to be fired because I enjoy the work."

"We'll see what happens. So, have you figured out what Mister Rodgers might be planning?"

"I still think you're right about the two trains, but I'm having a difficult time trying to imagine how he'll get the second train that he'll need to create the collision."

"I'm sure you'll come up with it. Maybe you just need to let it go and think about your bride for a while. She's been thinking about you almost exclusively for some time now."

Nelson smiled then said, "You're right again, Mrs. Cook. I do need to put it aside for a while. He only destroyed the bridge yesterday, so he'll need to ride to his next campsite before he does anything."

Cassie stood, took two steps, then sat on his lap and put her arms around his neck.

"This ought to take Jack Rodgers out of your mind."

Nelson pulled her closer and kissed her to express his appreciation of her mind and now her marvelous body that was pressed close to him.

Cassie felt the same rush she'd experienced the first time they'd kissed and wanted so much more. There was no doubt that Nelson had the same intentions, but they were going to be wed soon and there wasn't enough time to pre-consummate their marriage.

As soon as the kiss ended, she slid from his lap, let out a long breath and said, "That was close."

Nelson smiled and said, "Very," before he stood and had to restrain himself from scooping her back into his arms.

————

As they awaited the judge and their witnesses, Jack was still leading his band through the trees and around the rocky crags as they continued heading southwest. The others were chatting about the awesome display they'd witnessed yesterday, but Jack ignored them. He was calculating time and distance to arrive at the best possible moment for the horrific collision. He knew where he'd get his train and by the time that they realized it was gone, it would be too late.

He'd heard the stories that the newspapers had printed referring to his first job as a 'ghost train', and that had inspired him to add a touch of black humor to the next job. While the train he'd steal would be far from supernatural, he'd make some minor modifications to tweak the collective noses of the Union Pacific bosses.

———

Nelson may have been able to temporarily forget about Jack Rodgers, and Jack believed that Nelson was dead. But there was another man who had recently read later, expanded stories about both men and the ghost train in *The Rocky Mountain News.*

Tom Richardson had been about to leave Denver to return to Cheyenne and renew his interrupted relationship with Cassie Gray. But when he read her name among the list of passengers on the ghost train, he knew that Cheyenne wasn't going to be his destination.

The long article hadn't included where any of the passengers were going before the train was stolen, but he knew she'd been taken to Ogden with the others. He'd start his search in the Utah town and use his Denver & Pacific pass to get there. If he used his still valid Union Pacific pass, he'd have to go through Cheyenne but wasn't about to take the unnecessary risk.

Now he just needed to settle things and get rid of Anna. He expected to be out of Denver in three days at the most but hoped to be gone in two.

———

It was shortly after nine o'clock when Homer arrived with his wife and a very intrigued Judge Horace M. Bye.

Homer had stopped at his house and told Edith that not only was Nelson still alive, but they would be serving as his witnesses when he married Cassie. After she'd finished giggling, he'd asked her to join him when he went to the judge's house to help convince his honor that he was neither drunk nor crazy.

After Homer's explanation for his odd request, the judge at least understood Nelson's need to maintain his anonymity. The reason for the rushed marriage may not have been so clear, but he still agreed to perform the ceremony.

It was almost ten o'clock when Cassie and Nelson stood before the judge as he read from his small leather book. Neither of them even looked at the judge as they kept their eyes focused on each other. It was such an unusual setting and situation, but it seemed to be perfectly in tune with the tortuous path had led them to this occasion. Nothing about the collision of their lives' paths had been normal or expected. But no matter

279

how strange or fateful those events that resulted in them finding each other, Cassie and Nelson knew it was where they should be.

After he'd kissed Mrs. Cook, Nelson shook the judge's hand, then turned and shook Homer's. He kissed Edith while Homer planted a buss on Cassie's cheek.

It took another five minutes to complete the paperwork. As he wrote his particulars on the forms, Nelson handed Homer the telegram and asked him to put it on the wire sometime this afternoon. Some stations were empty on Sunday mornings while the operators were at church services. He still wasn't sure if Jack was listening because he didn't know how many batteries his operator had with the portable set. Even if he wasn't, it was still a necessary warning to expect another train hijacking.

He didn't take the time to explain his new theory to Homer because he still couldn't figure out how Jack would steal another train. The warning telegram he'd given to the station manager would make it almost impossible. He may not have told Homer, but he was still convinced that a head-on collision was Jack's next plot.

———

It was high noon and the only two occupants of the house were breathing heavily as they lay intertwined atop their marital bed bathed in perspiration.

Cassie gasped, "My Lord, Nelson! I was almost joking about making me cry out in ecstasy. I swear it must have sounded like a banshee's wail to anyone within a mile."

Between his deep breaths, Nelson replied, "If they didn't hear your banshee, then I'm sure I terrified them with my rutting giant imitation."

Cassie laughed before she kissed him and slid even closer.

Then she said, "I don't think Jack Rodgers' collision will be any more spectacular than ours."

Despite his intention of setting aside any thoughts of Jack for at least the rest of the day, Nelson replied, "It may be even noisier, but he won't enjoy it as much as I did."

But even as he let his left hand slide across Cassie's smooth damp posterior, his brain made an odd connection on its own that he would never understand.

He didn't bolt upright or even stop caressing his wife, but quickly said, "I think I know where he's going to get his train."

Cassie did begin to rise, but Nelson pulled her back down before she asked, "Which one will he steal?"

"I've been thinking about scheduled trains, but he doesn't need to pull off another stunt like he did to take your train. Jack himself even told me where he'd get his train even though he probably didn't realize he'd need it at the time."

"I'm listening."

"When we were talking, I told him the only mystery I hadn't solved was how he'd moved his stolen rails from the Park City warehouse. I envisioned all sorts of bizarre methods, but Jack laughed and told me that he had one of his contacts at the warehouse fake some documents so they could use the Union Pacific's own maintenance train. Because they have such a large warehouse, they have a long shed next to it to house an out-of-service locomotive and some flatbeds and boxcars."

"So, you think that his gang is going to steal that train to crash into another Union Pacific train?"

"It's become clearer to me the more I think about it. Taking the train itself wouldn't be hard to do if you had an engineer, which I'm sure he does. It's the timing that's difficult. Right now, that train is probably carrying loads of materials to the downed bridge, so it'll be busy for a couple of days at least. He'd have to steal it at night, probably after midnight. After it's fired up and rolling, all he'd have to do is get it onto the main line to meet a scheduled train."

"Won't he have to wait until the bridge is repaired?"

"Nope. Don't forget that you were going to take a Union Pacific train all the way to California. The line from Silver City to Pocatello that passes through Ogden is still open. He'd just need to check the schedule and find an inbound train to Silver

City and he's got his next victim. They'll be rerouting more U.P. trains down that route soon, too."

"How soon do you have to leave to stop him?"

"I have to do more planning, but I'm sure that if he's going to need that maintenance train in Park City, he'll have to wait until at least Tuesday night to make his move."

"So, you'll stay hidden in the house for at least another day?"

"I think so. I'll be sending you on errands tomorrow, but I believe we'll have time to enjoy our honeymoon."

Cassie smiled as she replied, "Calling this a honeymoon is like calling our house a cathedral."

Nelson pulled her onto his chest and kissed her before asking, "Shall we embarrass the congregation?"

———

Jack and his boys were still working their way closer to Park City. He still hadn't told them his plan, mainly because he was still dabbing the final strokes on his masterpiece. His idea about making the maintenance train into a spookier ghost train had been growing since it had first hatched.

As part of his original plan, the maintenance train's lamp would never be lit as it raced down the tracks, but now he would hang a red cloth over the light to give it an eerie and sinister appearance once they moved it out of Park City.

His new touches were to splash white paint on the locomotive if he could find any, but barring that, he'd have his boys hang light-colored canvas tarps in strategic spots where they could flap in the wind and make the engine seem as if it was flying on devils' wings.

Whatever changes he made in the maintenance train were all secondary to its primary purpose. He had the Union Pacific schedule and even though the routing would be changed for any eastbound trains, those heading for Silver City should still be on time. The U.P. would be using the Denver & Pacific's tracks for some of the redirected traffic and the Northern Pacific's for the rest. The only impact it would have on Jack's plan was if one of the trains that was going to take the Denver & Pacific's route might show up before the regular Silver City run. But even that only meant that the collision would happen earlier.

After they entered the maintenance train's shed, they'd load their horses and gear into one of the boxcars while Mick and Joe got the locomotive ready to move. He'd have Big Bob out front guarding the doors in case anyone showed up, which wasn't likely. If the train was back from delivering material to the downed bridge, everyone would be home in bed. He just hoped that they were diligent and filled the coal car before they retired for the night. They wouldn't need a full load but would rather have it topped off for a more spectacular show.

———

Nelson and Cassie had finally exited their bedroom and were sharing a long-delayed lunch or lesser-delayed supper.

Between their multiple sessions of lovemaking, they'd talked about many things, but were centered on what Nelson would do and when he would leave. For Nelson, it was a welcome bonus having such an intelligent and insightful wife to guide him when he was off track and to add her own helpful inputs. For his entire career, he'd never had anyone who could even keep up with his thought process, yet Cassie's mind was almost woven into his.

"You actually thought about using that dynamite?" she asked with wide eyes.

"It was just a passing thought. I hadn't used it when I should have and for just a brief moment, I wondered if it wouldn't be the way to end it. But that would probably mean blowing up more Union Pacific equipment and I don't want the bosses to be angrier than they probably already are."

"I still think you're wrong about that, but now that you've dropped that outlandish notion, where will you set up your ambush?"

"After they left their last disaster, they would have had to avoid being seen if they were headed to Park City. They might even have camped at the end of their temporary spur, but I doubt it. That would take them two days to make the trip, so if that's Jack's plan, then he'll arrive there tonight or tomorrow. That'll put them east of Park City. I'm familiar with the area and that same forest that hid the ghost train extends to less than a half mile from the Park City railyard."

"They'd have to cross a lot of open ground to get to the train; won't they?"

"Yes, ma'am. But they'll have a quarter moon that'll be waning, so there won't be much light, even if there aren't any clouds. I'll be waiting for them in the shed."

"Will you do anything to make sure that they still won't be able to take the train no matter what happens?"

Nelson shook his head then replied, "I don't think so. If they show up and I let them know that I'm there, Jack will know his plan has failed even if his boys manage to get the better of me."

"He won't though, will he?"

"No. I'll be in a well-protected position and even if they start shooting, all it will do is mark them as targets."

"You're going to use your crossbow?"

"Only for the first one or two, then I'll switch to my Winchester."

"Won't they just run away into the dark after you tell them you're going to fire?"

Nelson opened his mouth to reply, but then closed it again. He had envisioned the seven men entering the shed and once they were a good ten feet inside, he'd confront them. He suddenly realized that perhaps he'd placed too much importance on the shock value when Jack discovered that his massive assassination attempt had failed. Even if Jack was stunned, the other six wouldn't be. They'd probably do exactly as Cassie had just suggested and bolt for the protection of the darkness and the wide expanse of the open railyard.

Cassie watched as Nelson overhauled his plan but after almost two minutes, she stood, stepped next to him and set her hand on his shoulder.

He looked up and smiled at her as he said, "That was pretty stupid; wasn't it?"

"I'll admit that it wasn't one of your better solutions, but you're tired and we both need more sleep. I'll even be satisfied with just having you close."

"I don't think I have enough energy left to do anything else," he replied as he stood and took her hand.

"I'll clean up in the morning," she said before they began walking back to their bedroom.

The sun was about to set when they slipped beneath the quilts. Nelson wasn't the only one who was low on energy and soon the newlyweds were both unconscious to the world.

———

287

Homer had sent Nelson's telegram under his name without disclosing the source of its recommendations. His work crew was still out near the break, but he'd received a telegram from Omaha with an estimate of five days before the line was operational.

The same message had included a lengthy eulogy for Nelson Cook, which had tickled Homer to the point of making him giggle. He was lucky that no one was around when he read it because they'd think he was being incredibly insensitive. He wished he could have let everyone else in the yard in on the secret. He'd show it to Nelson when he could free up enough time to visit. He still had a lot to do as messages from Omaha kept arriving in a steady stream giving him even more work.

The crew that had used the maintenance train to move the material from the Park City warehouse was no longer needed. Most of the supporting lumber would be cut from the nearby forest and they now had enough rails and crossties to finish the repair.

It was just before sunset when the engineer backed the empty train into the long shed and shut it down. The last thing that the fireman did was to open the chute to fill the coal car. With the water tank full and the coal car loaded, the crew ended their day and went to their homes.

———

While he hadn't seen the maintenance train return, Jack had arrived at their campsite just fifteen hundred yards from the shed shortly after the big doors had been closed. His men set up the campsite while he headed for the tree line to make a brief reconnaissance. When he stopped, he was surprised to see men leaving the small side door. He kept watching to be sure that they were the train's crew and not just maintenance workers who were preparing the empty shed for the train's return.

He still wasn't sure after they'd all gone, but as he returned to the campsite, he decided he'd take a look in the shed later that night. It was two days earlier than he'd expected, but he'd still need to let the men get a good night's sleep. If the train was in the shed, they wouldn't be getting much rest tomorrow night.

––––––

Later that night, while Nelson and Cassie still slept, Jack left the campsite with Big Bob to take a quick look inside the shed. If the train was there and the shed was empty of workers, he'd have Bob stand guard. Then he'd make an inventory of what was available for the locomotive's makeover and check on its level of fuel and water.

When he slowly opened the side door in the light of the quarter moon, he grinned when he spotted the maintenance train just a few feet away. Then he listened for just a few seconds before stepping inside. He left the door open, but it was still almost completely dark inside. He walked to the locomotive and climbed into the cab. He was still smiling as he stared at the full coal car. He didn't check the water tank because if the coal car was full, the water tank had to be as well.

He stepped down on the other side of the locomotive and walked to the far wall where he could make out lines of shelves. He had to feel more than see what was on those shelves. He felt large tins but wasn't sure what was inside each one. But when his fingers touched folded canvas, he knew he'd found his devils' wings.

Tomorrow night, they'd light two or three lanterns before they began taking what they needed to convert the train then load them onto a flatbed car while Mick and Joe prepared the locomotive to get underway.

He'd checked the switch on the way to the shed and it was already set to get them on the line to Echo. After they reached that line, they'd have to change one in Echo to put them on the main line through Ogden and then one more to get them heading north toward Pocatello. Of course, their train would never reach the town, nor would the one heading for Silver City reach its destination.

They'd have to stop somewhere for a short time to make their modifications, but it would be worth it. He'd already added one last twist to his already twisted plan. He'd tap the outlet on the steam whistle to change it to more of a screech than a loud tone.

Satisfied that he'd be able to take the train tomorrow night, he walked around the front of the locomotive and soon exited the shed.

Fifteen minutes later, he and Bob had joined the others who were already sleeping. Bob quickly fell asleep himself, but Jack remained awake. He was too excited in anticipation of tomorrow night's adventure.

The scheduled night train from Pocatello would be due to reach the Ogden station at 2:20 in the wee hours of Tuesday morning. But it would meet his train just an hour earlier. After the collision, he'd send a telegram to the Ogden Daily News giving them a scoop on the story. He'd even suggest that they call it the Satan train, which was much better than ghost train.

He liked the name that the newspaper had given his first scheme, but wished he'd been able to use that dynamite to make it a real ghost train. At least there was no Nelson Cook to interfere with his Satan train disaster.

CHAPTER 8

While their energy may have been restored by their long sleep, Cassie knew that Nelson had to focus on Jack Rodgers today, although she didn't expect him to leave until tomorrow.

As she cooked breakfast, she renewed their last conversation.

"So, have you come up with a new plan yet?"

"Yes, ma'am. It's not as stupid, so it's probably much more to your liking."

"Well?"

"I think Homer will be pretty busy today, but I asked him to stop by when he got a chance. It's not critical, but I'd like to talk to him, so I can get a better read on the situation at the bridge. Regardless, I'm going to be leaving tomorrow. Because I'm still dead, I'll have you ask Sheriff Harris to stop by before I go. Park City is in Weber County, and even though I have jurisdiction because they'll be on Union Pacific property and have destroyed the railroad's property already, I'll ask him to come with me. If he wants to bring a couple of deputies, I won't object either.

"After Jack's gang sneaks into the shed, we'll cover the two exits and then I'll give Jack a chance to surrender. He probably won't. But if he doesn't, we'll just leave him inside until daybreak. Sooner or later, they'll probably have to shoot their way out. But they'll be at a significant disadvantage because they won't know where we are, while they'll only have two ways out. I imagine that the ex-railroaders will surrender, but Jack and Big Bob will probably die there."

"You're right. I do like that plan much better. Do you think that the sheriff will go along? He'll have to leave his office for at least two days."

"It's up to him, but even if he doesn't join me or give me one of his deputies, I can cover both doors without any problem. Even that wide door for the train won't give them enough room to avoid being hit."

"How will you be getting to Park City?"

"I'll take the morning train. It leaves just before ten o'clock, so I'll have Rowdy ready to go by eight. If the sheriff joins me, then he'll just need to saddle his horse and grab one of those Winchesters you brought to the office."

"So, we have most of the day to spend together?"

Nelson smiled as he replied, "Yes, ma'am. Do you have any plans on how to use that time?"

Cassie was smiling broadly as she nodded then said, "Yes, I do, sir. I think we should finally spend some time talking."

Nelson laughed but waited for Cassie to begin the conversation, as she must have something specific that she wanted to ask.

Cassie flipped the larger beef steak on the big skillet as she said, "I didn't know your middle name until I found your father's inscription in the book. He said that you'd appreciate it when you started your schooling. Why was that?"

"He was right, too. I took enough grief with Nelson. Boys would call me Nellie and dance like a girl while they did. I can only imagine what they would have done if my parents had christened me Horatio Nelson."

"Oh, I hadn't even thought about that. I thought it might have something to do with being an English hero. Did you get into many fights because of that?"

"Only a couple when I was in my first year. They still made fun of my name, but they stopped dancing."

"I can imagine why they stopped. You must have been a strong boy."

"I wasn't that much bigger than other boys my age, but my father taught me how to defend myself, probably because he knew that even Nelson would lead to fisticuffs."

"Are your parents still alive?"

"No. My mother died when I was five and my father passed in '71."

"You know about my family. Did you meet my uncle when you were in Omaha?"

"I might have, but I didn't know which one of the dark-suited, somber men at the table could have been him. I know about half of them by name, but the others, like your uncle, remain nothing but shadows in suits."

Cassie laughed then said, "That's one way of describing them."

They shared breakfast and an extended conversation before they left the kitchen and made their way to the bedroom. But it wasn't their marital bedroom. They entered the spare bedroom so Nelson could prepare for tomorrow morning's train ride to Park City.

———

"We're gonna steal that maintenance train tonight, boss?" Audie Scott asked.

"That's the plan. Once we're inside, we'll load our horses and supplies into the boxcar while Mick and Joe prepare the locomotive. Then we'll take those tarps and if there is any white paint on those shelves, we'll grab as much as we can. We won't

295

waste any time dressing up the locomotive while we're inside the shed. When we get it a few miles out of Park City, we can convert it into the Satan train. I have a couple of other wrinkles that I haven't told you about, too. They're both finishing touches that will add to the spooky nature of the train."

Pooch McGregor asked, "Where is the collision gonna be?"

"There's a hard curve just past Logan. The train from Pocatello will slow when it goes through that curve, but the engineer will open the throttle once they reach the straight track. They'll reach their top speed about five miles south of that curve. There isn't another stop after Logan until it reaches Ogden. That's more than thirty miles of open track.

"What we'll do is pull the train to a stop about ten miles north of Ogden where we'll unload our horses. Mick will wait in the engine by himself and once he sees the light on that oncoming locomotive, he'll open the throttle and jump out. The engineer on the other train won't spot our Satan train until it's much too late. We'll be riding on the road alongside the tracks and get to see the crash. It'll be about a mile in front of us, so we'll be safe. After the collision, we ride in and strip whatever we can find. We'll have at least four hours before they even start looking.

"After we have our loot, we'll ride due west to Brigham and follow the Central Pacific tracks and disappear for a few days. But before we leave the site of the wreck, Carl will set up his portable set and send a story to the Ogden newspapers. I'm going to write it out later today, but it'll make us famous and feared as well. The Union Pacific will probably send every agent they have to Utah, but it won't do them any good."

"Why not, boss?" asked Big Bob.

"Because we'll be done with Utah. After this job, we'll be heading north into Idaho to cause more destruction."

Jack grinned at his men but as he did, he took a measure of their commitment. There was no question of Big Bob's devotion, but he wasn't convinced that the others would be as willing to have the deaths of up to fifty passengers on their hands. The so-called ghost train job had only made mass murder a possibility and the collapse of the bridge only cost the lives of five Union Pacific employees, so they didn't count. But this one would end the lives of many innocents and Jack needed them to be dedicated.

After seeing some measure of reluctance in a few eyes, Jack said, "If any of you don't want to be involved anymore, then you're free to take the money you earned from the first job and ride out of here."

Joe Smith glanced at Big Bob who was sitting beside Jack and suspected that despite Jack's offer, if any of them stood and walked to their horses, he'd never set his butt in the saddle.

When none of the ex-railroaders stood, Jack smiled and said, "Thank you, boys."

Three of the five managed weak smiles but Joe Smith and Carl Brown couldn't even manage that level of agreement.

———

In Denver, Tom Richardson was packing for his long trip to Ogden. He hadn't told Anna because he couldn't face her weeping and whining. He'd be taking tomorrow's westbound Denver & Pacific and should be in Ogden in two more days. He didn't expect to find Cassie in the town, but someone would know where she'd gone. He'd have to use his Union Pacific pass when he left Utah, but at least he wouldn't have to worry about anyone in Cheyenne spotting him.

As he packed, he wore a grin as he imagined how excited Cassie would be when she saw him again. He wouldn't ask how much money she'd inherited from her fancy yet clumsy husband until after they were married.

———

While Jack worked out the final details of his plan, Nelson and Cassie continued to spend their first day as a married couple just getting to know more about each other.

Even though he had intended to visit Nelson earlier, Homer hadn't been able to break free of his duties to deliver his eulogy telegram. If he'd managed to find the time to make that short walk, the newlyweds' day would have been dramatically different.

Because they had so many topics to discuss, Cassie and Nelson's day passed quickly and soon she was preparing to make their supper. Nelson wasn't surprised that Homer hadn't visited but was going to stop by the Watson home later if he didn't stop by soon.

It was after six o'clock when Homer finally left the railyard and almost went straight home because nothing unexpected had happened, but the telegram from the Union Pacific bosses was too funny to ignore and he wanted to watch Nelson's reaction when he read it. So, after hurrying along Jackson Street, he soon made the turn onto Saint Street.

After reaching their home, he knocked on the door and waited with a grin on his face. He didn't have to wait long before he heard Nelson's loud footsteps cross the floor in the front room before he yanked the door open.

"I was hoping you'd show up, Homer. Come on in."

Homer was still grinning as he walked down the short hallway beside Nelson. Aside from the amusing nature of the telegram in his pocket, it was the first time he'd seen the couple since their almost impromptu wedding.

Cassie smiled at him as they entered the kitchen and said, "My new husband has been anxiously awaiting news of the outside world all day. He barely paid any attention to his willing bride at all."

Homer sat down at the table as Nelson stepped close to Cassie, kissed her and said, "I apologize for my neglect, Mrs. Cook. I'll be sure to make amends later."

Cassie laughed then Nelson stepped to the table and sat down across from Homer.

"So, what has been happening in the world outside these walls?"

Homer pulled out the telegram and before he handed it to Nelson, replied, "I got this early this morning. It's a system-wide message, but I figured you'd enjoy it more than the rest of us."

He then gave it to Nelson who unfolded the sheet and began to read his eulogy while Cassie stepped closer to the table.

He started laughing after the first line then continued chuckling until he finished the long message. He didn't tell Cassie its content but handed it to her without having to leave his seat. At least she hadn't read it over his shoulder.

She didn't react until she'd almost finished then smiled and gave it back to him.

"I guess that they're not going to fire you after your funeral after all."

"I didn't know that I was 'the noblest of men and the pride of the Union Pacific'. I wonder what they'll say about me when they discover that I'm still breathing."

Homer was snickering when Nelson asked, "Aside from this literary masterpiece, how is the repair job going?"

"They're moving along even faster than I expected. Have you figured out what Jack Rodgers might do next?"

"I think so. My very intelligent wife helped me figure it out. I'm pretty sure he's going to take control of another train then have it collide with a scheduled train during the night when the oncoming engineer won't be able to even slow his locomotive before they crash."

Homer exclaimed, "*Do you really think he'd do that?*"

"Why not? It's not much different than the bridge collapse, but it would take out two trains and stop traffic for another week."

"How could he get another train? I sent out your telegram and headquarters followed it up with a warning to all active crews to expect a possible hijacking."

"I know. That's what had me puzzled for a while. But it was only when I stopped thinking about scheduled trains that I believe we found the answer. Jack just shut down the main line from Ogden to Granger, so he'd want to do the same on another main line. He won't want to arrange his collision on a spur because it won't have nearly as big an effect on the Union Pacific's operations."

"So, where is he going to get his train?"

"I think he's going to steal the maintenance train from Park City as soon as it returns from the collapsed bridge."

"But it's already back in its shed, Nelson."

It was Nelson's turn to be stunned when he looked at Homer in disbelief and sharply asked, *"It's already back?* When did they leave Park City with those replacement rails and crossties?

"Yesterday morning. I guess they just loaded up, dropped off their load at the siding and returned to Park City. They didn't have to do any of the work, but the track was clear when I sent our crew out there this morning."

Nelson didn't panic, but knew the clock was already ticking. He had to get to Park City.

He quickly said, "Homer, I'm going to leave in a few minutes to ride down to Park City. I can't let that maintenance train reach the main line."

"Do you want me to send a telegram to the yard manager?"

"No. I could be wrong, but if he sends men to guard the train, they'd probably all be dead before Jack drove that train out of Park City. He won't try to take it before it's dark. I have another three hours of daylight and can make that ride in less than six hours. I'll be able to keep an eye on the tracks as I ride. I don't know how I'll be able to stop that locomotive if it's under power, but I don't think I'll see it on the tracks. I should get to Park City before Jack leaves those woods."

"Do you want me to tell the sheriff?"

Nelson thought about it for a few seconds. He'd like the added firepower but didn't want to delay his departure either. But more than that, he wanted to end Jack's scourge himself. He was the one who had let him go.

"Okay. But tell him I've already gone. Even if he doesn't follow, tell him to station one of his deputies near the main line to watch for anyone trying to fiddle with the switches. But if I were you, I'd throw the switch to send any traffic into the yard just in case I can't stop the maintenance train and it reaches Ogden."

"Alright."

Cassie watched him before he answered Homer's question and suspected that he might not even want the sheriff or anyone else to help. She believed that Nelson wanted to end this himself almost as penitence for letting the gang leave unharmed. Yet she wasn't about to interfere. Nelson needed this. All she could do would be to welcome him when he returned.

"Do you have any more information that I should have figured out?"

"Not much. They think that they'll have the main line open in five days. They're sending carloads of workers to inspect all of the bridges and trestles, but they won't start for a couple of days."

"Jack probably finds that amusing."

"Do you still want everyone to think you're dead?"

"I don't think it matters now. Even if he's got a man listening to the telegraph traffic, it's too late for him to change his plan. He'll want to act before that main line is repaired. I should have realized that in the first place. He's doing his utmost to shut the Union Pacific down. He knows he won't be able to stop it, but he wants to inflict as much damage as he can. I don't even think he cares if he dies as long as he's satisfied his need for revenge."

"How are you going to stop him?"

"I won't know until I find him. But I've got to go."

"Sorry I didn't come by earlier."

"It's okay, Homer. As long as we keep that maintenance train from reaching the main line, Jack Rodgers' plan will fail. I just need to make sure he doesn't have the chance to come up with another one."

Homer and Nelson stood, shook hands, then Homer turned and headed down the hallway.

Even before he reached the door, Cassie said, "I'll pack some of this food for you to take with you."

"Thank you, Cassie. I'm going to take my weapons out to the barn and start saddling Rowdy. I should be on the road in fifteen minutes."

They shared a brief kiss before Nelson hurried into the spare bedroom. He hung his crossbow case over his shoulder, then took his Sharps in his left hand and his Winchester in his right. He'd already moved his saddlebags with his spare ammunition into the barn.

Just ten minutes later, he waved to Cassie as he rode away from their house and headed for Jackson Street. Rowdy had him out of Ogden quickly and he set his gelding to a fast trot as he headed east. He'd have to go through Echo before he turned south. He could have cut a few miles off the journey by going cross country directly to Park City, but he didn't want to lose sight of the tracks. He could be wrong about Jack's timing.

The last thing he did before he left the house was to write a short note of thanks to Elmer Fincher for letting him borrow his horse. He gave it to Cassie and asked her to take the note and Boomer Wilson's horse and saddle to Charlie Nix at the U.P. stock corral. He'd written the Fincher ranch's location on the note and asked her to tell Charlie to ship both horses to the rancher on the next available train.

When Cassie had accepted the note, she didn't tell him that he could do it himself when he returned. She knew why he had given her the task and would do as he asked. She still firmly believed that he would be returning soon even if he had doubts.

———

Jack had either been watching the shed or had someone else keep an eye on it all day to make sure that it wasn't leaving to take more materials to the downed bridge. He knew that all of the heavy equipment needed to extract the heavy salvageable debris from the creek would come from Cheyenne. They'd use the nearby pines for the supports, so he didn't think that they would take more than one load of the rails and crossties from Park City's warehouse.

He was satisfied that the train wasn't going anywhere and headed back to the camp. He'd let them all take a long nap while they waited, so they would be alert when they entered the shed.

But the lack of activity in the railyard led him to believe that they could leave their camp just after sunset rather than waiting until midnight. It would give them time to prepare the train inside before they shifted it onto the main line. Then they wouldn't have to stop at all.

Even though he suspected that his ex-railroaders wouldn't be staying with him much longer, it didn't bother him. He only needed them to get the maintenance train rolling. He had been surprised that five of them had joined him after the theft of the ghost train. But he knew that if hadn't been for Big Bob's presence, each of them would have probably drifted away after the bridge job.

As he wound his way through trees, he decided that even if they didn't desert him, he'd go off on his own. He hated to admit it, but he felt as if he was almost cheating now that Nelson Cook was no longer there to challenge him. This may be his last spectacular assault on the Union Pacific's tracks. There was no point in creating intricate schemes that required detailed planning and added manpower. Once he was alone, he'd attack the monster in its lair. He'd go to Omaha and take his final measure of revenge at the headquarters building full of the bosses.

There was only one remaining issue. By the time he reached their camp, he still hadn't decided how to rid himself of Big Bob Pope.

———

After he left their house, Homer stopped at the sheriff's office but wasn't surprised to find that Sheriff Harris was already home. So, he headed for his house to pass along what Nelson had told him.

When he told the sheriff about Nelson's failure to die and his departure from Ogden, Don told him that he'd send a deputy to Park City on the morning train. It wasn't that he didn't want to help. It was just that he knew by the time he or his deputy could get there, it would be dark, and Nelson would have already met up with the gang. That was assuming that stealing the maintenance train was going to happen.

He also confided in Homer that he didn't trust Park City's town marshal or his two deputies to be anything more than a problem for Nelson, so there was no point in sending a telegram. Even if he had, he doubted if the town's lawmen would want to get involved in a nighttime shootout.

On his way home, Homer stopped to tell Cassie about the sheriff's decision and was surprised that she accepted it so well. He couldn't imagine how a woman who'd just been married the day before could be so stoic when her new husband was about to face seven men who'd already murdered two men and killed another two.

Cassie may have appeared to be unaffected by the news, but it wasn't because she didn't love her husband or was unconcerned about what might happen to him. It was that she understood his intense need to be the one to put a finish to Jack Rodgers and his gang. He felt responsible for that horrendous bridge collapse and loss of those railroad men and this was the only way to make amends. She also had her supreme confidence in Nelson to keep her worries in check.

She tried to return to a normal routine but knew it would be impossible. She'd still eat and visit the privy, but until Nelson returned, she'd be on edge. She knew that sleep would be difficult tonight, but she decided to use the spare bedroom when she tried to rest. She wouldn't lay her head on the other bed's pillow until her husband was with her again.

———

Nelson made the southern turn after passing through Echo and soon the town disappeared behind him. It was almost sunset, and he'd spent the entire ride trying to envision different scenarios when he arrived in Park City.

It made no difference if he was wrong about Jack attempting to steal the maintenance train. If he found no one there, he may look foolish, but he'd have to consider Jack's other possible targets. But Cassie's insights and support had convinced him that Jack was there.

He'd be arriving at night and had to allow that Jack might already be in the shed and preparing the train to move. He might already be on the spur line from Park City before he even reached the town. Those two situations would be much more difficult, but because they were, he'd been planning for them first.

The already-in-the-shed problem wasn't too bad, so he'd come up with his plan before he'd reached Echo. But the possibility that he'd be riding south when he spotted the maintenance train heading north was the worst possible scenario, and he was still pondering that issue after he left Echo behind.

He was losing his sunlight, but soon spotted an unusual natural feature that he'd seen many times before. When the Union Pacific's construction crews had cut through a small hill to clear a path for the tracks, they'd revealed a long, two-foot-high strip of white, powdery dirt. He thought it might be talc, but the local boys called it chalk and would scoop cups of it then get into all sorts of mischief.

As he looked at the stripe, he decided to use some of it to create his own mischief. As far as Jack and his gang knew, he was dead. While he may have considered the term 'ghost train' to be inexact, he planned to become a ghost special agent. Jack wouldn't be bothered, but Big Bob might be thrown into a real tizzy. Nelson didn't believe the ex-railroad men would be a danger, even if they started shooting at him. But if they even had the tiniest belief that they were dealing with Nelson Cook's spirit, then it might give him the edge he needed.

After rubbing the white powder into his hat, jacket and britches, he began tossing clouds of it onto Rowdy. He avoided getting any in his eyes, so when most of his body was at least partially covered with the talc, he rubbed some on his face.

When he returned to the saddle, he wasn't sure how effective it was, but the silliness of what he'd done at least lifted his spirit.

He still had another two hours before he reached Park City, and then he'd know if he and Cassie were right.

Ghostly Nelson then returned to the vexing problem of trying to stop a moving train that was carrying armed men. A lot depended on how fast the train was going. If it was moving at speed, it would be almost impossible.

He couldn't derail the train even if it was necessary. He didn't have the equipment or the time. Even the power of his Sharps wouldn't be enough to penetrate any of the critical parts of the locomotive. The wheel cylinders would have been his best option, but the cast iron was too thick even if he fired at close range. He might be able to crack the metal, but even that wasn't likely. Besides, he'd only get one shot as it passed.

He eventually settled on shooting the engineer and fireman if he had enough time. He didn't know if both men in the cab were capable of operating the locomotive, but most firemen were really engineers-in-training. He'd have to kill them both before he dealt with Jack or Big Bob.

———

Jack's men were sitting in their saddles while their boss stared at the shed in the dim light. He hadn't seen anyone near the building all day and wondered if most of the men had been left at the downed bridge to work as common laborers. That was the only reason for the lack of activity.

After a few more minutes, Jack walked his gelding out of the trees without looking behind him to see if the others followed. He could almost feel Big Bob a few feet away and knew the others were just a few feet behind him.

He kept his eyes scanning the dark railyard and didn't see any lights until he looked at the town. The nearest building with lamplight coming through its windows was a good eight hundred yards away. That meant they could light their own lamps in the shed and after boarding their horses, they could modify the train inside the shed, rather than on the rails. He expected the Satan train to be out of Park City within two hours. Then it would reach the main line at Echo forty minutes later and then on to Ogden. In five more hours, he'd watch the scheduled run from Pocatello to Silver City have its violent meeting with his train. The Union Pacific would suffer once again.

He planned to let everyone who was still awake in Ogden see his Satan train as it roared through town shrieking its banshee whistle. The southbound train would have already passed Logan and even if someone sent a warning telegram, it would be too late.

When they reached the south side of the maintenance train's shed, they dismounted and led their horses through the side door. Once inside, they lit four lamps and Mick and Joe bounded up the locomotive's steps while the others led their horses to the boxcar.

Jack soon had his men working to transform the old maintenance train into his vision of the Satan train.

There were only four cans of whitewash, but they were more than Jack could have hoped to find. While three of his men splashed the paint on the locomotive, he climbed onto the cowcatcher then stood on the platform below the light. He did the easier job first by hanging his red handkerchief over the locomotive's lamp. Because it was an older locomotive, the light wasn't as bright as the new ones, but it suited his purpose better. When they lit the lamp, it would be just enough light to give it an eerie, satanic look but not enough to warn the oncoming train's engineer.

His next modification required a more delicate touch, and he wouldn't be able to test his handiwork until the train was on the move. He pulled the small sledgehammer from his belt and reached up to the steam whistle. He had to bang it in the right spot and just enough to change its tone. He wasn't a musician and was unsure of the pitch he hoped to create, but he couldn't make it worse. If it didn't work, then he could live with it.

He began tapping the opening of the whistle where the steam escaped after creating its identifiable sound. After two or three taps, he felt the opening with his fingers then climbed down and tossed the sledge aside.

The final addition to the train was adding the tarps around the locomotive's drive wheels. If they were ripped as the train rolled over the tracks, it would be even more effective.

———

Even as the Satan train was being awakened, ghostly special agent Nelson Cook was approaching Park City. He was relieved that he hadn't seen the train yet, but that also made him wonder if he was on a wild goose chase.

He was still on the road beside the tracks as he passed to the east of Park City. The depot and railyard were well to the south of the town because of the noise, but he knew he was close. Not having seen any signs of the maintenance train were strengthening his belief that he'd been mistaken, and Jack had selected a different path and target.

He was at the south end of the town when he asked, "Was I wrong, Cassie?"

It was only when he saw the wide doors of the maintenance shed swing wide and seconds later, saw the bizarre apparition roll into the night that he realized Jack was there.

He wouldn't be able to reach the switch to prevent the train from reaching the tracks to Echo but the train wouldn't have enough time to pick up much speed before it reached him.

He walked Rowdy over the tracks and pulled him to a stop before he slid his Winchester free. He knew that the engineer would be looking at the tracks from the left side of the cab because his locomotive would be turning in that direction when it reached the switch. He just hoped that the man's attention would be on the tracks and not even see him until it was too late. He couldn't afford to give him or any of the others any warning. They'd already been warned once anyway.

He'd ignore everyone else until he'd eliminated the man driving the train. He expected that once the fireman saw the engineer fall, he'd either bail out of the cab on the other side or drop to the iron floor. Whatever he did, Nelson planned to board the locomotive right after taking that first shot.

He watched the strange iron beast roll out of the shed and noted the men sitting on the flatbed behind the coal car. He was

314

sure that they were armed, probably with repeaters. That changed the second part of his plan. He'd still shoot the engineer, but instead of trying to take control of the train, he'd have to engage the men on the flat car as it continued to roll. If the fireman was more committed to the crime than Nelson expected, that would pose another problem. If he stayed in the cab and opened the throttle, Nelson knew he wouldn't be able to match the train's speed for very long.

None of the men on the flatbed or in the cab had noticed the talc-covered agent yet. Nelson was still too far away in the shadows as they approached the switch. There were enough clouds in the sky to keep the quarter moon hidden for much of the time, which gave Nelson more time.

Nelson cocked his Winchester for the all-important first shot. It would probably set off a withering fire from the flat car, so he had to make it count. His big advantage was that the open firebox in the locomotive would illuminate both men. The throttle couldn't be pushed forward until the last car on the short train reached the tracks to Echo. He'd have to take the shot before that happened.

Mick was watching the tracks in front of his locomotive as it approached the switch. His head was out of the window because he was limited to just fifty feet in front of his leading wheels. He had his hand on the throttle as Joe continued to scoop heavy shovelfuls of coal into the firebox.

When he saw the switch and the cowcatcher began to turn to his left, Mick was relieved. They'd made it and soon he'd open the throttle. He had been horrified when he saw Jack and Big Bob shoot that engineer in the back, but he wasn't a criminal now. He was an engineer.

But even as his locomotive reached the straight tracks, what he was no longer mattered. He didn't hear the crack of Nelson's Winchester before he collapsed to the locomotive floor. His blood began to pool on the iron as Joe stared at him with his coal-filled shovel in his hands.

As soon as he fired, Nelson shifted his attention to the flat car.

Jack and the other four men were all shocked by the unexpected sound of gunfire but quickly grabbed their Winchesters to return fire. But they couldn't see Nelson clearly in the dark night.

Jack shouted, "Hold your fire until you see his muzzle flash!"

Even as he shouted, Joe Smith bounded out of the slow-moving locomotive and started to race away. But he exited the cab on the same side where Mick had been looking when he'd been shot. He should have bailed out on the other side of the locomotive where he would have been safe. But even as he leapt from his cab and began running, he soon had another problem. He tripped and began scrambling across the adjacent set of tracks.

Nelson knew he was unarmed and was probably just an ex-railroader who hadn't shot anyone. But he'd helped collapse that bridge knowing innocent men would die. That made him a murderer.

Even though he knew he'd be letting the men on the flatcar know where he was, he still set his sights on the fireman. There wasn't much light, but when the man crawled over some nearby tracks, Nelson fired.

Joe felt the hammer blow to his lower left side and screamed in pain before he tumbled to the cinder track bed.

As soon as he'd squeezed his trigger, Nelson had moved Rowdy to the right side just a few feet.

While the men on the flatcar were waiting for that muzzle flare, the train was still moving which affected their accuracy. The three remaining railroaders weren't good marksmen anyway, so there was almost no chance that their bullets would find Nelson.

Jack wasn't a much better shooter but was counting on Big Bob to kill the man on the horse. He still hadn't realized that the rider was Nelson.

All five Winchesters barked, sending their .44 caliber slugs whistling through the night air.

Nelson heard them buzz past, but none were close. The train was getting closer, so he wheeled Rowdy around and set him off at a canter on the depot side of the tracks. He had been there numerous times and knew that the layout gave him a clear path for another eight hundred yards or so. After that, there was a large warehouse. He had to set up before then.

After they'd seen the mysterious horseman ride away, the five men continued to fire at his shadow. Jack knew it was pointless and after another twenty rounds had been wasted, he had to stop the useless shooting.

"Hold your fire!" he shouted.

Three more bullets left their barrels before the repeaters fell silent.

The train had straightened and was now on the tracks to Echo, but Jack knew that someone had to get into the locomotive to open the throttle or they'd never get past that shooter. Jack still didn't know who he was, but he'd shot Mick and then Joe with just two shots, even in this light. If the train kept this walking pace, he'd shoot them all. While he may have been planning to rid himself of their company, he needed them to get the Satan train onto the main line to meet the Pocatello train.

He turned to Audie Scott and loudly said, "I need you to get into the locomotive and open the throttle. He won't be able to shoot you if you run on the right side of the train."

Audie nodded, but he wasn't about to take the risk. Even if he was able to safely leap from the flatcar, he'd probably break an

Audie nodded, but knew that if he even if he was able to drop off the flatcar without injury, he'd probably break his ankle trying to board a moving locomotive in the night. Even if he made it into the cab, that shooter would put probably put a bullet into him. He had a better plan.

He nodded then yelled, "Okay."

Audie set his Winchester on the flatcar's bed then sat on the edge before he pushed himself off.

He tumbled to the ground and screamed, "I broke my ankle!"

Jack didn't believe him for a moment, but Audie was already out of sight and that only left Carl Brown and Pooch McGregor to operate the locomotive. He suspected that if he ordered either of them to handle the throttle, they'd suffer similar faked injuries after they were off the flatbed, too.

He had to decide quickly, and it wasn't hard to take the next step. His Satan train plan was already a disaster. The lone shooter would have to stop the train soon and he'd only do that if he no longer had any shooters to worry about.

He exclaimed, "Bob, let's get out of here!"

Big Bob understood what his boss expected of him, so he just turned his Winchester at Pooch and pulled the trigger.

Pooch was stunned and didn't even move before Bob's .44 drilled through his chest and then exited his back before it disappeared into the night.

As Pooch wobbled on his feet, Bob quickly shot Carl Brown in the head. Bob didn't wobble but tumbled off the side of the car.

Pooch dropped to his knees before he fell onto the wooden surface of the flatbed while Big Bob and Jack Rodgers headed to the back of the car. They wouldn't be able to get their horses, but that was secondary to staying alive.

Nelson had been confused when he'd seen two more muzzle flashes after they had ceased firing. It was only when the train was closer that he noticed that no one was on the flatbed any longer.

He didn't see the bodies, but now he had a dilemma. *Did he try to find the others, or did he stop the train?*

He delayed the decision but quickly walked Rowdy back over the tracks before the train reached that warehouse. It would give him time and he'd be able to see if anyone was on the other side trying to climb into the locomotive's cab.

Nelson couldn't see anyone moving, so he slid his Winchester back into its scabbard and dismounted. He stepped close to the tracks and didn't have to wait long for the slow-moving train to reach him.

He quickly grabbed the handle on the side of the locomotive and jumped onto the lower step. If someone was in the cab, he would never get to see him or his muzzle flash. But the cab only held a dead body, so he had to slide Mick Gifford's body away before he reached for the throttle. He was about to pull it back when he thought it might be a good idea to put some space between the train and the town, so he opened the throttle and to alert the townsfolk, he pulled on the whistle's cord.

What came out of the steam whistle wasn't what he expected. It was a screech that almost made him want to cover his ears. He quickly released the cord as the train picked up speed. It wouldn't maintain pressure in the boiler without more coal for very long, but he just needed it another mile or so down the tracks. He was counting on Rowdy following the train on the road. But even if he didn't, if one of those men tried to ride him, Rowdy would show the uninvited rider how he'd earned his name.

Jack and Bob stood in the dark watching their Satan train disappear and the shriek of its whistle only heightened Jack's sense of frustration and stoked his anger.

Not only had his plan turned into a disaster; he'd also lost their horses and the money he'd given to the men. Before he did anything else, he needed a horse.

He turned to Bob and said, "We need to steal some horses."

Bob simply replied, "Okay."

Without any explanation, Bob began walking toward the depot. Only when the giant began stepping away in the direction of the station did Jack realize that the stock corral probably had some horses inside. They'd have their tack stored in a nearby shed, too. It was a standard setup for railroad stations.

While the gunfire didn't seem to disturb anyone in Park City, the loud screech of the Satan train's modified whistle did. For those few who looked toward the tracks, they saw a sight that they would never forget.

In the dim light cast by the few lamps still burning in the town, the onlookers witnessed the eerie passing of a devilish, ghostly spectacle that could never been crafted by human hands. Jack Rodgers had achieved at least one of his goals, but it wasn't one that really mattered.

By the time that Jack and Big Bob were off the train and heading for the stock corral, Audie had already headed in that direction with the same thought in mind. He passed Joe's body on the tracks and almost retched but managed to keep his stomach under control.

Audie had watched the train roll away and then accelerate which meant that someone had to be at the throttle. He assumed that Jack had convinced one of the others to run to the cab despite hearing the two gunshots. He thought that Bob had fired at the man on the horse.

He didn't look behind him because there was no reason to check. If he had, he would have seen two shadows trotting behind him and even in the low light, would have no difficulty in identifying Big Bob Pope.

Jack knew that it had to be Audie ahead of them. He focused all of his frustration for the final failure of his plan on the man who'd pretended to be hurt rather than reclaim control of the locomotive. He was going to have Bob shoot him, but his disgust with Audie drove him to aim his cocked Winchester at Audie's back just fifteen yards away and fire.

Audie felt the bullet rip into his back just below the right shoulder blade. The .44 broke one rib before ripping through his lung's middle lobe then fracturing two more ribs before it created a hole in the front of his jacket.

Audie crashed awkwardly to the ground and as his blood soaked his jacket, he watched Jack and Big Bob step close to him. Before he could even ask why they shot him, Jack put his second shot through his left eye.

Bob never said a word before they started jogging toward the stock corral.

Nelson had driven the train a good mile past the northern edge of Park City before he brought it to a stop and began shutting down the engine. He didn't believe that any of them would be able to get it moving again, but he didn't want to take the chance.

It wasn't a normal, controlled shutdown, but it was good enough for Nelson. He stepped down from the cab and checked the flatcar for any shooters. He noticed the two bodies on the empty bed but knew that neither was Big Bob. He was pretty sure that the other wasn't Jack simply because Big Bob was his protector.

He then searched for Rowdy. If he hadn't coated his horse with talc, he probably wouldn't be able to find him very easily. He was jogging past the boxcar when he heard the sounds of dancing hooves from inside. They had to be the gang's horses, which meant the survivors were afoot. He'd killed two and there were two on the flatbed. That left, at the most, three more wandering in the dark.

He started moving again then spotted Rowdy trotting towards him. He didn't whistle but just shifted to the road to wait for his gelding to reach him.

When Rowdy stopped, Nelson patted him on his chalky neck, then climbed into his saddle. He pulled out his Winchester then wheeled him about and started him walking back toward the depot.

He hadn't heard the gunshots as he was shutting down the locomotive. But it didn't take a genius to figure out where the first place Jack, Bob and the other one would be going. They weren't going to try to hide but they needed transportation.

Jack and Bob had quickly saddled two of the six horses in the corral and made trail ropes for two more. Jack wanted to get away from this debacle that he attributed to the lackluster performance of his ex-railroaders.

They had just ridden out of the corral and were preparing to cross the tracks to return to the protection of the trees when Bob spotted Nelson. Nelson's ghoulish appearance disturbed Bob enough that he didn't even mention seeing him. He simply stared.

Nelson had barely noticed their movement and almost lost sight of them after he glimpsed their shadows. But it had been enough for him to keep his eyes focused where he'd seen the movement. He soon saw two riders leading two other horses. One was obviously Big Bob which meant that the other was Jack Rodgers. Nelson no longer cared if the last man had escaped. It was time to end Jack's campaign of death and destruction.

He had his cocked Winchester in his hands as he walked Rowdy closer. He didn't leave the road because he knew they'd have to cross it to reach the safety of the trees.

When Jack finally spotted Nelson, he wasn't as spooked as his big partner, but he was disturbed. After all the talk of a ghost train and his desire to create the Satan train, the sight of the ghostly rider on a mottled white horse seemed to be a creation of his own imagination.

Imaginary or not, the man on that horse had appeared out of nowhere and destroyed his plan. Jack pulled his Winchester and cocked the hammer.

He then glanced at Bob who was still staring at the rider and exclaimed, "Bob! Get your rifle ready! We need to kill that guy!"

Nelson was less than eighty yards away and was close enough to hear Jack exhorting Big Bob.

As Bob slid his Winchester from his scabbard, Nelson shouted, "Hello, Jack! I've come back to kill you and Big Bob. You aren't going to hurt anyone else."

Bob hadn't recognized the voice but was still unnerved enough to forget to cock his repeater.

Jack may have identified Nelson but found it almost impossible to believe that he was not only alive but had somehow miraculously discovered his plan.

For just a brief moment, he thought that Nelson had somehow risen from the grave, but then his logic intercepted and eliminated the very concept. The only rational explanation was that one of the men with him had betrayed him. Instead of answering, Jack quickly examined each of the other men's actions and finally settled on the most obvious choice – Carl Brown.

He'd sent those telegrams and no one else understood what he had transmitted. He'd been monitoring traffic on his own, too.

Jack was satisfied that Carl had not only warned Nelson about the weakened bridge but had kept him informed of the plan to crash the two trains. There could be no other explanation.

Satisfied that he was dealing with the mortal Nelson Cook, Jack finally yelled, "You're not going to kill anyone, Nelson! I know that Carl was telling you what I was planning. You probably never even got on that freight train. You let the bridge collapse and didn't care if those men died."

Nelson kept Rowdy walking as he shouted back, "I was there, Jack. I felt the weight of those cars crush me, but then I rose above the dust and saw you and Big Bob shoot the engineer in the back before you had one of your boys drive that locomotive back into the creek to make the explosion you had hoped to see the first time."

Bob had begun to believe what Jack had shouted because he still thought that his boss was the smartest man he'd ever met. If he said that Carl was a traitor and the special agent hadn't even been on the train, then Bob knew it had to be true.

Then Nelson said things that only someone who'd been there would have known and his opinion quickly reversed.

He still didn't cock his Winchester as he watched the spirit rider grow closer. He was expecting the ghost's eyes to turn into red balls of fire and start shooting beams of burning light into his face at any moment.

Nelson pulled Rowdy to a stop and set his Winchester's sights on Big Bob. He was a much bigger target and was probably the better shot. He just wasn't sure if his first .45 would put Bob down or just make him mad. If he'd known the effect his talc makeup was having on the giant outlaw, he would have shot Jack.

Jack had already shifted his horse another three feet away from Bob, expecting that Nelson would want to eliminate his protection first. Once he fired, Jack would have a clear target and aim at his muzzle flare.

Bob hadn't noticed the shift or Nelson's choice of targets. He simply stared at the shadowy figure waiting for those blood-colored bolts of killing lightning to erupt from the ghost's eyes and send him to hell.

Nelson wondered why neither man was making any attempt to either escape or fire. He knew that he was plainly visible by now and Big Bob should have fired.

He couldn't spend any more time thinking about it. He squeezed his trigger.

Big Bob saw the burst of light and even as the .45 punched into his massive chest, he still waited for the demon's eyes to fire their bolts of killing lightning.

As soon as Nelson's Winchester flared, Jack settled his sights on the muzzle blast and fired.

Nelson was already levering in a fresh round when Jack's .44 arrived. It didn't hit him, but ricocheted off the barrel of his Winchester, ripping it from his hands. Just a second after it hit the ground, Nelson turned Rowdy then dropped to his gelding's neck to escape Jack's next shot.

Jack fired two more quick shots without effect but turned to Bob who finally realized he'd been shot. He'd felt his wet shirt and was now staring at his massive, blood-covered hand.

Jack was awed that the man could take a bullet to the chest yet still act as if he'd been bitten by a squirrel.

"Bob!" he shouted, "He dropped his rifle! You need to kill that bastard!"

Big Bob turned to Jack and asked, "He ain't a ghost?"

"No, he's just a man and you need to kill him, or he'll kill me. You don't want him to kill me; do you?"

Bob's anger that the rider might hurt his only friend overpowered his concerns about ghosts or having a .45 buried in his chest. He nodded then started his stolen horse after the rider who threatened to kill Jack.

As soon as Bob began to move, Jack wheeled his horse to the right and walked him and the trailing horse across the tracks to reach the trees.

After Nelson had ridden for a minute, he sat straight and looked behind him. He didn't see anyone but could hear a single set of hoofbeats in the distance. He suspected that Jack had sent a wounded Big Bob Pope to either kill him. Even if Big Bob failed, he'd still give Jack time to make his escape.

He pulled his Sharps and cocked the hammer. He only had one shot, but if the power of the Sharps couldn't stop Bob, then he'd have to depend on the six .44s in his Remington.

Bob may have acted as if he wasn't suffering any ill effects from being shot, but he knew better. He was losing blood and knew that he had to kill that special agent if it was the last thing he ever did. He didn't see Jack run off but wouldn't have cared if he had. Jack was his friend.

Nelson spotted the big man and leveled his Sharps at the giant. He waited and wondered when Bob would start firing. He was just sixty yards away yet still hadn't leveled his Winchester. He'd wait another couple of seconds to make sure that he didn't hit the horse.

Bob hadn't fired because he believed that he could survive another shot, at least long enough to kill the man with his bare hands. It was his way. It was the best way.

Nelson had already released his Sharps' first trigger, then when Bob was just thirty yards away, he squeezed the second. The heavy rifle rammed against his shoulder and a long stream of bright light erupted from its muzzle.

Bob saw the flash at the same moment that he felt the power of the Sharps when the .45 crushed his sternum. He rocked in the saddle before he slowly dropped off to the side and plunged to the ground. His massive body created a large, shadowy cloud as it struck the dirt then stopped moving.

Nelson wasn't sure if Bob was dead, but he was out of action and now he had to find Jack Rodgers.

He still stopped by Bob's body and grabbed his Winchester. He wasn't sure if his '76 was functional and didn't want to chase Jack with only his pistol and crossbow. He wasn't sure he could trust Bob's repeater, either. It might be empty which would explain why Bob hadn't fired it.

Jack had entered the trees and slowed once he was among the pines. He had the advantage now. Nelson would have to find him or let him go. There were at least six more hours of darkness, and he could be miles away before sunrise.

Nelson was well aware of the situation. Jack not only was well hidden in the trees, but there was a real mess behind him that needed to be addressed.

But while he may have granted that Jack had an advantage, he also had a problem. He had no supplies and only the spare ammunition he had on his gunbelt. But the ammunition was secondary. Jack would be able to find water easily, but he didn't have any food. He couldn't hunt, either. He couldn't risk letting anyone hear the gunshots.

He looked to his left and could barely see the maintenance train in the distance. He suspected that Jack might swing around through the trees to get to his supplies, including the remaining cash from the ghost train's express car safe.

Nelson kept the train in sight, but turned to the town and shouted, "I'm Union Pacific special agent Nelson Cook! I need to talk to Tom Jeffries or any other U.P. worker!"

He could have ridden to the railyard manager's house which was on the southern edge of the town, but he didn't want to give Jack a chance to reach the boxcar.

Jack had no intention of returning to the train. He'd also changed his mind about getting as far away as possible. He had ridden just a few hundred yards into the trees before he dismounted. He tied off the stolen horse and his spare mount then walked more than fifty yards away. He expected Nelson to arrive shortly, so he set up with his Winchester, then waited and listened.

———

It was more than five minutes before four men left town and reached Nelson, who never left his saddle.

Tom Jeffries led the small group who all carried either pistols or Winchesters. Nelson was relieved that town marshal Larry Eppley wasn't one of them.

Tom looked up at him and loudly said, "We heard you were killed in that bridge collapse, Nelson. You sure look dead."

"I was sitting on the caboose stairs when it went over and was thrown off the side. I don't have much time to talk. The gang that collapsed the bridge was going to steal your maintenance train. They decorated it to make it look spooky for some reason but were planning on crashing it into a scheduled train. They didn't damage anything, but I stopped it about a mile north of town.

"All of the gang is dead except for their leader. He escaped and is in those woods to the east. I need to go after him, so he doesn't build a new gang and keep going. There are five bodies scattered on the ground behind me. Four are ex-railroaders and the giant is Big Bob Pope. There's another one in the locomotive cab.

"What I need you to do is bring the train back and load those bodies onto the flat car. Don't let anyone enter the boxcar. They put their horses and gear inside. Send a telegram to Homer Watson and Sheriff Harris to let them know what happened. After that's done, I need you to clear the track to Ogden and use the maintenance train to take the bodies to the sheriff. Oh, when you find a Winchester '76 on the ground, that belongs to me. It's probably useless now anyway. Do you have all that?"

Tom nodded then replied, "Bring the maintenance train back, put the bodies on a flat car, send the telegram to Homer and Sheriff Harris, then get the train to Ogden."

"That's it. Oh, the two horses running loose were stolen from your stock corral. Jack had two others that I'll return after I kill him."

"You need any help, Nelson?"

"You're already helping more than enough, Tom. One more thing, if you don't mind. Add a line to that telegram to have Homer tell my wife that I'm okay."

"When did you get married?"

Nelson grinned, replied, "Yesterday," then wheeled Rowdy around and set him east across the tracks.

Tom watched him for a few seconds, then turned and snapped, "You heard the man! Ed, you and Joe go get that train ready to roll and bring it back here. And don't blow that damned whistle!"

The two men trotted away, then Tom took charge as more men arrived. He didn't have to ask Nelson why he preferred to leave Marshal Eppley out of the recovery. He probably would prefer to stay in his bed anyway.

Nelson's only concern now was Jack Rodgers. He may not have worried about his lack of food when he'd made his escape, but he must have realized his problem by now. He wouldn't risk returning to Park City, but he might try to reach one of the two smaller towns between Park City and Echo.

Even before he entered the trees, Nelson discarded that notion. Jack would head northeast. When he'd led his men from the bridge collapse to Park City, he had probably passed the end of his temporary spur line. If so, he probably discovered that his tents were still there. The tents that were still full of supplies. It was an oversight that didn't seem important at the time, but now it might be a lure for Jack Rodgers.

That mistaken belief made him less attentive as Rowdy carried him into the pitch black of the pines. The trees blocked most of the quarter moon's light, but some of the weak rays still made it to the ground.

While he wasn't as prepared as he should have been, that didn't mean that he was ignoring the possibility that Jack was setting up for an ambush. He didn't bother taking Big Bob's Winchester from his scabbard. Even if it was loaded, he hadn't had time to inspect the carbine and there was a good chance that it had become fouled when it fell to the ground. He couldn't trust the weapon.

He still had his Remington and his Sharps, but the rifle's single shot was a real liability in this situation. As Rowdy snaked his way around tree trunks, Nelson turned and pulled out his crossbow case, then hung it over his shoulder. He couldn't load it on horseback but having it available was another option.

After waiting for minutes without hearing anything, Jack had decided that Nelson wasn't going to come for a while. So, he left his ambush site and began to walk back to his horses. He still hadn't given a thought to his lack of supplies as he tried to guess what Nelson might do. After he'd overcome his shock that Nelson was still alive, he'd let his reincarnation refuel his need for a challenge. Granted, it wasn't the intellectual contest he'd originally considered after the theft of the passenger train, but it was still a challenge.

He had only walked twenty feet when he stopped. For some reason, he suddenly recalled that Carl had told him Nelson was going to marry Ned Gray's widow. He couldn't imagine that Nelson hadn't been familiar with the woman before she boarded that train. She must have been on her way to Ogden to join him. If he'd known that tidbit of information, he could have made good use of their hidden affection.

He grinned then said, "You weren't a very good boy, Nelson. I wonder if you blew up her hubby to make her widow?"

After he posed his rhetorical question, he snickered, then started walking again.

Nelson may not have expected to find Jack, but when he'd heard Jack's voice, Nelson pulled Rowdy to a stop. As Jack snickered, Nelson tried to pinpoint the direction. It was difficult among the trees, but he knew Jack had to be close.

He slowly dismounted, then tied off Rowdy's reins to keep him from following. Now that he was on the ground, he opened his crossbow case, removed one bolt and the weapon.

After sliding the bolt under his gunbelt, he set the stock of the crossbow on the ground, set his boot on the cocking lever and pushed down until the string was taut and held in place by the releasing pin.

He lifted the crossbow and inserted the bolt. The weapon was ideally suited for this situation. It may not have the range or the power of a pistol, but it didn't produce a muzzle flare. He'd have one shot which wouldn't give Jack a target. If he hit Jack anywhere, then he would have the time to draw his pistol.

As he crept slowly forward, he listened for more sonic evidence of Jack's presence.

Jack was still smiling at the thought of an immoral Nelson Cook, but just when he was almost to his horses, he heard a sound that didn't belong in the woods. He didn't know what it was but froze in place as he listened.

He didn't hear it again but looked at his horses just twenty feet away. Even in the darkness, he could see the whites of their eyes as they both seemed to be afraid of some wild critter. While he wasn't concerned about a bear or wolf, he suspected that the horses had sensed an approaching human. A human who should be dead. Now Jack was determined to finish the job.

He began sidestepping to the closest pine trunk for safety. He expected Nelson to appear where the horses were staring.

What had attracted the horses' attention wasn't the human, but the gelding he'd ridden. The problem for Jack was that Nelson wasn't with Rowdy anymore.

After Nelson had prepared his crossbow, he'd set off toward the sound. But Jack had spoken when he was a good distance from his horses.

Nelson was stealthily making his way past where Jack was hiding in wait. He was just past Jack's ambush site when he stopped to listen again.

The usual noises of the night in the forest were silent as the two men prepared to kill each other; one with a modern rifle, the other with a relic of history.

Jack made his second mistake when he decided to make use of his superior intelligence rather than patiently wait for Nelson to come into view.

He wanted to taunt Nelson into revealing his location. Jack hoped to get the special agent to take a shot in his anger but would settle for an angry reply.

With his cocked Winchester still level, Jack shouted, "I know you're out there, Nelson! I'm kind of surprised that you left Gray's widow alone. I'll bet that she's already let another man into her bed!"

Nelson was startled, but not by the taunt. He was stunned when he realized just how close Jack was. He didn't bother giving Jack the angry response he obviously expected and was almost disappointed that he'd used such a simple tactic.

But this wasn't a time to ponder Jack's reason for making the blunder. He slowly stepped to his right until one of those elusive moonbeams illuminated Jack's light gray shirt sleeve which was outlined against the dark bark. Nelson could barely make out anything else on Jack's body, but it was enough.

He aimed his crossbow at the sleeve and pulled the release. The pin dropped, releasing the bowstring. The bowstring twanged as the bolt shot from its slot and whistled across the thirty-one feet of darkness.

Jack heard the distinct sound but before he could determine its source, he felt the sharp tip of the bolt penetrate his left bicep then punch almost two inches into the pine. He screamed as his Winchester dropped to the ground.

Nelson dropped his crossbow and was pulling his Remington as he ran toward Jack.

After his arm had been impaled to the tree trunk, Jack had quickly grabbed the bolt to pull it free. The tip wasn't barbed, but it was buried so deeply into the wood that he couldn't budge it before Nelson reached him.

Nelson pulled Jack's Colt from his holster and tucked it under his waist before picking up his Winchester, releasing the hammer and setting it down behind him.

He then holstered his Remington and without saying a word, grabbed hold of the bolt. He didn't expect Jack to try anything because any movement would be incredibly painful and cause more damage to his arm.

Jack was already in too much pain to even look at Nelson when he grasped the shaft. He'd felt Nelson remove his pistol, but it didn't matter.

When Nelson began wiggling the bolt to loosen the pine's grip, Jack cried out but didn't dare move.

After he thought it was free enough, Nelson ripped it out of the tree and through Jack's torn bicep. Jack screamed again, then collapsed to the ground and grabbed his bleeding arm.

Nelson just tossed the bloody bolt away before picking up the Winchester. He then looked down at the man who'd caused so much trouble for the Union Pacific and himself.

"I'm going to return to my horse to get something to bandage your arm, Jack. Don't be stupid and try to escape. You won't get far."

Jack managed to sit against the trunk but didn't reply as he stared at Nelson before he turned and soon disappeared into the darkness. He knew that Nelson believed that he'd won, but Jack wasn't about to let him have his victory so easily. He looked at his two horses and thought he'd be able to get into the saddle and then disappear again. But he had to act quickly and couldn't afford to worry about his bleeding wound.

He used the tree to help him stand then walked quickly to the horses. He untied the reins, then climbed into the saddle just as Nelson reappeared carrying a towel.

Nelson pulled his Remington, cocked the hammer and pointed it at Jack.

"Get down, Jack. You're going to Ogden to face trial."

Jack grinned then said, "You're not going to shoot me, Nelson. You want our little game to continue as much as I do."

"It's not a game, Jack. We both knew that it's been a war for some time now. Don't make yourself the last casualty. I'm warning you for the last time. Dismount, or I will shoot you."

Jack honestly believed that Nelson wouldn't pull his trigger, so he just smiled and turned his stolen horse to the right. He tapped the gelding's flanks and the horse started to move. He was still smiling when he felt Nelson's .44 slam into the left side of his back. The report echoed through the silent forest as Jack rolled to his right side and slowly dropped onto the pine-covered floor.

Nelson holstered his Remington, then walked through the darkness and soon reached Jack. He was still alive, but both men knew it wouldn't be for much longer.

"I didn't think…you'd shoot me…in the back," Jack wheezed when Nelson knelt next to him.

"I warned you, Jack. I wish that I didn't have to shoot you in the back, but there was no other way. I couldn't run the risk of you surviving to kill more people."

Jack felt life receding from his mortal body and wanted to say something more profound, but he couldn't find the words as his mind began to fade. He began gasping for air as Nelson stood and waited for him to take his last breath.

When his chest stopped moving, Nelson reached down and closed his eyes. He then left his body and retrieved the stolen horses. After he returned them to Jack's corpse, he tied off the saddled horse then lifted his body and laid it face down over the barebacked gelding.

He led the horses back to Rowdy and mounted. He didn't think that Jack's body would fall off if he kept Rowdy at a walk, but it no longer mattered to Jack. Nelson didn't think that the engineer was busy building castles in the air. He was probably doing a fireman's work and stoking hell's fires by now.

He had taken Jack's Winchester, but he'd left his crossbow and its case in the trees. It had served its purpose, and he'd stick with weapons that made loud noise.

He emerged from the forest and saw a lot of shadows moving in the distance. They hadn't even had time to get the maintenance train moving yet. He'd only been gone for about thirty minutes. He thought he'd be chasing Jack all night if not for a few days. Now he'd be able to return to Ogden with the train. He'd send a telegram just to Cassie before he even set foot on the train to let her know that it was over.

———

Cassie had slipped between the sheets in the spare bedroom hours ago but hadn't come close to finding sleep. So, after she realized that rest wasn't possible, she lit a lamp, dressed, then walked out to the kitchen to make some coffee. She expected to hear something from Park City shortly after daybreak. If she finally did feel tired enough to sleep, she'd revisit the spare bedroom.

She had just poured her coffee when there was a loud knock on the front door. She popped to her feet, then raced down the hallway, crossed the front room and yanked the door open.

She wasn't surprised to find Homer standing in front of her and quickly read his face to get a hint of what he was about to tell her. He wasn't smiling, but he didn't seem distressed either. But whatever the reason for his coming to the house at this hour must have been important. It also had to be something about what Nelson had done in Park City.

Homer and said, "We just got this telegram from Park City, Cassie."

He handed her the sheet and she read:

HOMER WATSON UPRR OGDEN UT
SHERIFF HARRIS OGDEN UT

NELSON STOPPED THEFT OF MAINTENANCE TRAIN
KILLED ALL EXCEPT RODGERS
CHASING HIM NOW
SHOULD HEAR MORE SOON
NEED TRACK CLEARED FOR TRAIN
WITH BODIES AND THEIR PROPERTY
EXPECT DEPARTURE IN TWO HOURS
REQUESTED RELAY TO WIFE
WILL NOTIFY UPRR HQ

TOM EPPLEY UPRR PARK CITY UT

She handed it back to Homer and asked, "Do you think that Nelson will be returning with that train?"

"He might be, but if he's chasing Jack Rodgers in the dark, he might not find him until sunrise."

She smiled as she said, "You should have more faith in my husband, Homer. I'll bet you a dollar that he'll be on that train and another dollar that Jack's body will be coming with the others."

Homer was surprised by her reaction as he expected her to be worried after learning that Nelson was chasing a killer in the dark of the night.

But he still smiled and replied, "Okay. You have a bet. I expect the sheriff will be waiting for me at the station when I get back, so I'd better skedaddle."

"Thank you, Homer," Cassie said before kissing him on the cheek.

344

Homer smiled as he nodded then turned and headed back to Saint Street.

Cassie closed the door and soon returned to her coffee. After she'd read the telegram, she felt a surge of pride and relief. She believed every word that she'd told Homer. She would finish her coffee, then take a bath and await the arrival of another telegram from Nelson telling her that he'd join her in their bed within a few hours.

She had no doubt that by then, she'd be more than ready for sleep and Nelson would be even more exhausted. But knowing that the constant threat that Jack Rodgers created was finally over gave her hope that they could finally spend much more time together.

———

She had taken her bath, dressed and had just finished drying her hair when there was another knock on the door, but not nearly as loud as Homer's.

Cassie tossed the towel onto the bed then left the spare bedroom. When she opened the door this time, she smiled at John Hipper who had a telegram in his hand.

"I suppose I could have waited until the morning to have my boy deliver this, but Homer said you were still awake, and I figured you'd want to read it. Me and Ollie were both in the office because it was so busy, so I told him he was in charge until I got back."

Cassie almost didn't have to read the message after seeing John's face but accepted the sheet and while the telegrapher watched she unfolded the page.

CASSIE COOK SAINT STREET OGDEN UT

ALL OVER NOW
WILL BE RETURNING WITH MAINTENANCE TRAIN
SHOULD BE HOME BY SUNRISE
HAVE THINGS TO DO
BUT WILL JOIN YOU FOR BREAKFAST
AND SLEEP
LOTS OF SLEEP
WITH LOVE RESPECT AND GRATITUDE

NELSON COOK PARK CITY UT

She was smiling even more inside than the broad smile she wore on her face as she said, "Thank you for bringing me this wonderful news."

"You're welcome, Mrs. Cook."

Cassie appreciated hearing him call her Mrs. Cook, but still said, "Call me Cassie. I'm going to be living in Ogden for a long time now."

"I reckon that's so, Cassie. Good night," John said before he tipped his hat then left the short porch.

Cassie closed the door and slowly returned to the spare bedroom. She sat on the edge of the bed and reread the telegram. She laughed when she reached the 'lots of sleep' line but was deeply touched by his inclusion of those two simple words 'respect' and 'gratitude' that ended the message. She knew that he loved her, but the others meant almost as much.

She'd spent the last six years of her life believing that she was a horrible person and lost her self-respect in the process. In just a short time, Nelson had restored her belief in herself. He not only allowed her to be herself; he loved and respected the

346

real Cassie. And now, he even expressed his gratitude for her being the woman she'd hidden from everyone for so long.

When he finished what he needed to do, she'd make sure he understood that she was just as grateful. Nothing would ever drive them apart.

CHAPTER 9

The cleaned maintenance train rolled out of Park City at 3:25 in the morning. While they finished preparing the train, Nelson had washed Rowdy and dusted off as much of his own talc as possible. They'd found his damaged Winchester and left it with the bodies, but he knew it would be nothing more than a conversation piece. While it looked serviceable, the deep crease along the barrel was enough to demand its replacement.

Tom Eppley had them attach a caboose to the train before it departed, so Nelson was sitting on one of the bunks telling the conductor and brakeman what had happened. It was a way to pass the time and to prepare the report he'd be sending to the Union Pacific. He suspected that another summons was in his future, but his departure would be delayed until the bridge was repaired. So, he should be able to spend a few days with Cassie before he made that long journey again. He didn't think that they'd give him a fast passage either way this time.

———

As the sun broke over the horizon behind them, the maintenance train slowed as it neared the Ogden station. Nelson had already moved to the caboose's platform in anticipation of seeing Cassie again. He wouldn't be surprised if she decided to wait for him at the house because he'd added that line in his telegram to her that he'd have things to do once he arrived. But he still hoped to see her before he put the final touches to the end Jack Rodgers' reign of destruction.

He may not have spotted Cassie on the platform but there were many others waiting whom he did recognize. As he'd expected, he found Homer and Sheriff Harris in front of the crowd, but he also saw Joseph Reynolds, the mortician with his assistant and his two gravediggers. He assumed that the two big men who dug the holes would be the ones moving the bodies to Joseph's waiting hearse.

He had a set of saddlebags over his shoulder when he hopped down from the steel steps just before the train came to a stop then hurried to the platform. Homer and the sheriff both stepped down to the ground to meet him halfway.

After both men shook Nelson's hand, Homer said, "We already got a reply from Omaha, but that can wait."

Nelson nodded as the sheriff asked, "Do you have time to come to my office and tell me what happened? Don't worry about the bodies. The horses, including yours, will be kept here until we sort things out. I reckon that you're pretty spent by now."

"I'll admit that I'm at the end of my rope, but I can I tell you and Homer in his office?"

"That's fine."

Nelson then walked with the sheriff and the station manager to Homer's office and once inside, Sheriff Harris closed the door.

After they'd all taken a seat, Nelson dropped the saddlebags on the floor and said, "Before I start, I need to let you know that I took all of the cash they had left and put it into these saddlebags. There was only fifty-four hundred dollars, but between that and the other two thousand, it's more than half of what I let them take from the express car."

Sheriff Harris replied, "I'll take it to the bank, and they can put it in their vault. Now give us a quick rundown of what happened."

Nelson began his narrative with his preparation and discovery. He didn't claim to have shot any of the gang in a fair shootout when he reached that part of his report. He explained how he'd shot the man driving the locomotive without warning, then shot the fireman as he crawled away. Big Bob was a mysterious encounter, but Nelson couldn't explain the giant's reason for failing to fire his repeater. He attributed the other three deaths to Jack and Big Bob but then had to spend more time talking about the fatal encounter with Jack Rodgers.

When he finished, the sheriff said, "I hope you don't feel bad about shooting those boys in the back, Nelson. They were all going to hang anyway and if you didn't stop that train, who knows what would have happened?"

"No, I'm all right. I knew before I left that it had to end no matter what it took. I was surprised that Jack Rodgers honestly believed that I'd just let him ride away."

The sheriff said, "You'll be getting another reward for Big Bob, but I don't think that's important to you; is it?"

He replied, "No. It's not. I haven't seen the others yet, but you can hang onto them until this one arrives."

Then he smiled and said, "I have to provide for a wife now."

Homer laughed then said, "I reckon she'll be happy to see you even if you do like something that even the cat refused to drag in."

Nelson grinned then slapped his thigh creating a small dust cloud.

"If you'll have Charlie take care of Rowdy for a while, Homer, I'm going to head home to see my bride."

"Hang on. You have to read the latest telegram from Omaha."

"Oh, I forgot about them. I guess they'll be wanting me to visit again, but at least they have to wait until the bridge is repaired."

"Not exactly," Homer said as he handed him the telegram.

Nelson sighed as he took the page. He knew that they'd be rerouting rail traffic using other company's tracks but had hoped that they would at least wait until the bridge was repaired. But the look on Homer's face told him that they weren't going to give him a day or two to recover.

He opened the sheet, and his suspicions were confirmed when he read:

NELSON COOK UPRR OGDEN UT

RECEIVED THE WONDERFUL NEWS
TAKE NEXT DIVERTED RUN TO REPORT
EXPECT YOUR ARRIVAL IN THREE DAYS

WILLIAM BURNS UPRR OMAHA NEB

"That gives me about six hours to spend with Cassie before that train arrives," Nelson said quietly.

Homer replied, "Sorry, Nelson. They should have given you a break after all you did for them."

"They have a railroad to run, Homer. They don't have time to think about such things. I've got to get home, get cleaned up and get ready to leave again. You haven't shown this to Cassie; have you?"

351

"No, sir. I wasn't about to incur her wrath. But give her these and tell her I'm glad to pay off our bet."

He handed Nelson two silver dollars as he said, "She bet me a dollar that you'd be on the train and another dollar that you'd have Jack Rodgers' body with the others."

Despite his disappointment, Nelson smiled, slid the two large coins and the short telegram into his dusty jacket pocket then stood.

"I'll tell her," he said before he walked quickly out of the office.

As they watched him leave, Sheriff Harris said, "That isn't right, Homer."

"Nope. I don't think so, either. Well, I'll go talk to Charlie to have him take care of Nelson's horse and the other ones. I reckon you've got a lot of work ahead of you, too."

"Not as much as Nelson does. I think we both need to catch up on some sleep, too. Maybe we can all return to a normal life now."

"That would be different," Homer said as the sheriff stood then left the office.

————

Cassie knew that the maintenance train had arrived and was anxiously waiting for Nelson to walk through the door. She already suspected that another summons to Omaha was probably waiting for him. But just as Nelson had believed, she expected that the downed bridge would delay his departure. But she already decided that she wasn't going to let him travel alone. She no longer worried one bit about what the Grays thought of her. She was Mrs. Nelson Cook now.

She had fresh coffee and a big breakfast waiting for him. He could tell her what happened as he ate, then after he finished, they'd both go to their bedroom, strip off their clothes and go to sleep. She may have wished that they could remain awake for a little while, but knew he had a greater need for a prolonged rest.

———

But even as she paced in their front room, five hundred miles away, Tom Richardson boarded the morning Denver & Pacific train.

While it was five hundred miles to Ogden as the crow flies, the tracks followed a wide curve through the southern half of Colorado then Utah before it turned north. The train would take two days to cover the almost seven hundred miles, but then Tom would begin his search for Cassie Gray.

He hoped that she had remained in Ogden but was determined to find her sooner or later. He only hoped that in the interim, she hadn't tried to find him in Denver. He'd read about the bridge collapse, so the only way to make the journey was to take the Denver & Pacific. He thought how ironic it would be if she'd taken the train from Ogden to Denver while he was traveling in the opposite direction. Maybe they'd meet at a small station near the Colorado-Utah border.

———

Tom Richardson wasn't even Cassie or Nelson's mind when he opened the door to their home.

She was so excited to see him that she ignored his appearance and threw her arms around him. Nelson didn't try to stop her and soon held her close.

When she looked up him, he kissed her before she could even let a syllable pass her lips. She wasn't about to say anything even if he'd given her the opportunity.

After the long kiss ended, she said, "I have coffee and breakfast for you on the table. You can tell me everything while you eat."

"Alright," he said as he released her then took her hand.

The newlyweds walked down the short hallway and Nelson sat at the table while Cassie began filling his plate.

After she placed his loaded plate in front of him, she set two cups of coffee on the table then sat on the closest chair.

Nelson took a sip of the much-needed coffee but delayed having his breakfast until after he'd given her the bad news.

"I gave my report to the sheriff and Homer. Before I left, Homer gave me a telegram from my boss."

"I expected that they would want to see you again."

He nodded then said, "So, did I. But I thought I'd have a few days before I had to leave because of the downed bridge."

"But you don't?" she asked with arched eyebrows.

"No. I have to catch the afternoon train that's been rerouted on the Denver & Pacific line. It'll take more than three days to get there, but they didn't give me any leeway."

He had expected to see serious disappointment in her eyes after he'd told her, but it wasn't there.

Before he could say another word, Cassie said, "I guess you'll have to pack and get cleaned up quickly then. I'm almost finished packing myself but didn't expect that we'd be leaving so soon."

He gawked at her as he asked, "You're coming?"

"Do you believe I'm going to let you leave me alone? We've only been married for two days and we've been separated for most of that time. I'll come with you to Omaha and we can call it our honeymoon."

Nelson smiled then began to wolf down his breakfast while he told Cassie the last act of the ghost train play.

———

There hadn't been enough time for either of them to get any sleep as they bustled to prepare for the long trip. While they would be traveling on Denver & Pacific tracks for the first half of the journey, they'd be using a Union Pacific train. That was an advantage for Nelson. While Cassie finished her packing, Nelson paid a short visit to Homer and had him add a second caboose to the train. It would serve as a rolling honeymoon cottage.

So, when they boarded the late afternoon train, instead of entering a passenger car, Cassie and Nelson climbed onto the first of the two cabooses. The one at the end of the train still belonged to the conductor and brakeman.

———

The Union Pacific train crossed onto Denver & Pacific tracks before leaving Ogden and headed for Provo. Then it would soon turn southeast and begin the same curving route that Tom Richardson was taking in the opposite direction.

It wasn't long before the train's crew began making off-color comments about Nelson and his lady sleeping together in the spare caboose. They were right about it, too. Cassie and Nelson were in fact together…sleeping.

———

It was almost noon the next day when their train had to pull off to a siding to allow a Denver & Pacific train pass on their company's tracks. It was one of the negatives of having to use another company's rails. Their own trains always had priority.

As he looked out the window of his passenger car, Tom spotted the Union Pacific train sitting on the siding and grinned. He knew that it had to have passed through Ogden and wondered if Cassie was on the train heading for Denver to find him.

He was still grinning when he noticed the odd double-caboose arrangement which made him tack on another snicker. He had no idea why the Union Pacific would use two cabooses. Then he figured they probably had armed guards in the second one in case that gang who stole the ghost train struck again.

He soon forgot about the other train but grew more anxious about finding Cassie. He shifted to his second favorite topic as he tried to calculate how much money she had inherited from her disintegrated husband.

———

Neither Cassie nor Nelson had looked out of the caboose's window at the passing train. It was already the third time that their train had to leave the main line. For most of the passengers, it was annoying, but for the newlyweds, it just extended their rolling honeymoon.

Traveling on trains was practically ingrained into Nelson, so he did all he could to make the long journey more comfortable for Cassie. It helped that she had packed well. While she hadn't taken nearly as much as she had when she left Cheyenne, she still had two large travel bags.

By that the next day, they were back on Union Pacific tracks, so the rest of their trip would be more predictable.

Because of their almost invisible courtship, the couple spent most of their time talking. Nothing shocking nor even surprising was revealed in those long conversations. They simply confirmed what each of them had already beleived from that first day. They were destined to find each other.

———

It was two days after crossing onto U.P. rails that their train rolled into Omaha at 4:50 in the afternoon.

They were met at the station by Mister Sullivan's secretary, James Dillingham. He was surprised that Nelson had arrived with a woman and stunned when he was introduced to Mrs. Cassie Cook. But he took it in stride. He guided them to Mister Sullivan's waiting carriage and then escorted them to the Chase Hotel.

When they were alone in the very well-appointed room, Cassie said, "I may be wrong, but I believe that the president of the Union Pacific is very pleased with you, Mister Cook."

Nelson wrapped her in his arms before he replied, "It's either that or this is the equivalent of a last meal."

"He didn't even put us in the Railway Hotel. This is quite fancy. It even has a bath with hot and cold running water."

"That isn't a very subtle hint, Mrs. Cook. I'll start unpacking while you enjoy a nice hot bath."

She smiled, kissed him then quickly took her nightdress from one of her travel bags before she waltzed into the bathroom.

Nelson began unpacking his bag knowing he had a long wait before Cassie left the luxury of a hot bath.

Passing through Denver had reminded him of Tom Richardson. Even though he recognized the chance of the man suddenly reappearing in Cassie's life was remote, he wished he could have found the man. He'd just strongly suggest that he remained in Denver.

But Tom Richardson and Jack Rodgers were both in the past now. Cassie was his present and his future.

She'd told him that she was barren and after six years of marriage to Ned Gray, he believed that she was right. In their long talks, she had expressed a melancholy for that condition but there was nothing he could do. He hadn't mentioned adoption yet because even talking about children seemed to have a depressing effect. They could discuss it when they returned to Ogden if it became necessary. There was no rush.

As he placed his clothes into one of the drawers in the large, polished chest of drawers, he was curious about tomorrow's nine o'clock meeting with the directors. He wasn't worried about their questions or even their answers. He wondered about the lady who was about to slip into the tub. *When he met the bosses, did she want him to keep their marriage secret?*

He hadn't asked her to describe her uncle yet. But after she finally left her bath, he'd have her give him his description. At least he'd know who the second person was at the table he needed to avoid. The first, of course, was his boss, William Burns. He wished he could ask Mister Sullivan what Mister Burns' told them when they'd learned of the bridge collapse. Maybe he could ask the secretary who took the minutes of each meeting.

His travel bag was empty, and he wasn't about to open either of Cassie's bags. So, he walked to the large window, opened the heavy green embroidered drapes and looked out at the still growing city of Omaha. In the distance, he could see the Missouri River flowing south where it would eventually join the Mississippi at St. Louis. He had often wondered how that worked. When the two rivers met, the Missouri had crossed more miles, but the Mississippi had a bigger watershed. He never had asked the question. But if they had called the river from St. Louis to New Orleans the Missouri, *what would the state of Mississippi be called?*

He was smiling at the silliness of his question when he heard the bathroom door open. His smile grew larger when he beheld

Cassie wearing her nightdress that clung to her still damp body. He wondered if she had intentionally not dried herself completely but didn't waste much time pondering the mystery.

———

An hour later, Cassie was no longer wearing her nightdress and was even wetter than she'd been when she left her bath. Nelson hadn't taken a bath yet but looked as if he'd swum across the Missouri River.

Nelson had his arm around his wife and asked, "Cassie, when I meet with the bosses in the morning, do you want me to keep our marriage secret?"

"That would be difficult; wouldn't it?"

"Why would it be difficult?"

"How would you explain the woman sitting beside you?"

Nelson hadn't given her attendance a thought, so he rolled onto his side and looked into her eyes.

"You're coming with me?"

"Are you ashamed of me, sir?" she asked with a smile.

"Now that's a silly question, ma'am. Of course, I'm ashamed to be seen with you. Why, you're the same woman who stole my Winchester right out of my hand. No other man could tolerate such behavior from a mere woman!"

Cassie laughed then smacked him on his behind.

"Maybe I'll buy you a nice new Winchester '76 to make amends."

"I'll be forever grateful, ma'am. So, you'll come to the meeting tomorrow morning. What do you think your uncle will say?"

"I don't care what he says or how long he glares at me. If he collects all of Ned's family to march on our hotel room, my husband and I will send them packing."

Nelson kissed her then said, "I already thought tomorrow's meeting would be interesting. Now, it will be much more intriguing."

Cassie slid closer to him and after kissing him much more passionately, whispered, "Now, where were we?"

———

At promptly 8:30 the next morning, James Dillingham arrived with Mister Sullivan's carriage to take him to the meeting. He may have raised an eyebrow when he watched Nelson assist his wife into the carriage, but he said nothing.

When they entered the large headquarters building of the nation's largest railroad in terms of track laid, Nelson and Cassie were escorted to the conference room by Mister Sullivan's secretary.

As they entered the room, Nelson, even without Cassie having described him, instantly identified which of the men was Ned Gray's uncle, John M. Fitzpatrick. While the others, even William Burns, smiled when the couple entered the room, Mister Fitzpatrick's face shifted from shock to scowl in seconds. But Cassie wasn't affected in the least.

There was only one open chair, so Nelson pulled it back and let Cassie sit while he stood behind her. He didn't have to stand for long when the recording secretary popped to his feet then dragged one of the chairs that lined the back wall and set it next to Cassie.

Nelson sat down then waited with everyone else for Edgar T. Sullivan to start the meeting.

The president smiled as he said, "Nelson, you really outdid yourself this time. I thought your actions with the ghost train were extraordinary, but just the brief outline of what you did in Park City to end Mister Rodgers' scourge was beyond belief. Before you give us the details, I assume that there's a reason you brought Mrs. Gray with you. I know she was one of the passengers on the ghost train. Can I guess that she's here for a very different reason?"

Nelson smiled then replied, "Sir, I'm sure that Mister Dillingham has at least already given you an answer to your question. But for those board members who haven't met Cassie when she lived in Omaha, she is now my wife. We were married in Ogden ten days ago. She was the widow of Ned Gray, one of the Union Pacific engineers. I believe Mister Fitzpatrick was his uncle."

Several heads, including the president's, turned to John Fitzpatrick which forced him to convert his scowl into a poor excuse for a smile.

Nelson glanced at Cassie long enough to see a genuine smile cross her lips before he returned his eyes to the president.

"We had met years earlier but hadn't been introduced. When I released the passengers from captivity, we talked, and I asked her to take charge after I returned to the train. We knew almost from that first conversation that we belonged together."

Mister Sullivan smiled as he said, "We should all be so fortunate. Congratulations, Mrs. Cook."

"Thank you, sir," Cassie said as she smiled back while ignoring Ned's uncle.

"Now, tell us what happened in Park City, Nelson," the head of the railroad said from the other end of the long table.

Nelson began his long narrative by explaining how Cassie had been instrumental in determining Jack Rodgers' next plan and target would be. After that, it was just a timeline report of events as they happened. He didn't make it sound brave or even honorable when he explained the gunfights or shooting Jack in the back as he rode away. Nor did he express any remorse in the way he had to kill any of the others.

When he finished, he spent another hour answering questions before Mister Sullivan ended the meeting, but asked Nelson and Cassie to stay after the board members and recording secretary left.

After they'd gone, the president asked them to come to his end of the table. As they walked down the left side, Nelson wondered what was on Mister Sullivan's mind. He hoped that he wasn't going to ask him to take William Burns' job.

Cassie sat down then Nelson took a seat between her and the president.

"I wanted to thank you personally for what you did, Nelson. I know that William Burns is worried that you want his job, but I know better. Am I right in assuming that the very thought of sitting behind a desk is nauseating for you?"

Nelson smiled as he nodded and replied, "Yes, sir."

"I thought so. I'm not going to tell him, though. I'd rather just watch him wallow in his discomfort. He had that position before I was put in charge and it's easier to leave him there than to fight his sponsors. That being said, what I am going to do is have him create a central security district. It will encompass Union Pacific property in Utah, Colorado, Idaho and Wyoming Territory. I want you to be in charge of that district."

Nelson didn't see any difference between sitting at a desk in Omaha and doing the same job in Ogden, so he shook his head.

"Thank you for the offer, sir. I wouldn't be content with sitting behind a desk even if it was a thousand miles from Mister Burns."

The president laughed then said, "I'm not about to stick you behind a desk, Nelson. But we have a problem with our special agents that should come as no surprise to you."

"Too many of them are crooked."

"That's it. The head of the district will just be the senior agent. He'll have an office manager to handle all the paperwork, but the senior agent will have the power to hire and fire the special agents in the district. As the senior agent, you'd be able to rid the company of men who cause as much grief as those they're supposed to stop. You could train good men to be good special agents, Nelson."

Nelson looked at Cassie for her approval and saw her answer in her smiling eyes.

"I'd enjoy doing that, Mister Sullivan."

"Good! Good! I'm glad to hear it. I've already had the paperwork done, so before you leave, I'll have a set drawn up for you. I also had a new badge created just for you."

"Thank you, sir."

"You'll get a big pay raise as well. Lord knows you've earned it. Your decisions and actions saved this company much more than just money."

Nelson let out a deep breath then said, "Mister Sullivan, my decision to let Jack Rodgers and his gang leave when I could have blown them all into oblivion was horribly wrong. If I'd pulled my trigger, then that bridge would still be standing, and the freight train would have reached its destination with its crew still alive. I let my hubris lead me to make the wrong choice."

Mister Sullivan studied Nelson's face for a few seconds before he said, "No, it was the right decision. I believed it when you told us at the first meeting and I still do. You couldn't kill railroad men who hadn't murdered anyone any more than I would have."

Nelson quickly said, "But the bridge and the freight train…"

The president interrupted him by waving his hand and saying, "Nonsense! You even warned us about that possibility. Besides, bridge collapses and derailments are inevitable costs in this business as the tracks continue to flow across the West. Why just a couple of days ago, the Denver & Pacific lost a train to a derailment that killed all the passengers, too. You probably passed it on the way to Denver. So, don't go blaming yourself for what happened. Hell, if you want to blame anyone other than Jack Rodgers, blame me."

"I wouldn't do that, sir."

"I know you wouldn't, so don't blame yourself, either."

Nelson smiled as he nodded then felt Cassie take his hand before he replied, "I'll take your advice, sir."

"That's not advice, senior agent, that's an order."

"Aye. Aye, sir."

When Mister Sullivan began to stand, so did Nelson and Cassie.

As he shook Nelson's hand, he said, "Take my carriage back to the hotel. Then, tomorrow morning, you will board the executive train with your bride. This time, you are not returning to Ogden on another freight train or even a passenger train. Is that understood?"

"Yes, sir," Nelson replied with a grin.

The president shook Cassie's hand and said, "Keep him safe, Mrs. Cook."

"I'll do more than that, sir. I'll keep him happy."

"I'm sure you will."

Nelson still held Cassie's hand as they turned and left the conference room. Mister Dillingham was waiting in the hallway as if there was an invisible telegraph wire between him and Mister Sullivan.

The return trip to Ogden used a much more luxurious and comfortable mode of travel and took thirty fewer hours now that the bridge had been rebuilt.

When they'd boarded the executive train, the paperwork authorizing Nelson's new position was waiting for him with his new badge. He'd need to find an office in Ogden and find a manager to run it. But he was already excited about getting a chance to replace the bad agents with men who were dedicated to the job. He'd offered the position of manager to Cassie, but she declined.

Aside from the hint of nepotism, she said that she'd prefer to travel with him when they investigated the bad special agents. She wouldn't get involved in the confrontations that Nelson expected but she'd offer her insights. Nelson was more than happy with her decision.

Because she had been so pleased to be joining him, Nelson decided not to broach the subject of adoption. He'd let Cassie be the one to ask about it, assuming she ever did.

When their special train arrived in Ogden in the middle of the afternoon, the travel-weary couple stepped down onto the platform and were greeted by Homer Watson.

368

As they shook hands, Nelson said, "We're going to head back to the house to unpack. I'll tell you what the bosses said tomorrow."

"I didn't reckon they'd fire you, Nelson."

"They gave me a new job that I'll tell you about when I see you."

Then he turned to the corral and asked, "Did Charlie send the two horses back to Mister Tincher?"

"Yup. But he's got another horse waiting for you."

"I told the sheriff that I didn't want any of the gang's horses."

"It's not one of them. Come along with the missus and I'll show him to you. He's got a bit of a story."

Nelson took Cassie's hand as they stepped across the platform heading for the corral.

As they walked, Homer said, "There was this Denver & Pacific train derailment south of Provo."

"I heard about that. What is it doing here and not in one of their stockyards?"

"That's part of the story. All the passengers were killed because the train rolled down an embankment after it left the tracks. All of the horses in the stock car were killed, too. All of them except this one who didn't even have a broken bone. The

369

boys who found him called him the ghost horse. The foreman figured that because you found the ghost train, that he belonged to you and sent him here. I reckon they were a superstitious bunch."

"It sounds like it," Nelson said as they approached the corral.

Charlie had been expecting Nelson, so he already had the ghost horse waiting.

Despite the afternoon heat, Nelson had goosebumps erupt on his arms as he rubbed the horse's neck.

"He's one lucky critter," Charlie said as he opened the gate.

"I guess so," Nelson replied as he took the reins.

Cassie took his free hand as they left the station to reach the welcome embrace of their small home.

Nelson wasn't sure what to think as he led the pinto with its black face, two white ears and a white muzzle. All he knew was that the pinto's original owner's identity would be the only secret he ever would keep from Cassie.

EPILOGUE

Over the next two weeks, Nelson found his office and hired a manager for the new security district. He'd stolen Homer from his job as station manager because he was able to offer him more money and better hours. It was up to the U.P. to find his replacement.

After the office was operating, he and Cassie began their investigations of other special agents. Nelson already had a good understanding of which ones needed to be eliminated. It was the hiring process that was more time consuming. Cassie's input on that part of the job was invaluable.

But after just two months of their joint investigative trips, Cassie threw a wrench into the works. She was stunned but incredibly excited when she discovered that she was pregnant. She wasn't sure what Nelson's reaction would be to the news because he'd never even mentioned children. When she told him that she was unexpectedly expecting, Nelson practically exploded with joy. She had been very happy herself, but once she saw that he was just as pleased as she was, it pushed her into a level of happiness she believed she would ever experience.

All those years believing that she was barren had led her to accept that she would never become a mother. Now her wonderful husband had given her the one gift she believed God had denied her. The joyous revelation was just the final proof that they were destined to find each other.

———

Nelson was making excellent progress on recreating the entire structure of his newly established security district. While Cassie still joined him on the shorter trips, she accompanied him less often as their baby grew.

He was having Homer send regular reports to Mister Burns about the changes, more as a courtesy than a requirement. He rarely received a reply.

While the stories about the ghost train and Jack Rodgers' other crimes diminished over the winter months, other gangs decided to use some of his tactics, which kept the new special agents busy. No Union Pacific trains were derailed or even robbed during the winter of 1882-3, but other lines weren't so fortunate.

When Cassie's pregnancy entered her ninth month, Nelson stopped handling any problems on his own. Despite his dread of sitting behind the desk, he remained in the office to be there when his beloved wife went into labor. She hadn't shown any signs of difficulties, but Nelson still felt the need to stay with her.

On the beautiful spring evening of May 11th, Cassie went into labor. She endured the extraordinary pain that all women experienced bringing new life into the world. And like most of those women who'd preceded her, she wished it would end. To Cassie, it seemed that those twelve hours and thirty-six minutes lasted for days. But when she heard the wail of her newborn child, she wept with relief and unrestricted joy.

When her daughter was placed into her sweaty arms, Cassie let her fingertips slide across the baby's cheek. She looked at the tiny face letting her love wash over her child. She was still in a world of disbelief and wonder. She was now the mother of a beautiful daughter.

When Nelson was allowed into the room, he sat in the chair next to her and smiled down at his wife and daughter.

"We have a little girl, Cassie," he whispered.

Cassie nodded as she touched her husband's face. She wished she could have said something meaningful to the man who'd saved her and the other passengers. The man who had given her the chance to be herself. He had given her happiness and now the incredible gift she never thought was possible. But there weren't any words to express how grateful she was.

But even as she failed to find the words, she could see in his eyes that he understood. It was because he was just as grateful for finding her.

33	Virgil's Herd	12/14/2017
34	Marsh's Valley	01/01/2018
35	Alex Paine	01/18/2018
36	Ben Gray	02/05/2018
37	War Adams	03/05/2018
38	Mac's Cabin	03/21/2018
39	Will Scott	04/13/2018
40	Sheriff Joe	04/22/2018
41	Chance	05/17/2018
42	Doc Holt	06/17/2018
43	Ted Shepard	07/13/2018
44	Haven	07/30/2018
45	Sam's County	08/15/2018
46	Matt Dunne	09/10/2018
47	Conn Jackson	10/05/2018
48	Gabe Owens	10/27/2018
49	Abandoned	11/19/2018
50	Retribution	12/21/2018
51	Inevitable	02/04/2019
52	Scandal in Topeka	03/18/2019
53	Return to Hardeman County	04/10/2019
54	Deception	06/02/2019
55	The Silver Widows	06/27/2019
56	Hitch	08/21/2019
57	Dylan's Journey	09/10/2019
58	Bryn's War	11/06/2019
59	Huw's Legacy	11/30/2019
60	Lynn's Search	12/22/2019
61	Bethan's Choice	02/10/2020
62	Rhody Jones	03/11/2020
63	Alwen's Dream	06/16/2020
64	The Nothing Man	06/30/2020
65	Cy Page: Western Union Man	07/19/2020
66	Tabby Hayes	08/02/2020
67	Letter for Gene	09/08/2020
68	Dylan's Memories	09/20/2020

Made in the USA
Columbia, SC
08 February 2021